THE PARIS CONSPIRACY

JEANA KENDRICK

CONSPIRACY SERIES BOOK 2

Also By Jeana Kendrick

St. Abient Run Conspiracy Series

The Last Bridge across Mostar

Memoirs of a Bible Smuggler

THE PARIS CONSPIRACY

JEANA KENDRICK

CONSPIRACY SERIES BOOK 2

Northridge Press

USA

Northridge Press

Copyright 2022 by Jeana Kendrick

Library of Congress cataloging in publication data
Library of Congress Control Number: 2021922382
Kendrick, Jeana
The Paris Conspiracy / Jeana Kendrick – First Edition.
pages; cm
First Printing 2022

ISBN: 978-1-952406-08-9 (trade paperback). ISBN: 978-1-952406-09-6 (e-book).

Northridge Press
P.O. Box 2562
Conroe, Texas 77305
Printed in the United States of America

To Jeff, my knight in shining armor
and to my sister and family for
their love and support

"For by grace ye are saved through faith; and that not of yourselves: it is the gift of God:" (Ephesians 2:8).

ACKNOWLEDGMENTS

I greatly appreciate the friends and authors in my weekly writers' critique group, Jacqueline Pelham, Beverly Butt and Joy Zeigler, who have edited and proofed my manuscripts and inspired me year after year. Special thanks to our mentor and author extraordinaire Guida Jackson, my copy editor Jode Hestand, my sister Kathryn Kendrick, my niece Shelly Boyd, Anne Campbell, and family and friends for their encouragement and support. Any mistakes are my own. Last, thank you to my husband Jeff who makes it all possible and has cheered me on throughout this endeavor.

PROLOGUE

Dominic Trudeau stood in the sweltering forest and watched the burning plane as the emergency crew fought to dampen the blazing inferno. The pilot and copilot were dead. Fahid's terrorist minions had wired the hydraulics to malfunction during landing. The crash had destroyed most, if not all, of the evidence. The stench of melting metal and exploding fuel permeated the air.

Dominic didn't want the Americans involved. The situation was complicated enough without entering into charades with the FBI or, should the crisis escalate internationally, the CIA.

He could see the death of his relationship with Gayle reflected in the wreckage. To return to Paris was out of the question. Too many of his suspicions had become reality. And he had his orders.

Dominic turned, and though his step was light and sure, his future weighed heavily upon him as he cut back to the road where he'd parked.

1

Gayle Regan strode into Transway Airlines' Paris HQ, unable to keep from smiling at everyone she passed. In a few days, she and Dominic Trudeau would be married. She wore a two-piece silk suit and heels, the champagne color matching the promise of their future. Maybe the thought was silly but she was in love. Dom's tender gaze, his mouth barely turned up at the corners, letting her see how deeply he loved her was heady stuff.

She caught the elevator to the third floor, then walked down the hall and greeted her PA. "Good morning, Helen. How are you on this gorgeous day?"

"Someone's happy. I can't believe you're here with the wedding so close."

"I'll enjoy the honeymoon more knowing my work's caught up." Gayle entered the adjoining office, settled in at her desk and began slogging through the enormous pile of paperwork to be resolved. She was in the middle of it when Helen buzzed her on the intercom.

"*Madame* Trudeau is on the line."

"Thanks, Helen. I hope she isn't calling to add more guests to the reception but put her through." Gayle picked up the phone as it rang. "Madame, I don't think there's room for even one more guest."

"That's no longer a problem."

The woman's voice was tight and unfriendly, but Gayle knew Dom's parents had never warmed to her.

Madame continued, "Dominic has finally come to his senses and terminated the wedding. He's been called out of town and asked us to let you know how things stand."

Gayle was stunned. "There's some mistake. You must have misunderstood."

"I'm sorry, but to marry an American, especially one without any background . . . Well, enough said."

"No. Dom wouldn't leave without speaking with me, and he certainly wouldn't cancel our wedding."

"Perhaps it would be best for you to go home to Texas."

There was the click of the phone as his mother rang off.

Her heart in freefall, Gayle dialed Dom's mobile but got a recording in French. "We're sorry, but you have reached a number that is no longer in service."

She phoned Dom's home next and spoke with his butler Ives, who regretted to inform her that *Monsieur* Trudeau had left town indefinitely and could not be reached. "He asked me to give you his apologies for the inconvenience and said, 'The marriage would have been a mistake.' I'm so sorry, *mademoiselle*."

Gayle closed her laptop without bothering to save the unfinished letter. What was the point? Susan was in Houston, too far away to help.

If only Gayle could believe Dom had willingly disappeared. A month had passed since he left. She rose and crossed to the window, gazing out at the Paris night. Spring had cast its spell on the city. Roses, honeysuckle and clematis twined about the wrought iron fence below, the fragrance wafting through the open window, testifying to renewal and new beginnings.

Yet she was mourning the surrender of a dream, even as she clung to its remnants. Why couldn't she accept that Dom had abandoned her before their wedding? The media and everyone Dom knew would assume he'd fled rather than marry an American nobody.

Gayle couldn't come to grips with his alleged desertion and doubted she ever would. Not while her heart warned her that he was in trouble and needed her.

In what seemed like another life, she recalled their first meeting two years earlier. As the new marketing general manager with Transway Airlines' Paris office, she'd attended a party for the company's premier accounts. Her assistant Clyde Mort had pointed Dom out as an important client. "Come on, I'll introduce you."

Gayle glanced at the elegant man across the room and followed in Clyde's wake. She winced as he halted next to Dom and interrupted his conversation mid-sentence.

"Dominic Trudeau. I'd like you to meet Gayle Regan."

"How do you do?" Dom murmured, the twinkle in his eyes setting her at ease. They shared a smile of amusement, in complete agreement over Clyde's crassness without ever having spoken a word.

She knew that Dominic often flew with Transway, and that several of his holding companies shipped with the airline as well. At first, her reserve had presented a challenge to Dom. Yet they soon discovered a similar taste in books, plays, and shared an absolute fetish for the ballet.

Then Gayle's best friend Susan had arrived in Paris to investigate a student's disappearance from an exclusive French school. For a period, Dom appeared to be the chief suspect. Gayle had worked with him to clear the school and his name. In the process they fell in love.

Now she feared Dominic had been kidnapped or was being prevented from contacting anyone. There was no one she could think of to turn to except— She shook her head slowly.

Did she dare call Interpol Agent Francois Rodiet, Susan's friend and former fiancé?

Impulsively, she grabbed her mobile and dialed his exchange, but quickly hung up as she'd done on a dozen occasions. Why should he believe Dom was in trouble when no one else would?

Her phone rang, and with a start she picked it up.

On the other end of the line, Francois said, "Mademoiselle Regan, I am curious why it is you keep ringing me and hanging up? Your name and number are on my caller ID."

"Monsieur Rodiet, I'm Susan Pardue's friend. I've been trying to gather the courage to ask for your help. Dominic's in trouble."

"Mademoiselle, as much as I could wish it, there is nothing I can do to bring your fiancé back. One must face reality, no matter how difficult."

Gayle grimaced. She coped with Dom's seeming desertion daily with much of Paris looking on.

As if he had read her thoughts, he said, "Reporters are not known for their sensitivity. Better perhaps to return to your country and family."

"For Susan's sake, won't you meet with me and hear what I have to say?"

After a few moments of silence, he sighed. "Now it is you who have left me no choice. I will be there shortly. What is the address?"

She gave it to him and hung up. While she waited, Gayle struggled to order her suspicions about Dom's disappearance, which must be logically assembled and examined.

Dominic had been three days from happiness, when his aspirations burned into hot ashes on a foreign field in East Texas. They had vanished like smoke, as he surely must.

Once again, he would cling to duty, burying his emotions in the cause. "For unto whomsoever much is given, of him shall much be required; and to whom men have committed much, of him they will ask the more," Dom murmured in his native French, quoting Luke 12:48, the scripture that had become the mantra of his life at an early age.

With a soundless groan for what he'd lost, he treaded onto the blacktop road where he'd parked the older model Camry caked with mud from the recent rains. Sweat beaded on his forehead and trickled down his back from the Texas heat and humidity. It was only spring. What must summer be like?

He climbed into the car and drove toward Houston. If fantasies had wings, he would catch the afternoon flight to Paris, leaving this debacle for Guy, his Interpol colleague, to clean up. Instead, Dom would have to hunker down in East Texas and cover the mistakes of others before engaging in the important job ahead.

He exited I-45 onto the Hardy Toll Road. From the corner of his eye, he caught a glimpse of curious brown spots crawling on his trouser leg. A swift glance down as he crossed three lanes of traffic to angle into the right lane caused him to shudder. Ticks. He was surrounded and besieged in more ways than he had imagined possible.

Dom whipped onto the 610 Loop and set the car on cruise control to allow him to see how much damage the insects were doing. He was shocked to see he was covered with the bloodsuckers. Nothing to do but continue to his meeting and deal with the problem there.

To take his mind off the ticks, Dom focused on the tranquility of the blue sky, wishing a measure of its serenity could drop into his life. His existence of late had become an unrewarding exercise in patience and control.

Twenty minutes later, he pulled into the shaded garage behind Guy's home in the Heights and entered the servants' quarters in back where he often stayed. With a grimace, Dom stripped and tossed his clothes outside, then began removing the offensive pests before stepping into a hot shower.

If only his relationship with Gayle could be resolved as efficiently as the delicate removal of these parasites. Dispirited, he dressed and strode outside, crossing to the house and into the study.

Guy, as dark as Dom was blond, sat behind a massive walnut desk, hard at work on his laptop. Dom grabbed a soft drink from the small fridge in the corner and sank into a leather chair. "Everything went as you expected."

Guy quirked an eyebrow. "I merely ran the analysis."

"I wanted the pilot and copilot spared. We could have warned them."

"Hassledorf's hands were in the till like the rest. He died because of his own greed."

"Yes, he was criminally responsible for his actions. But was it wrong of him to want to give his dying wife the medical care she needed?"

"We don't make those calls, Dom. If you're going to feel sorry for someone, how about Hassledorf's copilot. He was entirely innocent." Guy spread his hands in a gesture of frustration.

Dom knew Guy was right. If Interpol had intervened, Fahid would have been warned of their surveillance, inevitably leading to more deaths.

Dom was letting his emotions intrude on the job, and the situation with Gayle was distracting him. He'd have to quit thinking about how wounded she must be feeling, or he'd never be able to concentrate. He schooled his features to a practiced impassiveness. "Have we zeroed in on the cargo the plane was carrying?"

"Diamonds. Fahid had paid the pilot to smuggle them, while overtly contracting with Carey International to transport a shipment of semiprecious stones to make the transaction appear legit. The working theory is Fahid is using illegal profits to fund his brand of terrorism."

"The trip to Tulsa must have been a diversionary tactic to get the stolen diamonds out of Houston, until they could safely take them to New York."

"Yeah. Stealing jewels in Amsterdam and flying them directly to New York would be a red flag the thieves would want to avoid."

"There is a remote possibility, the gems might be on the plane or in the remaining rubble."

"If so, the investigation into the crash will uncover them."

Dominic still questioned the aviator's guilt. He didn't fit the profile of a thief or a traitor. Dom mulled aloud, "Maybe we're looking at this wrong. What if the pilot had planned all along to report the smugglers for the reward, using the diamonds as evidence, and Fahid got wind of his intentions?"

"Imagine anyone having the guts to betray Fahid?"

Dom frowned. "You've got a point. Would a man trying to save his wife turn his family into targets for terrorists?"

"Not likely. Unless they were going into witness protection."

"Or he thought Fahid was running contraband. Smugglers are not nearly as scary as terrorists," Dom said with satisfaction, his mind turning to the next question. "Any other leads on Fahid's motive in engineering the pilot's death?"

"Why else but to silence him? If there's more, it's up to you to pinpoint the connection."

"All right. If there is nothing else, I'm leaving."

Guy nodded. "Watch your back. Your game is off lately."

Dom's smile was mocking, "I didn't know you cared."

His attention shifted to his laptop. "Get out of here so I can get back to work."

With a wave, Dom slipped from the room.

From her third-floor apartment window, Gayle watched Francois pause outside the weathered saffron building before entering. When the bell rang, she opened the door with an uncustomary hesitancy.

"Monsieur, won't you come in?" She led him to the living room. "May I get you some coffee?"

He declined as she waved him to a chair and sat across from him.

His gaze moved from the autumn landscape with shimmering aspens above the fireplace to the antique furniture, and then to the gold tapestry rug on the marble floor. "The room makes a stunning backdrop for you as it would for any redhead," he said, with a lift of his brow.

"Thank you, if that's a compliment?"

"*Oui*. Despite the obvious awkwardness, I mean to be frank. Dominic and I have been friends for years."

"Yes, he told me you've been close since childhood."

Francois's expression became grave. "Dom contacted me before departing Paris to explain he had changed his mind about marrying you. He believed it would be kinder to you both if he left for a period. He made it clear there's no place for you in his life. It would be better if you accepted this."

Her eyes prickled with tears and hurt clawed at the back of her throat. "Why, for heaven's sake, didn't you tell me this on the phone? You could've spared us both—" She rose, not waiting for an answer, and he accompanied her to the door.

"I am sorry," he said, turning to face her with one hand on the handle. "I meant to be kind, and it seemed cruel to relate Dom's regrets on the telephone. Go home, mademoiselle. Find yourself a nice American and marry him. You will be much happier." The door closed behind him with a snap.

Gayle grabbed a tissue, wiping the dampness from her face. How could she be sure he'd told her the truth? That he wasn't another person trying to separate her from Dom. Had Francois spoken with Dom? Gayle knew how to find out.

She picked up her mobile and dialed the number of her friend and colleague Abby Verrater. "Abby, remember back on the Riviera when you said to call if I ever wanted help?"

"Yes. You saved my life that day. I meant every word."

"I need a copy of Dom's phone records ASAP."

"I'll move on it immediately."

"Thanks for not asking any questions. Now, I owe you."

It was raining when Gayle turned onto the long sweeping drive leading to the Trudeaus' residence. A sense of desperation impelled her to make one more attempt to discover if Dominic's parents had learned anything since his disappearance. The rain came down in long sheets, obscuring the formidable estate. She shivered, dread of confronting the Trudeaus' snobbish contempt congealing her stomach to *blancmange*.

She forced herself from the Porsche, nearly oblivious to the water beating against her hat and trench coat, sloshing its way down her black fashion boots.

Gayle rang the doorbell. The butler answered promptly, sympathy and exasperation in his stern gaze. "Mademoiselle, the Trudeaus are not home to you."

"Please, Yves, is there any news?"

He shook his head and started to close the door.

"Wait. I know you care for Dominic. He told me how special you were to him. How growing up he spent more time with you than his father." Yves face softened, and she pressed on. "You saw him the day he left. Was he troubled? Did any visitors drop in who might have disturbed him?"

Yves hesitated. "He seemed happy, but he did receive a call, which had him frowning. He left shortly after."

"I knew it. Dominic's in trouble and needs us."

The butler swallowed and said gruffly, "Mademoiselle, there is nothing more I can tell you, but should pertinent information surface, the proper authorities will be notified."

"Will you phone me?" She reached out to give him one of her cards, but he shook his head regretfully and closed the door.

Gayle let the card drop to the ground and walked away disheartened. She climbed back into the emerald-green Porsche that Dom had given her as an engagement present and drew a deep breath. She swiped at her tears. Though she tried to overlook it, his parents' treatment of her wounded Gayle.

It was time she returned to Transway, but the thought of facing everyone tempted her to delay the inevitable. At Dom's suggestion, she had arranged a month off for their honeymoon and some space for adjustment. When the wedding was canceled, she agreed to deal with departmental emergencies from her apartment in the interim, but her leave was almost up. A part of her wanted to pack her bags and fly home to America. Yet she needed to work and focus on the successes in her life.

She could endure smirks and innuendos more than the pity of the kindest of her colleagues, and Gayle knew it might get worse. Still, it was fortunate she'd insisted on keeping her job for the first year of their marriage despite Dom's protest.

The discussion had marked their first serious disagreement and it was one she had been determined to win. With a final glance at the Trudeaus' unyielding mansion, she dug her keys from her purse and started the car. It was yet another reminder of Dominic's kindness and care for her, which made it difficult to move on and cut the past.

When she had told Dom that she didn't want a new automobile, that her Citroën was fine, he had quietly taken her hand. "*Chéri*, let me do this for you. It gives me such pleasure."

He had kissed her then, telling her how much he loved her. "You won't refuse my gift, will you?"

Her independence at that moment had seemed unimportant and she'd agreed. Gayle stared at the engagement ring on her finger. There was so little of Dominic left to her, a few letters, a message on her answering machine that she played every night, dried orchids, this car and all the memories that sent her grief spiraling out of control.

Angry, she shook off the self-pity and absorption that characterized her lately, determined to get through the rest of the day without breaking down and making a further spectacle of herself. She backed the car out of the driveway and exited onto rue Chanoinesse glad the ordeal was done.

It was not quite dark when Gayle arrived home. She let herself in quietly and stood wondering what she was going to do. "If you love him, you'll follow him." She heard the words so clearly in her mind, they could have been spoken. She loved him enough to follow him, but how to begin? It was time she quit acting like a fool and became the investigator she'd been trained to be.

Gayle had sources, though she'd never considered using them for personal reasons. She could call in some favors. She sensed whatever had taken Dom from her went much deeper than their personal relationship. An innate purpose in his life, she'd perceived—a life separate from her. Strange, she'd never realized it until now. What other signs had she tuned out?

Abby Verrater was perplexed about how to proceed, which was unlike her. She was nearing forty and had been at manipulative spy games for two decades. She tried to remember when the turning point had occurred, but there were too many twists and too many cases.

Her friendships through the years were as predictable as volcanic meltdowns. Chiseled out of cold, hard lava, they incinerated into ashes. The eruptions of these relationships were wrenching but necessary to do the job.

She ran a trace on Dominic's phone records per Gayle's request, although Abby already knew what she'd find. During operations, she made a point of keeping all the players on the board in view.

2

Magnificent snow-covered Alps stretched as far as Dominic could see, their purity creating a yearning inside him. Poised beneath a mirror of brilliant blue sky, the slopes appeared transformed into glistening sheets of Bohemian cut-glass.

For a blinding minute, he stared at the crystal reflections, the repercussions of his past crowding in. Then he regained his composure. His mistake lay in forgetting his commitments. When Gayle had whirled into his life, he'd tossed logic aside. Caught off guard, he failed to anticipate the approaching collision. Torn between duty and love, his imploding intentions fragmented, dividing him from Gayle for good.

Dominic would do his duty. He hated wounding Gayle. The bottom line—he had no choice. None whatsoever.

He swung around and walked into the plush hotel, traversing the marble foyer to the private conference room reserved for the morning's meeting.

Dom paused on the threshold, absorbing the state of affairs before greeting the five men there. "Gentleman, I am told you have urgent information." He eased into the remaining empty seat at the round table where the others sat.

Lance gave him a measured look, the weathered pockmarks on his face receding into his corded turtleneck sweater. With a disgruntled air, he handed Dominic an agency briefing. "Read the report and then we'll talk."

He agreed with a meekness that caused Lance to regard him with suspicion.

Dom focused on the update, seeking any links to the fiasco that in effect had hijacked his life. Intelligence had picked up chatter of a three-pronged attack on Paris, London and New York scheduled for the end of summer or early fall. Nothing was concrete but as a precaution he would investigate further. Paris was his home.

In the brief, Dom noted a curious reference to Walter Helmut, the German ambassador who was murdered in the United States five years ago, along with a reference to his wife's subsequent disappearance. He found the document raised more questions than it answered.

He set it aside. "Okay, what's this about?"

Lance nodded to the suited man wearing dark horn-rimmed glasses across from him and said, "I'm going to relinquish this portion of the briefing to special analyst Kern Jacobs."

Kern, a middle-aged, lanky redhead, emitted a sense of suppressed energy as he strolled to the front of the room and pulled down some analytical charts. "The data here was compiled by experts from several fields before it was transferred to our department for processing. My team has put together a scenario of coincidences that we believe led to the death of Walter Helmut."

He took a moment to study the men, then nodded to Lance. "Go ahead and dim the lights, and we'll run through the video clips."

Dominic's attention was captured at once by the images on the screen.

The video time stamp showed Walter Helmut, looking weary and anxious, entering the Washington D.C. German Embassy parking garage at 11 p.m. He paused beside his black Mercedes, drew out his keys and opened the driver's door. Helmut slid into the seat and started the engine, activating the automobile's hidden camera surveillance and sound unit.

Three dark-skinned men leapt from the shadows and climbed into the vehicle, two in the rear and one in the front, surrounding Helmut. From behind, a knife pressed against his back and a hand covered his mouth.

"*Sprechen Sie nicht,*" one of the men warned in German. The man in the front passenger seat inched closer, pointing a gun at Helmut's chest. "When my colleague removes his hand, you must remain silent or else."

Helmut nodded and murmured into the camera, "Kidnapping—possibly terrorists. German Muslims."

The man scowled, raising his weapon menacingly. "What are you mumbling? I said silence."

"I was praying."

"Drive home as you routinely do. Maybe this prayer to Allah will help you, and then maybe not."

"My wife is at home. She is expecting our first child." He glanced sideways. "But you already know that."

"Quiet. You Germans think aloud too much!"

"Why are you doing this? I'll pay anything you ask."

The man beside Helmut spat at him, then jerked his right arm from the wheel and twisted it behind his back.

Helmut lost control of the car.

"Drive, you German infidel. This is for Fahid."

"*Gott in Himmel,*" Helmut whispered.

"Slow down," the man ordered in a raised voice. "It is not yet time to die."

The video cut to a street cam clip of the car swerving onto the sidewalk, scraping the downtown buildings. Sirens sounded from behind as two police cars approached.

"*Gut,*" grunted Helmut. Then a bullet plowed into his chest, and the steering wheel was wrenched from his hold. "*Meine Liebling, Ich habe dich im Stich lassen.*"

Dominic's chest tightened as he translated those last words: "My love, I have failed you." God, how he could identify. If only he could make amends to Gayle. He blinked as the lights came on.

Kern resumed speaking. "This is what we have: Summer 2005, the ambassador and his wife Pia recognized Fahid Ally, a terrorist with dual citizenship, at a Denmark hotel." Kern pointed to the site on the map.

"Later, perhaps innocently, the Helmuts observed Fahid meeting with Sequor, a prominent French politician, outside the Burger King in downtown Copenhagen." Kern directed everyone's attention to the place on the map.

"That evening the Helmuts came across Fahid and Ari Mslam, an identified member of al-Qaida, at a nondescript café." He indicated the location. "As you can see, the sightings occurred in spots seemingly unrelated."

He gave the men a searching glance. "In our line, we don't buy into coincidences and neither do the terrorists who witnessed the Helmuts near them on three unlikely occasions in less than twenty-four hours. Subsequently, a contract was put out on the couple. His wife's body has never surfaced. Some believe she was snuffed out, others that she helped orchestrate her husband's death."

Kern introduced various displays with photos and intelligence on the terrorists and the politician. After a brief rundown, he concluded, "Now we'll open for discussion. Dominic, you look as though you have a question."

Dom shifted in his seat, wishing the day were over. "Why the interest in Helmut five years after his murder? And is his death or his missing wife linked to the **alleged** threats on Paris, London and New York?"

"Excellent questions. I wish we could answer them all. There has been recent chatter that leads us to assume the events of five years ago might be related to these threats or have a significance we've yet to uncover. But five years have passed, making it even more difficult to get at the truth."

Kern responded to several more queries, then motioned his colleague to the front. "Lance is the agency's lead investigator on the missing wife, and he'll bring you up to speed."

Lance passed out copies of Pia Helmut's picture and bio. "As you can see, Pia was born in Connecticut. Her father served a lengthy term as the former United States ambassador to Germany. His family lived with him abroad which is where his daughter met Helmut.

"Pia's mother is French and her relatives remain active in political circles. Her third cousin is the French politician Sequor whom you witnessed meeting with Fahid in Copenhagen."

He paused. "Pia's schooling and associations appear unremarkable, except for her American college roommate Sara who married Ari Mslam, a Syrian and an al-Qaida operative. You may recall earlier in the video the Helmuts observed Sara's husband Ari meeting with Fahid at a small café off the beaten path. Like Pia, Sara vanished about five years ago."

Dominic's pager went off. He signaled an apology to the other men, unlocked the door and stepped out of the room. Ari had neglected to inform him of the meeting with Fahid that the Helmuts had observed. Dom sent Ari a text: "Urgent that we talk." Only about three people knew Ari Mslam was working undercover for Interpol, and Dom was his handler.

Dom rang Francois back and listened intently.

"The plane search came up empty. Where could the diamonds be?"

"On their way to New York via Oklahoma?" Dom queried. "To think Fahid would leave them on the sabotaged plane was a forlorn hope. Any success at tailing Fahid?"

"No, but we've simply got to crack his organization and stop any attacks," Francois said. "Can you imagine the devastation if Paris, London and New York were hit?"

"I don't want to. Interpol has to prevent those jewels from being sold to fund more atrocities," Dom said.

3

Clyde Mort slowly closed his office door, the pressure of his tenuous position causing him to hyperventilate. From the start he knew there was one sure means to handle the problem, and that was to undermine Gayle Regan and force her out.

It hadn't been enough. Here she was, back again. He needed to get rid of her before she toppled the walls of his deception. He couldn't afford to have her stumbling onto evidence, leaving him vulnerable to criminal investigation, or worse, incarceration.

When Clyde failed to make general manager of marketing, and Transway brought Gayle into the company, he realized he might be in trouble. He couldn't imagine what had led them to suspect his department of embezzlement in the first place. If it weren't for that, he would have been promoted, and she wouldn't have the position, which should be his.

He forced himself to calm down. The situation was controlled. Tonight, her end was in sight. He'd made sure of it. The brotherhood had promised to help, and Clyde had accepted the offer, despite his preference to work alone.

Gayle paused in the middle of the report she was compiling and drank in her surroundings. This morning she'd taken the plunge and returned to work. It felt wonderful to be back in her element. She sat behind the ornate walnut desk she'd found in a dusty second-hand store during those early days in Paris.

A smile flickered as she recalled her pleasure in redoing the modern, sterile office the company had assigned her. The room's present warmth and tasteful elegance were a contrast to the impersonal workspace she'd first beheld.

The intercom buzzed. "Clyde is here to see you."

"Send him in, Helen."

The door burst open and Clyde entered, cloaked in self-importance. She waved him to a seat but he hovered over her, seemingly agitated at not being there to welcome her.

She looked up at him. "No one knew I was arriving this morning. I preferred to slip back into my routine without a lot of fanfare."

He adopted an ingratiating smile, his hazel eyes shadowed with disapproval. "If there's anything I can do . . ." he began.

"Thank you. Not at the moment. I am rather busy . . . if there's nothing else you wanted . . ." She gave him an inquiring look. Gayle understood he coveted her job. His lack of subtlety, though amusing upon occasion, was especially irksome today.

He squared his shoulders, his chest puffed out. "About the CI matter—"

"Is there a problem with Carey International?"

He appeared nonplussed. "Nothing that need concern you much. I wanted you to know I have the situation covered." He began reversing out of her office. "I've got to go. See you later."

Gayle suspected Clyde was entangled in some imbroglio. But how did it involve CI, a private airline carrier they often used? Any scheme he devised was bound to be awkward for her. He'd made it his mission to place her at a disadvantage whenever possible.

In the past, with hopes of upsetting her, Clyde had even escorted Chantal, one of Dom's former girlfriends, to events Dominic and Gayle attended. Chantal had vied for Dom's attention, clinging to him while attempting to oust Gayle. Though she sympathized with the woman, it was disconcerting to be the object of her jealous harassment. After all, Chantal was married to a reputable doctor who seemed to adore her. Still, she had been hurt by Dom, too. Gayle reflected with bitter irony on the foolishness of love.

> If music be the food of love, play on . . .
> O! It came o'er my ear like the sweet sound
> that breathes upon a bank of violets,
> Stealing and giving odour. Enough! No more:
> 'Tis not so sweet now as it was before. . . .

How well Shakespeare comprehended the follies and intricacies of love. If life were but a play, like *Twelfth Night*, she'd write herself a happy ending.

Gayle pressed the intercom. "Helen, bring me the Trudeau files."

"All of them?"

"Yes, I want a comprehensive overview of their business with Transway. And I need the CI files to catch up on what's been happening during my absence."

While she waited, Gayle reached into her purse and brought out the notebook she used to record Dom's movements. She then put in a call to Francois.

She greeted him. "I have a quick question. When did you last speak with Dominic?"

His voice tight with annoyance, he asked, "Does it matter?"

"Yes, to me."

"If you insist, the week he disappeared."

She noted the dates in the ledger. "Before or after our canceled wedding day?"

"I wasn't keeping record."

Good, she'd managed to upset him. Maybe now he'd let his guard slip. "I suppose not," she said, placating him. "Have you heard from him lately?"

"No, and you?" he asked with the smugness of one who has no doubt as to her answer.

"Nothing."

"I did warn you."

"Hmm. I wonder what you aren't telling me."

"There you go, imagining things again. There are no secrets to uncover here." His reply was too smooth and practiced.

She hung up, sensing he was lying. His reasons puzzled her. Was he acting in friendship to Dom or was his agenda more sinister?

Helen brought in several boxes containing the Trudeau files and set them on the drop leaf table against the wall. She placed the CI files, the morning mail and several letters requiring signatures in the middle of Gayle's desk.

From the size of the stack, Gayle knew she would be working late. "Thanks, Helen. There's one more item."

"Yes?"

"Have you noticed any activities in my absence that should be brought to my attention?"

"Like what?" She failed to meet Gayle's gaze.

"I'm well aware of Clyde's plotting to get my job, and I imagine that he dared even more with me conveniently gone."

Helen gave her a relieved smile. "Clyde is forward, isn't he? He instructed me to pull all the CI files and then get the attorneys on the phone. I'm not sure what it was about. Though I did hear him say that the contract was made on the basis of your personal relations rather than sound business practice."

"I appreciate your telling me, and don't worry, your confidences will stay between the two of us."

"Thank you. I hope you get it straightened out. I much prefer working for you."

"Helen, you are a treasure."

After Helen left, Gayle dug into the CI records. While it was true that her brother Seth had referred Mitch Carey, his friend and CEO of Carey International, to her, the relationship was purely professional.

CI's initial contract was set up on solid business principles. Any further negotiations would be based on the same, as far as she was concerned. Unfortunately, one of CI's pilots, allegedly intoxicated, had crashed, killing the flight crew. The investigation was ongoing. Negligence charges were pending against the company regarding their alleged failure to screen the pilot for drugs or alcohol. The families of the deceased were also suing the firm for damages. CI's bottom line had to be suffering.

She logged onto their website and studied the financial records and prospectus. Clyde was right to be concerned, but CI's insurance should handle liability from any lawsuits. Government fines and rulings were another matter.

If Transway canceled CI's contract, the business would be left in a more precarious situation. Clyde had overstepped his authority by engaging in negotiations without consulting her. She may have been officially on vacation, but it was understood she remained available and should be contacted for emergencies and special problems.

Gayle considered how best to handle CI and Clyde, both potentially dangerous. She studied the files, creating projections and analyzing the company's future viability. It soon became clear Transway had nothing to lose, and continuing its relationship with CI would be advantageous. The original contract's provisions protected Transway from any failure on CI's part to perform, as well as any liability.

She pressed the intercom. "Helen, can you come in, please?"

"Be right there."

The door opened and her PA said, "Also, Kara from Legal called and will try to drop by, if that's convenient."

"I'll ring her in a bit. Meanwhile, I'd like you to draw up a renewal contract for Carey International, same terms, new dates."

She gave Helen several moments to complete her notes. Next, Gayle dictated letters to her immediate boss Jeff, president of the marketing division; the legal department; and Clyde, summarizing her conclusions and subsequent renewal offer to CI. "I'd like these to go out this morning with a copy of the tender to both Legal and Jeff. And get Mitch Carey on the phone, please."

"I'll jump right on it." A conspiratory gleam in her eyes, she left.

After Gayle had a chance to learn more about what had transpired in her absence, she'd deal with Clyde directly. If he continued to work with her, Clyde would learn he needed to become a team player.

Helen buzzed her. "Carey's on the line."

Gayle picked up the phone. "Mitch, how are you?"

"Middling to fair, and yourself?"

"Back to work at last, after a long vacation. Terribly sorry to hear about the crash. I thought you'd want to know I'm getting a renewal contract out to you today."

"That's great news. Any modifications I should be looking for?"

"No, the documents are status quo with mere date changes. I wish I could have offered improved terms, but that's impossible now."

"Understood. I appreciate your handling this personally. Frankly, I was concerned."

"Well, relax. It's on its way. I've got to run, but good luck, Mitch."

Gayle decided to tackle the files on Dom's import and export businesses next. Emotionally, she'd been delaying the inevitable. A line from Dickinson flitted through her mind: "Hope is a thing with feathers that perches in the soul." *Au contraire*, any feathers of hope in her life had taken wings and flown to a far-off land buried in her past.

She didn't anticipate unearthing much of interest but she crossed the room to the stacks on the table, tracking Dom's long association with Transway. Some days she hated him. If only she could forget him. Her anger and resentment swelled. She had to get a grip. In an effort to concentrate, Gayle scanned the box tags, muttering aloud, "Contracts, renewals, financials, flight plans." She stopped. "Hmm. That sounds promising." She opened the lid and thumbed through the flight manifesto records of several of Dominic's holding companies that were routinely shipping with Transway. The info seemed prosaic.

It would help if she knew what she was searching for. Maybe she should start with cargo shipped to troubled hot spots. She wavered. What did she expect to find? This self-inflicted torture must stop. God, help me let go of Dominic.

Helen buzzed her on the intercom. "Kara's here to see you."

Relief whooshed through her. "Fine. I need a break. Send her in."

Kara entered, slim and athletic, her short pomegranate curls bouncing as she moved to hug Gayle. "It's positively great to have you back. I've missed you."

"Me too."

"Everything going okay?"

"Yes, as you can see from all these files, massive catch up is in progress. Have a seat."

Kara sank into a chair and studied Gayle with concern. "How are you really?"

"Continuing on the best I can, step by step."

"I'm glad to hear it. Relax, I'm not about to ask any more awkward questions, but I want you to know I'm here for you."

Gayle smiled her thanks, relieved to move past the issue of Dom's desertion. "Say, have you checked the Carey contract renewal I sent over?" Gayle knew Kara's carefree and sunny nature might lead some to underestimate her keen intelligence, but Gayle relied on her sound legal counsel.

"Yes, it looks viable. Clyde's nose is going to be bent out of shape about this. He's been trying hard to get at you."

"Yeah, I've noticed. Wouldn't it be nice to get rid of him first? Any ideas?"

Kara rose. "Shall we wait for a dark and stormy night to do the ugly deed?"

"I wish we could." Gayle chuckled. "You're good medicine."

"Duty clamors. *Au revoir*, my friend."

"Thanks for stopping by." Much encouraged after Kara's visit, Gayle realized she'd laughed for the first time since Dom's disappearance.

She directed her thoughts back to work where yet another cloud hovered on her purview that must be dealt with. It was why she'd accepted the airline's initial job offer per the agency's instructions. Her personal crisis with Dom had distracted her from the mission.

Gayle moved to her desk and logged onto Transway's pension plan for the company's Marketing Division, which effectively traded as a mutual fund. She studied the stock's recent movements, noting an abnormal volume of buying and selling as well as irregular activity in accounts that were usually dormant. Even more of a red flag, most of the transactions occurred after hours.

She punched in several keys, trying to follow one of the smaller deals to the broker. Someone had covered their tracks well. Next, she went to the auditing software to discover who was in the system at the time of the exchange. The search led to Clyde.

Gayle quickly forwarded a report confirming what she'd found to Elliot, her agency liaison with the CIA. His response was swift. "Stay on it and set up traces on the larger acquisitions too."

Gayle decided to skip lunch and study the logs, a tedious process, which revealed zilch. Someone had to have been online when the shares were sold and then, to hide their identity, must have tampered with the audit files. These were notoriously difficult to hack, so the suspect list could be narrowed to employees with the security clearance to gain access.

She exited the software and turned to tackle the mail, thumbing through the pile. Her gaze fell on one envelope in particular, postmarked Paris. With a shaky hand, she picked up Dominic's letter.

Chéri,

We were not meant to be. I loved you, but not enough. Forgive me for playing the coward, but it seemed more fitting for the two of us not to meet. Enjoy life and forgive me if you can. Until then, please relinquish any attempts to find me.

Au Revoir,

Dominic

She swallowed past the lump of pain in the back of her throat. A tremor ran through her. He didn't love her. How cruel of him to wait and tell her now. What everyone had said was true. She'd been a fool. Gayle struggled for composure.

Somehow, she got through the rest of the day, a forced smile in place, while the inner axis of her being wobbled off course and spun out of control.

The sun hung low in the sky when Gayle reached the Latin Quarter. It had been Dom's favorite haunt. He brought her to Louis's Bistro on their first date. He said it was stimulating to escape from the snobbery and the reporters for a whiff of realism.

There was rarely a spot in front. She parked a few blocks down and walked the relatively peaceful streets to the place where they'd eaten often. What was she doing here? His letter made his feelings brutally clear. Why couldn't she give him up?

Instead, she had driven to their restaurant on automatic pilot, inventing excuses for him at every turn. His kidnappers forced him to write the letter. He wanted to spare her feelings. Gayle wanted to believe he would never willingly leave her.

Yet she was torn. Was it her imagination that they had shared a great love? That she could still feel the beat of his heart and his will to be with her? What an idiot she'd become.

Louis, the short and balding owner, greeted her with a compassionate look and a hearty, "*Bonjour.*" He paused in the act of whisking a cloth over one of the tables. "Mademoiselle, you must not come to this part of the city alone. Whatever would Monsieur Trudeau say?" He stopped, aware of his gaffe, then continued with a shrug. "I'm sorry. Come, now that you are here, sit and eat."

He seated her next to the window rather than in their usual secluded alcove.

Gayle squirmed at the doubts and insecurities leading her to question Dom's motives and actions. Yet they had taken up residence, refusing to budge until she examined them. "Louis, did Dominic ever bring anyone else here?"

He shook his head. "No one besides his old school friend, Monsieur Rodiet."

Dom had mentioned they were close. She waved aside the menu Louis offered. "Bring me a salad and roast chicken. Yours is the best in Paris."

After he left, Gayle brought out the bulky envelope she had received from Abby and pulled out Dom's phone records. On the calls to and from his home, she noted Francois's number appeared frequently. His exchange, however, did not pop up on the day Dom went missing. Though there was one from Houston matching the approximate date and time the butler had given. Who did Dom know in Texas? Most likely a business associate, except the call was to his private line.

She examined both the office phone and cell activity but saw nothing remotely interesting. Her earliest attempts to trace Dom through friends, family, internet, airlines and other avenues had failed. The individual in Houston was the closest she had to a lead.

Louis brought dinner, and she picked at the food. In the backdrop of her mind, Gayle heard Dom's gentle laugh and felt the touch of his hand holding hers. Outside, the sunset, a glorious haze of rose and purple, seemed a stark contrast to her loneliness.

She drew out her mobile and dialed the Texas number.

A male voice answered tersely, "Yes."

Gayle said, "This is the operator. Am I speaking with seven-zero-eight-seven-zero-five-one-seven-seven?"

"Yes. Yes. What do you want?"

"I have a call for Dominic Trudeau."

There was a slight telling pause. "I'm afraid you have the wrong number." The line went dead.

She immediately contacted Abby and asked her to trace the exchange and get back to her.

Gayle paid for her dinner, bid Louis a fond farewell and left. She started down the street, whirling when she heard someone call her name.

Chantal, sophisticated and beautiful as always, hurried to catch up.

Gayle knew Dominic had never been interested in Chantal despite the lady's arsenal of witchery aimed at him.

"We can walk together," the woman huffed as she reached Gayle, pausing to catch her breath.

"This area is a bit out of your league, isn't it?"

"Yes, I had to deliver some papers for Troy."

Gayle knew Chantal had wed Troy, a wealthy and reputable doctor, months before Gayle arrived in Paris. Gayle resumed walking. "You, running errands? Seems most unusual."

"Perhaps. Stranger yet, have you heard anything from Dominic? It's the most delicious scandal."

Gayle increased her pace, striving to outstrip the hurt barreling within, but then, she slowed, squared her shoulders and, ignoring Chantal's inquiry, said determinedly, "Isn't it time you got a life of your own, instead of haunting mine?"

"What kind of existence does a jilted nobody have? Certainly not one I'd want." Chantal stopped next to her car, unlocked the door and got in. "Au revoir."

Gayle experienced a rush of pure rage at the woman's continued harassment. The situation was troubling enough without bumping into a parasite like her. Perhaps she was being unfair and unchristian. She might even have provoked her nemesis's attack, but in this instance, she couldn't summon the least desire to reign in her temper. Chantal had exerted considerable effort to wound her.

Gayle blamed Clyde in part for fanning Chantal's animosity. She and Dom had frequently encountered him squiring the woman to social events in her husband's absence. Clyde's conversational tidbits never failed to direct his companion's wrath at Gayle. His compliments to her, while appearing in the best of taste, invariably inflamed her adversary, much to his amusement.

Gayle climbed into her Porsche and drove in the twilight to the Left-Bank. She sat there as night set in, thinking. A couple holding hands strolled past. With a sigh, she got out of the car and gazed at the river as though the rippling waves could conjure answers. She supposed her connection with the water came from growing up near the Gulf Coast. The Seine, splayed with moonlight beneath the canopy of stars, was stunning.

Still, she shouldn't be there alone in the dark. Though she wasn't strictly alone. The couple sauntering nearby had passed her earlier. A frisson of unease hit her. They walked by once more, pausing to embrace. The man shifted the woman in his arms, drawing her closer. Gayle looked away, embarrassed and relieved. The next moment an arm clutched hers.

Startled, she whirled and saw a man wielding a club. Gayle

screamed as he struck her repeatedly, the searing pain plunging her into unconsciousness.

The couple shared a congratulatory glance. The woman helped her companion drag Gayle to the edge of the bank. She drew out a prepared syringe, stabbing it into Gayle's arm. "That should end it."

The man brushed against her. "Fantastic."

"We'd better grab her stuff and get out of here." She knelt beside Gayle's inert body, sliding Dominic's diamond engagement ring off her finger and removing the sapphires from her ear lobes. She picked up Gayle's purse and rifled through it, removing a set of keys.

They stepped back, studying the body and the surrounding area to ensure nothing was forgotten. The two ambled off, keeping to the shadows.

"That was hot," he whispered, heavily.

His excitement surprised her. She had expected him to be a wimp when it came to his actual involvement in the crime, but clearly the thrill of danger revved his inner engine. Had she misjudged him in other areas? Could he be cleverer than she'd thought? For both their sakes, she hoped not.

When they reached Gayle's Porsche, he unlocked the car and they climbed in. She tossed Gayle's purse onto the back seat. As he sped through the lighted streets, a smirk on his face, she revised her opinion of him. Any novice with a bit of intelligence, cruising in a stolen car, the owner's body a few miles away, should be wary. Something was amiss.

She flinched as a police siren whined from behind, blue lights whirling as it approached and passed. She relaxed, maintaining her silence until they pulled into the rented garage and he shut the door, blocking out the city.

They stripped off their flesh masks and slipped them into a paper bag which would later be dropped into the incinerator, along with the gloves and outer layer of clothing they were wearing.

Her instincts screamed that he was the wrong man for the job. If she'd only realized sooner, another death might have been avoided. Before she could think of how to accomplish his demise, she felt his hands on her shoulder, moving to caress her neck. He increased the pressure as she struggled, gasping for breath until life ceased.

Satisfied, the man thought back over the evening. He had tailed Gayle from the office to Louis's Bistro, then phoned the assassin to meet him, setting in motion the plan to get rid of Gayle. The woman assassin worked with al-Qaida affiliates but wasn't entirely trusted. No one would miss her. He had guessed her interest in Dominic Trudeau was purely operational. He also knew Dominic was with Interpol.

He needed Gayle out of the picture and tonight he had achieved that. He'd rid himself of the woman as well. She knew too much, and he couldn't risk her talking. All in all, it had been a productive evening.

4

American Airlines pilot Seth Regan rushed down the tarmac. He had barely enough time to drive home and change. His mobile rang and he slipped it off his belt, peering at the caller ID before he answered. "Mitch. What's up?"

"Believe me, you don't want to know."

"Bad, huh?"

"Yeah. I'm wondering if you could talk to your sister for me. Gayle assured me a week ago a renewal contract was in the mail, but I haven't received it yet, and she isn't returning my calls."

"This about the crash?"

"I guess. I don't know anymore. I was hoping you could find out."

Seth was silent, debating what to say. He trusted Mitch but didn't like being made the go-between. "I'd like to help, though I'm doubtful anything I could say would make a difference."

"Maybe not," Mitch conceded.

Seth wanted the problem resolved for both their sakes. "You've had some tough breaks. How is the situation at CI?" Mitch had invested most of his capital into his baby, Carey International, a fledgling airline that had shown impressive growth until one of their planes crashed, killing the pilot and crew.

"We're in survival mode, trying to figure out what happened. Our inquiries keep running into strange U-turns. It's almost as if someone is out to sabotage the company. I simply can't think of any motive."

"Scary stuff."

"You've got that right. Thanks anyway. Gotta go, pal."

The phone went dead in his ear. He'd let Mitch down. Seth rubbed the back of his neck distractedly. If Mitch knew how deeply Seth's finances were affected by CI's problems, he'd feel even worse.

It couldn't do any harm to touch base with Gayle and see what was happening. He punched the memory dial for her mobile and got a recording. "We're sorry, the number you are calling is no longer in service." Why would she disconnect her phone without giving him the new number? She wouldn't. He had an uneasy hunch that escalated when he dialed her home number and received the same message. This wasn't like her.

He rang her at Transway and was told she was unavailable. When he insisted this was an emergency, her assistant Clyde came on the line and said Gayle was on leave and he was unable to give out her current address.

"This is her brother, Seth Regan."

"I'm sorry. I didn't realize you were family. Your sister had a minor accident a few days ago, but she's recovering."

"Was she badly hurt?"

"No, she fell and sprained her ankle. I haven't spoken with her personally, but a friend called in to say Gayle would be staying with her until she recovered."

Relieved, Seth said, "I'd like that number, please, if you have it."

"Hold a moment and I'll connect you with reception."

"Thanks for your help."

"Glad to be of service."

Seth wrote down the exchange the receptionist gave him. When he phoned, there was no answer. He kept trying to no avail and by evening he was thinking of worst-case scenarios. He called his parents and casually asked if they'd talked to Gayle lately, and found they were also unable to reach her.

His dad sounded anxious. "She'd contact us, even if she were busy. One of you boys needs to go check on your sister."

Seth contacted his brothers next, explaining, "Gayle seems to have gone off the radar. Mom and Dad are stressed and that's not good for Dad's heart. I'm hoping one of you might fly over and visit her."

His brothers all replied in almost the same terms, "Nice try, but you're the one with a week's leave. Hightail it to Paris and locate Gayle, or else."

Their reaction was a foregone conclusion. Seth closed his eyes in an attempt to stay calm, fearing Gayle's uncharacteristic inaccessibility might prove serious.

5

Ray Regan set the phone down on the desk in his study and stared at the photo of his wife and children taken last Christmas. Gayle and her three brothers had been able to get home for a rare visit.

Gayle kept in touch better than any of his boys, calling and emailing often. It upset him that he hadn't heard from her for several weeks. Seth was concerned too, though he'd tried to hide it on the phone.

Lately, she was never at work or at home when they rang. The canceled wedding had been a sorry business that devastated his darling youngest.

He looked up as his wife Deanie came in with a smile and asked, "Not too busy, are you?"

"Not a chance."

His petite wife was still a whirlwind of motion after forty-four years of marriage. "You're in here brooding about Gayle, aren't you?" she asked.

"What makes you think so?"

She sank into the chair across from him. "Maybe because we all are. I've put off talking about it. I didn't want to distress you. The doctor said you were to relax as much as possible."

"We'll have no more protecting me, please." His blood pressure was fine though the medication he was taking seemed to slow him down. His dear wife was as dramatic as ever and needlessly anxious. Her care for him and the children was a part of who she was, and seeing her left him feeling warm, tender, and more vulnerable than he'd once imagined possible. As they often did, Ray's thoughts strayed to the past and the day they met.

She gazed into his eyes and he knew she was remembering as well. A flight attendant with a competing airline, she had literally bumped into him at the airport, spilling a cup of coffee down his pilot's uniform.

Before long they were married and raising a family. Across his ash paneled study, through the large window to the backyard, he could picture Gayle, his little ballerina, twirling past the azaleas as if she couldn't contain her joy while breaking into a series of somersaults. She was the only one of the children with the curly red hair and blue eyes he'd inherited from his Irish father.

With three protective brothers, she complained that everyone in the family still thought of her as the baby. The siblings remained close despite their busy careers and the distance separating them.

James Owen, the eldest of the boys, was a hotshot pilot in the Air Force. He went by the nickname of J.O. Jason, was perhaps the steadiest of the three, and he owned a small airline in Anchorage. Seth, in the family tradition, his dad liked to think, was an American Airlines pilot. He was the youngest and closest to Gayle in age.

Like her brothers, Gayle's love of aviation came naturally. As a former senior pilot, now retired, Ray maintained a small aircraft which he flew for pleasure. His children it seemed had followed in his footsteps, not precisely, but he had never wanted carbon copies. They were too fine for imitations.

He turned his thoughts back to his wife and the present. "Let's talk about what's worrying you."

"I wondered when you were returning to earth," she teased, then grew serious. "Jason told me that last year Seth referred Mitch Carey, his nice friend with the freight airline, to Gayle at Transway. Apparently, she signed a contract with him to handle part of Transway's surplus freight and has since canceled the renewal option."

Ray shrugged. "Hon, these kinds of things happen every day."

"Yes, but Seth invested some money in CI and neither Gayle nor Mitch knows."

"Let me do a little research. Seth wouldn't invest in a business that wasn't solid. And though Gayle wouldn't intentionally hurt her brother, she has to put Transway's interests first."

"Ray, maybe we should fly to Paris and find out why she's not answering her phone. After all, we're retired. Unless you think the trip might be too much for you?"

"If we don't hear from her soon, we'll go. I wouldn't be surprised, however, to learn one of her brothers is already headed there." He squeezed her hand. "Especially as I asked them to go on our behalf."

Dom boarded his private jet, relieved to be leaving Switzerland. He fastened the seat belt and looked out at the snow-covered mountains as the craft treaded down the tarmac. A ski down those slopes would have been sublime. Not a chance. The agency had hijacked his life and Dom wondered if he'd ever recover.

As the plane approached cruising altitude, he noted black storm clouds. They were in for a bumpy ride. Dom regrouped and mentally ran through the case facts. Ari's wife Sara, known as *the package* for security reasons, had disappeared about the same time as Pia Helmut. Strange how no one had linked the two incidents when they occurred. Possibly a closer examination of the cases had eliminated any association. Helmut and Ari, both foreigners, married Americans. Their wives who were former college roommates had similarly vanished. Ari never mentioned the connection. Could he have missed it in his quest for Sara?

Dom disliked the implications. The two women might be dead, working together, or even be one and the same. Tests would have to be run before he could put the last theory to rest. He had telephoned forensics and ordered a comparison of the two women's fingerprints. If his suspicions were correct, it would narrow the search.

Few knew Ari was one of Dom's covert assets. When they last talked, Ari was distraught after reading a Russian newspaper report he'd received about an unidentified woman found dead in an outlying Moscow park. The anonymous sender of the article had attached a typed note which read:

You can stop searching for her now.
A Friend.

Ari's Russian contacts were already hustling to check out the story, but as the woman had been cremated, any evidence would be difficult to verify. Meanwhile, Dom struggled to link Fahid to the terrorist plots.

Fundamentally, he didn't believe in coincidences. Why would Helmut and his wife engineer meetings with two known terrorists and a prominent French politician? What possible connection could the Helmuts have to Fahid and Ari? Ari claimed he was unaware of the Helmuts until Fahid, disturbed by their presence, had pointed them out.

The contract Fahid allegedly put out on the couple suggested they were not in league, unless the Helmuts had planned a double cross. Dom had placed calls to department moles in Germany, France and Syria and set them all on the task of gathering the answers.

He was still investigating the CI crash and Fahid's involvement in the diamond smuggling, but it was hard going. He'd hoped for answers from Ari, but Fahid was keeping him out of the loop on the jewels.

Did Fahid suspect Ari was working with Interpol? Fahid might even suspect him of bringing in German Intelligence. No, all of that happened five years ago. Ari had proved his allegiance to the terrorists' satisfaction. Fahid and his lot would have checked and found there was no connection between the Helmuts and Ari.

Fahid was on the move. Recently, Dom met with one of the dealers Fahid had allegedly robbed. The diamonds stolen were valued in the millions. Interpol investigations to date suggested Fahid's men had perpetrated the theft at a watch and jewelry trade show in Basel. The problem was the agency's inability to produce evidence linking Fahid directly.

The diamond industry faced new challenges in securing its wares. With the dramatic improvement in the capabilities of jewelry stores to protect stock, most heists had shifted to off-premise locations. Courier and trade show robberies were common. Organized crime and lone thieves liked to strike the couriers who served the stores. Fortunately, every diamond was unique and therefore identifiable, and the FBI and Interpol's recovery network was colossal.

Video surveillance at the Basel trade show had captured the faces of the thieves. They were now being tailed in the hope that they would lead Interpol to Fahid so he could be implicated and charged. It was imperative to trace the profits Interpol suspected were being diverted to fund the three eminent attacks that intelligence had picked up chatter on. Dominic was frantic to make sense of the conundrum he feared might rip the globe apart.

6

Gayle awoke in a panic to strange surroundings. She thrust the covers aside and attempted to rise. Her head pounded and her limbs refused to cooperate. She ached all over. With a moan Gayle fell back on the bed.

She forced herself to concentrate. The luminous dial on a table across the room gave the time as 12:15. As her eyes grew accustomed to the shadows, she sensed the room was small and clean. She sniffed, recognizing an odor of disinfectant much like that in a hospital. Had she been in an accident?

She lay on a soft full-size bed. There were no windows and Gayle was much too lethargic to investigate, almost as if she had been drugged. Worse, she had no recollection of how she came to be there.

Earlier in the evening, she recalled eating a dinner of roasted chicken and salad at Louis's Bistro. Strangely, her last memory was of a woman walking beside her down the street.

Try as she might, she remembered nothing after that. She strained to unravel the mystery. Had she become ill? She put a hand to her hurting head and closed her eyes, shutting out the dark unknown. She soon gave up and drifted back to sleep.

Gayle awoke to an indistinguishable murmur of voices. She felt hot and clammy. Deep languor overcame her as she slipped back into an uneasy drug-like sleep. Then the dream came.

She was running through a field when she fell headlong,

cushioned by a sea of green four-leaf clover. The wind caressed her and an ensuing sense of sweetness engulfed her.

Like a whirling kaleidoscope, the scene changed. She lifted her face heavenward and saw herself standing before a great cathedral. She hesitated, then entered and knelt at the back pew. Her lips formed a soundless prayer, her mind filling with new purpose.

The majesty of a still, soft whisper welled within, "Fear not, for I am with you."

Gayle bowed her head and wept for the grace which had been shown to her.

7

Doctor Langston hummed along with the Beatles' tune, "Something" on the taxi radio. Who would have thought the French liked the Beatles? Then again, why wouldn't they? He was merely surprised to hear a familiar song in English.

That evening Perry was anticipating having dinner with Gayle Regan, a girlfriend from his college days who needed perking up, according to Susan. Thus far his schedule had been packed, and he was looking forward to his first weekend off.

The driver stopped at Perry's hotel. He paid his fare and got out. Still humming, he strolled through the lobby and up to his room. Although he'd officially begun work for Cremont Sanatorium two months earlier, he had yet to find a flat. His new job in Paris included lodging, so he was in no rush to set up housekeeping. The hotel was convenient and comfortable.

He checked his messages, noting with regret that Gayle had not returned his call, then dealt with a few emails from his former secretary and the nurse back home regarding his patients' cases.

Perry grabbed a bottle of *Badoit*, his favorite sparkling water, out of the small fridge and dropped down into a striped, overstuffed chair. His thoughts turned gloomy. He was no closer to a decision now than last week.

He reached into his pocket and pulled out the letter, though he'd memorized the words. Five days to decide whether to try to save or, in effect snuff out a life.

8

Cremont Sanatorium

Leah Weller entered Doctor Langston's office, one hand clutching a long limp strand of her dull brown hair. She sat in her usual seat, resentment and fear burgeoning as she watched the doctor shuffle through the folders on his desk.

Maybe the truth would stop the emotional turmoil. Suddenly, she blurted, "I was not happy last night."

The doctor eyed her with a concern she didn't dare trust. "No? Why was that?"

She reminded herself to be patient and explain, not to act crazy and fall into any trap. "Does there have to be a reason? Maybe I was feeling overwhelmed, like everyone wants a part of me, and I can't make the pieces stretch far enough to fit. Haven't you ever felt similarly?"

"Did something occur yesterday to set off this sense of desperation?"

Tension gripped her. "Hold on there. I never said I was desperate. That's your word, not mine."

He looked at her as if he were soothing a child. "What word would you choose?"

"Can't you leave this alone and move on?"

"Yes, if you're able to."

"Well, of course I can. Isn't that what I've been saying?"

"What do you want to talk about instead?"

"Oh, never mind, nothing. I don't know why I persist in coming here. You're not helping."

"I'm sorry, but perhaps if we give it more time."

"I suppose it's my fault and not yours. It usually is," she said.

"Aha! You are pessimistic." He smiled, inviting her to laugh at the irony and admit the truth.

"Don't be smug. I'm not confessing to guilt about my feelings. Discouraged is more the term I'd choose."

"Discouraged?"

"I hate it when you treat me like I'm insane and use that coaxing voice."

"All I want is the truth."

"The truth. How rich! I've been trying to tell you what happened ever since he died. No one listens to me."

"I am."

"So everyone says, but no one believes me."

"How can you be certain?"

She closed her eyes for a moment and then stared around the drab office, envisioning the cubicle someone would soon lead her back to. The compressed box had constricted her life since her husband's death five long years ago—her only flight these talks, daily showers and walks around the grounds.

Leah wanted to trust that this doctor, who was new on the job, would be different and understand she hadn't murdered her husband. Yet she was afraid to hope, and as the years passed, a new fear, twisted and gnarled, spread like cancer. What if the doctors were right? What if the truth were her greatest enemy?

She gazed across at the man, forlornly. "I'm here and neither of us can change that unless we believe in who I once was. And I'm afraid she no longer exists."

"Why do you think so?"

"She's been away from home too long. I can't find her anymore."

"Does she ever visit?"

"Oh, yes, sometimes in my dreams and every morning when I first wake up. Then I open my eyes and . . . It's hopeless, you see."

"I'm beginning to."

She rose. "I guess I'm ready to go back."

He pushed a button and the attendant in the hallway came in. "Mrs. Weller would like to return to her room." He stood, reached across the desk, and shook her hand. "Leah, there's always hope."

"Hope." A ghost of a smile, unfamiliar and untried, pressed at the corners of her heart and with it the memory of a long-forgotten poem. She spoke its healing words in a soft and raspy voice:

'"Hope" is the thing with feathers –
That perches in the soul –
And sings the tune without the words –
And never stops – at all–'

She paused and glanced up in surprise and wonder at herself.

As if wanting to protect the fragile moment, the doctor continued in a hushed voice in his effort to reach her:

'And sweetest – in the Gale – is heard –
And sore must be the storm –
That could abash the little Bird
That kept so many warm–'

His gaze invited her to continue the poem. It brought light to the storms in her life and she heard herself whisper:

'I've heard it in the chillest land –
And on the strangest Sea –
Yet, never, in Extremity,
It asked a crumb – of Me.'

"Emily Dickinson, 1861," he said in a voice, a bit too hearty as if intentionally breaking the magic thread that had bound doctor and patient. "It's a great favorite of mine."

She nodded, too overcome to speak. It was time to go back. Still, there had been a glimmer, a moment of rare communion. She walked from the room, her head bowed, the attendant's hand on her arm, until she was safely locked in her cubicle.

9

remont Sanatorium

A week later Langston leaned forward in his chair with boyish excitement and turned off the tape recorder on his desk.

His assistant Abby Verrater gave him a curious look. "Leah said yes, when she meant no."

"How could you tell?" The thrill of a possible breakthrough brightened his ho-hum existence, which normally submerged him in duties, charts and patients who rarely responded to treatment.

"I heard it in her voice. There was never any question." Abby smiled, as if sharing in his triumph.

Reality surfaced and with it the too familiar statistical probability of failure. "Let's bring her in and see."

Abby rose to leave but Perry motioned for her to remain seated. "She might feel less threatened with another woman here." He picked up the phone on his desk. "I'd like to meet with patient Weller now."

A few minutes later Leah walked in, aloof, yet he could somehow sense an underlying exhilaration. Could it be their session last week with the poem had signaled a breakthrough? He had been afraid to hope. Perry winced at the doubt weighing him down. The old saying, "Physician heal thyself," was apt.

Leah looked startled, and he perceived her withdrawal.

He willed her to hold his gaze. "I wasn't reacting to you. I had an unpleasant realization about myself."

She nodded her understanding and sat in her usual chair in

front of the desk, seeming to notice Abby for the first time. "Why is she here?"

"As my assistant, she sits in on some cases to observe. Do you mind?"

Leah lowered her head. "My wishes as regards policies here are seldom consulted."

"I don't suppose they are. During our last visit you confided to me the person you once were no longer exists except in your dreams. Did you feel different after the poem?"

"Oh, yes, but only briefly."

"Why do you believe that is?"

Leah shuddered. "Because you changed. It was like you helped open a window and then slammed it shut in my face."

"I try to remain neutral. It's what makes our conversations safe."

"Safe for you."

"Abby has a different theory. She thinks you can no longer be who you were because what you did before frightens you too much."

She shot Abby a venomous look. "Perhaps."

Perry shifted uneasily in his chair. "Does this mean you're ready to discuss the possibility?"

She shook her head furiously. "I can't. I loved my husband. Why won't anyone believe me?"

"I want to trust you, but you need to help me understand. What happened the night your husband died? Can you tell me in your own words?"

"I've told you people and told you. I didn't kill him. Leave me alone, just leave me alone." She started to sob. "You manipulated me, posing as a friend. Take me back to my room. I won't stay here and listen to this, not another word."

"I want what's best for you and that means facing the truth whatever it is and moving on."

Leah rose. "It's no use. I might as well have confessed. No one has ever believed in me but him, the sweetest man I ever knew and loved."

Perry rang for an attendant. "I'm not giving up on you."

"As a murderer or a person?" Leah cackled, an underlying hysteria in the sound. Then she began to speak.

Perry, sensing a breakthrough, leaned forward, listening carefully. The madness had left her voice.

'I felt a Cleaving in my Mind —
As if my Brain had split —
I tried to match it — Seam by Seam —
But could not make them fit.

The thought behind, I strove to join
Unto the thought before —
But Sequence ravelled out of Sound
Like Balls — upon a Floor.'

Then, mimicking his tone from their previous interview, she said in a voice which managed to be both hearty and distancing, "Emily Dickinson, 1864."

Perry clapped. "Bravo! Very apt." He caught the answering gleam in her eyes and on impulse quoted:

'Heavenly Hurt, it gives us —
We can find no scar,
But internal difference,
Where the Meanings, are —'

As if intrigued against her will, she said, "I don't recall that one."

"It's the middle verse from one of Dickinson's poems. Next time I'll recite it in its entirety, if you like?"

The attendant came in and took hold of Leah's arm to lead her out.

"I . . . I'd like to hear it," Leah said, as she turned and left.

10

Gayle regained consciousness with the realization something was dreadfully wrong. The drugged euphoria that had engulfed her seemed to have evaporated, leaving in its place the feeling of a wretched hangover. Thank heavens, she could think and see. For too long everything had been hazy. A glance around the room revealed she was not in a hospital, which troubled her. If she had been in an accident, wouldn't someone have taken her there? Why couldn't she remember?

Before she could panic, the door opened and a young boy peeked in, then raced away, shouting, "*Maman*! Mademoiselle has awakened."

He soon returned with a woman who appeared to be in her early thirties. "Bonjour," she said, her concerned gaze running over Gayle. "I am pleased to see you are a little better."

Gayle's tension eased seeing the kindness in her face. "Where am I? What's happened to me?"

The woman smiled reassuringly. "You have been ill." She turned to her son and spoke in rapid French, "Run get your uncle, quickly." As the boy scampered from the room, she asked, "You understand French, *oui*?"

"Oui. How long have I been here?"

"Two days."

Gayle gasped. Her family, friends and colleagues at work must be frantic. No, surely this kind woman and the doctor would have notified them. But if so, why was she in the care of virtual strangers?

Of course, she wasn't working a regular schedule and no one would have known she was missing.

As if she understood Gayle's bewilderment, the woman explained, "My son found you unconscious on the Left *Quai* and I called an ambulance. There was a wound on the back of your head . . . as if you had been struck. Could you have fallen?"

"I can't remember."

"Perhaps you were mugged. You were bruised and beaten up. Your legs were scraped and you had no purse or identification. The doctor in the emergency room said you were assaulted and drugged."

"I feel as if I've been drugged but how . . . and why . . . and with what?"

Madame sighed. "Someone gave you an overdose of heroin, enough to end your life. The doctor said you were fortunate that heroin works slowly. He administered Naloxone to counteract it. You almost died. If my son hadn't found you when he did. . . . "

"I don't understand." Gayle winced. The strain of thinking about her near-death experience only worsened the pounding in her head.

"You are much too weary for this." The woman handed her a glass. "Drink this for your headache. My brother, who is also a doctor, lives here, which is why you were permitted to return home with us. He has a clinic through the back entrance. The hospital was full, too many cases of the *grippe* this time of year."

Gayle swallowed the mixture, the moisture soothing her parched throat.

"Rest and you will feel better."

Despite her efforts to delay the inevitable, Gayle's eyes closed. "Please, I need to go home," she whispered, lapsing into a deep sleep.

Her dreams returned:

Gayle stood in the market next to the lemons, where she'd run into Chantal who was determined to have her say.

She studied Gayle, appearing to search for a center to spring from, and peering into that core, said, "I'm pregnant."

"Congratulations. You and Troy must be incredibly happy." Finally, Chantal's harassment would end.

The woman inched closer and tilted her head like a haughty prom queen accustomed to the cosmos adapting to her terms. "But the baby is Dominic's."

Gayle experienced the sensation of diving into a backward flip and landing smack on her stomach. Yet in the glaring light of Chantal's smugness, she pulled herself together. "However, will you break it to Troy?"

Chantal seemed to squirm at the idea of her outrageous comments reaching her rich, complacent husband. Then as if dismissing the thought as beneath her, said, "Troy need never know, just you, me and Dominic." She let her words sink in and, having succeeded at delivering the intended blow, walked away into the milling crowd.

Gayle awoke to a sound from deep within, keening and terrible. She struggled to consciousness and realized the dream, horrible as it was, had jogged her memory. Chantal was the last person Gayle remembered seeing. Was it preposterous to imagine a social butterfly like Chantal attacking her?

She knew her to be a vindictive woman whom Dominic had appeared to have little use for. A month ago, she would have discarded Chantal's words as mere spitefulness. Yet in the current upheaval of her own life, nothing was routine or transparent, not even a dream.

She needed to analyze the data. Start with Dom's disappearance, even go back a few months. Use her training.

She'd have to confront her growing suspicions that Dom was a government agent on a mission. And somehow Francois was involved.

Her headache resurfaced and she closed her eyes. How well had she really known Dom? He had waltzed her into a fantasy and like a naive adolescent she'd followed. Yet what was his purpose in pretending to love her until just days before their wedding?

Gayle frowned at the throbbing in her temple. She should rest. Tomorrow, she would think about it. Tomorrow.

Perry got out of the cab in front of the sanatorium, the postmodern building appearing curiously out of place in Paris. Inside, he strolled to his office. For the last three months, he'd been working in the American facility, which was charitably maintained for difficult cases abroad.

His friends had questioned his decision to leave his position in a lucrative medical practice. Perry had never considered himself overly enterprising or greedy but realized he couldn't abide shuffling about this facility indefinitely.

The patients were mostly forgotten by their families, the ocean separating them consisting of more than water. The horror left some relatives reluctant and ashamed to face the breakdown of one of their own. Many acted as if they secretly feared their acknowledgment of mental disease would make it contagious. Was it wisdom or folly on their part to dread association with the darkness that placed others in such institutions?

Perry opened Leah's file, regretting he'd ever agreed to treat her. His curiosity had led him astray. Initially, her case had seemed paradoxical. An elusive, intelligent and sensitive woman who was in the prime of life yet gripped with psychotic delusions. She was possibly schizophrenic and capable of brutal murder.

And somebody wanted her dead.

The records on her background were sketchy. Where had she come from? What had her formative years been like? Interestingly, her history provided few answers. Perry flipped through his notes and read: patient cold and withdrawn; poetry the exception; relates to Emily Dickinson.

Abby, his assistant, walked into his office with a harried look. "So sorry I'm late."

The sight of her cheered him. He'd never noticed how pretty she was. His innate optimism rising, he smiled. "It's nice of you to postpone your vacation."

He absentmindedly ran his hand through his bushy brown hair. Perry turned on the tape recorder. He and Abby went through Leah's sessions together, checking for anything he could use to reach her.

An hour later, Perry switched off the recorder. "Sadly, there's nothing new here."

Abby said, "I'm not surprised. Still, we went the extra mile. Many patients never progress."

"I'm not sure why Leah's case is fascinating. Perhaps it's her complexity which intrigues me. There is a hardness certainly, but in the center of her is this soft core of poetry. I sometimes feel as if it's unfurling, bit by bit healing her wounds."

"She's intelligent. The gentleness could be an act."

"Yes, there's the rub. Her situation is curious. Why must her identity be hidden from even her doctors? Where did she come from?"

Abby glanced around as if to ensure no one was listening. "Careful Doctor. You haven't been here long but making inquiries about *Miss Insanity* will only upset the cart."

He gave her a skeptical look and noticed she'd paled. "You're frightened. Why?"

"Forget I said anything. Please. I'm going to get the research on the Lazlo case taken care of. Besides, they'll be bringing Leah in soon." She rose and left.

Perry shook his head. What was that about? His phone buzzed. "Yes."

"Doctor Langston, Leah is ready now."

"Send her in." Mentally, he prepared himself for the session.

She stepped into his office, long straggly mud-brown hair framing her pinched face, a wiry strength in her tall, slight form.

"Hello Leah. It's good to see you again. How have you been?"

"I've been waiting too long for you to send for me," she accused.

"Our weekly meetings have always been on Wednesday."

"I'm not stupid. I was afraid they'd take you away."

"To where?"

"Never mind." She glanced down with a sigh. "I'd like the rest of the poem now, please."

"Let's talk first."

Softly, as if speaking to herself, she said, "Always you must work if you want to move forward and be free."

He sensed the intensity of her disappointment and reflected on how best to respond. "Are you working to get ahead and be free?"

She laughed, a pitiful sound. "Ahead. That's a good one. Since when do we speak in rhymes, telling jokes to those who can't get a line?" She nodded as if to herself. "If I must. Yes. I admit it all. I killed him. What else can I say? It must have been me. Who else?"

"Leah, do you comprehend what you are saying?"

She gave him a pensive look. "Yes, let's get on with it. Am I dead yet or dreaming? God, I want to be saved from this place. I thought I loved him. But you've convinced me at last . . . except . . ." She hung her head as if an immense load weighed upon her shoulders. "How could I have done it? I loved him. Don't you see? Every day and minute. I didn't know where his needs ended. I couldn't think or drink or move without his needs, his care consuming me. I never complained. I waited on him with the greatest love. Now he's gone and I have this space—this emptiness only. Oh, how could I have done it?" she sobbed.

Perry couldn't tell whether the entire scene was real or enacted but decided to quote the rest of the Dickinson poem as promised:

'There's a certain shaft of light,
Winter afternoons –
That oppresses, like the Heft
Of Cathedral Tunes –'

'Heavenly Hurt, it gives us –
We can find no scar,
But internal difference
Where the Meanings, are –'

'None may teach it – Any –
'Tis the Seal Despair –
An imperial affliction
Sent us on the Air –
When it comes, the Landscape listens –
Shadows – hold their breath –
When it goes, 'tis like the Distance
On the look of death –'

Leah glanced up, her hazel eyes glowing with fresh knowledge. "Thank you." Without a word, she stood and walked to the door.

Perry pressed the button for the attendant, letting her think she was in control, that she had won. Then she pivoted and stared at him, and he realized she understood. Her piercing stare conveyed that neither of them were winners, but losers caught in someone else's game.

Did he imagine the meaning behind her gaze? Or was he, like she, ensnared by someone from afar sealing his fate?

Sara imagined her life was like a spider's web, the net spinning tighter until the constricting threads strangled her. Her various identities confused even her. In the beginning, everything had seemed simple. A first-year student in college, ripe for rebellion, she supposed any cause would have done. Yet, it was the Muslims' call to prayer and arms that invaded her very life and existence, creating such a diversity of images and shadows in which to lose herself that it was only lately she'd experienced regrets.

The present, which was entwined with her father, and whom she would become, disallowed individuality or nostalgia or any drifting from the avowed purpose. Her pity for her estranged husband Ari and her old friend Pia was wasted. They were the prominent stars of her glorious youth and in part the product of her ultimate rashness. Their destinies were set long before she entered their spheres.

She had traveled far, and now there was no stepping back from the possibility of implosion. No one knew who she truly was except for one man and one woman. It was safer for her and for them. The American family she had once held dear were dead to her, and should she ever attempt to contact them her mother and grandparents would die. Her father had warned her, and there was no softness in him.

11

Gayle awoke to an urgent tapping. Thankfully, the throbbing in her head had eased. "Yes?"

Madame put her head around the door tentatively and then stepped in. "Mademoiselle, you have a visitor."

Gayle tried to collect herself, feeling puzzled. "Who knows I'm here?"

Madame smiled. "I contacted the American Embassy. You had some questions when you regained consciousness, and you fell asleep before I could ask your name."

"*Pardon.* I'm Gayle Regan and most grateful to you, your son and the doctor for taking such diligent care of me. As you can see, I'm much better. I'm not sure how I'll ever be able to repay you, Madame . . . "

"Elroy, but please call me Thea."

Her hostess was not precisely pretty, but striking, with a trim figure and cropped black hair. Her eyes, a warm shade of brandy, held kindness. Gayle alluded to yet another detail bothering her. "It's strange you haven't notified the police."

Thea gave a throaty laugh. "I did, almost immediately. There were no missing reports on anyone fitting your description. The officer suggested I inform the American Embassy, as the local *gendarmerie* are too overworked to deal with your case. Finally, after haranguing them almost daily, the embassy has responded."

Another tap at the door caught her attention. "It must be the man from the embassy. I have left him too long. May he enter?"

"Naturally, but I prefer to be sitting. Would you hand me the robe?" Gayle had her petite hostess to thank for the too small cotton gown she was wearing. She rose and slipped on the wrap Thea passed to her. Though a bit wobbly on her feet, she was strong enough to move unaided to the chair.

Thea opened the door and Gayle masked her surprise at seeing Elliot, one of her colleagues with the CIA. Few people knew she was an undercover agent. It was a secret Gayle kept from family and friends.

Elliot greeted the two women and then took charge. "*Madame, s'il vous plâit excusez-moi.*" He held the door for her to leave. "We have official business to conduct. It is better if we are private for now."

"Certainly." She looked at Gayle, and feeling reassured, left.

"Well Elliot, however, did you find me?"

"Believe me, it wasn't easy. And it was twice as difficult to sidetrack the embassy on this."

"Let me guess, there's a girl you happen to know."

He grinned. "How else?" He reached for her hand. "Are you okay?"

"I am. Do you suppose this might be connected to—"

He placed a finger to her lips. "Shh. We can't be too careful. How soon can you be ready to leave?"

"Give me a few minutes to get dressed."

"Good girl. In the meantime, I'll see what I can learn from your rescuer."

After he left, Gayle summoned the strength to move. Weak and a bit faint, she slid one leg and then the other into her pantsuit, which Thea had laundered and pressed. Gayle stumbled, nearly falling, catching herself before she crashed into the chest by the bed, determinedly pulling the pants to her waist and fastening them. *Lord, how many more jolts are there in store for me?* Gayle made an effort to block the radiating uncertainty. She needed to get back to work and focus on preserving her job. Transway's arrangement regarding her temporary leave wasn't etched into the company's granite walls.

She grasped her blouse and swayed, fumbling with the buttons, then slipped on the matching lime-green jacket, drawing strength from its cheery color. Ready at last, she followed the house sounds to the others. Gayle entered a room jam-packed with ill-chosen furniture.

Thea glanced up. "Don't mind this mess. I'm collecting for the church rummage sale. You can step around it."

Streams of brown crepe paper and plastic bags of clothing overflowed onto the dark wooden floor, contradicting Gayle's newly formed sense of who she assumed Thea was. "Wow. You've been busy."

"This sale happens once a year. It's nice to be able to help in some small way."

While Elliot spoke into his cell phone, the two women chatted briefly. Gayle said, "You'll be glad to hear I'm leaving. Elliot is going to give me a ride home."

Thea appeared concerned. "Let me get the doctor to examine you first."

"Truly, I'm fine."

Thea argued, "You must eat to build your strength. Please, it is my pleasure to feed you."

Outmaneuvered, Gayle meekly acquiesced as Elliot joined her.

Her hostess gestured to the mahogany dining table. "Please sit."

He seated himself across from Gayle. "*Merci*, but I've eaten. I'll have a coffee though."

Thea nodded and left.

Gayle raised her eyebrows. "Well?"

"Some sustenance will be good for you," Elliot said.

Thea entered carrying a tray with coffee, soup and a basket of bread. Gayle picked up the polished silver spoon by her place and dipped into the porcelain bowl of steaming broth. "Mm. This is good."

She bit into the crusty French baguette with a murmur of pleasure, realizing she was ravenous. "This tastes like it's fresh from the oven."

Thea smiled at the compliment and embarked on a rambling dialogue designed to draw Gayle and Elliot into the conversation and set them at ease.

Finished, Gayle pushed her bowl back, set the spoon beside it and rose, leaning on the table for support, but feeling more like herself.

She met Thea's worried gaze. "Relax. I'm far from ready to keel over." The food had helped the dizziness pass and the thought of going home was a comfort to which she clung. Gayle murmured her appreciation to Thea again, making sure she had Thea's address and phone number. A few moments of chitchat brought the three of them to the front door. She clasped her hostess's hands and, kissing her cheeks, promised to keep in touch.

There were no bags or purse to gather as she stepped outside. For a moment, she forgot her problems. The crispness of Paris in the spring soothed her, seducing her with the beauty of flat maples leafing out and apple trees washed in delicate white blossoms, their perfume mingling with that of diesel fuel and people and the faint smell of rain in the air. With a final wave, Gayle climbed into Elliot's sedan, a feeling of expansion in her chest.

He glanced at her before setting the Peugeot into gear. "You, okay?"

"Yes. A few battle scars and a bit of indignation that I slept through the siege. Still more curious than hurt. Do you have any idea what this is about?"

"The investigation comes to mind."

"What would be the benefit of getting rid of me? The agency would simply replace me with someone else. Unless the assailant needed more time. The disruption caused by my death would buy several days or possibly weeks."

He appeared pensive. "You're lucky to be alive. It was a mistake to bring you in on this case. It's too close to home."

The CIA had transferred her to Paris to ferret out two security brokers suspected of running a scam. Both had access to the airline's marketing department's 401(k)s. Initially, Gayle found no supporting evidence and recommended closing the case. Then, on her last afternoon at the office, several red flags had popped up, causing her to reconsider.

The agency suspected the two culprits of using false identities to make fraudulent trades. An accountant with undisclosed ties to the department had set off the alarm. The CIA became involved because the transfer of large funds overseas could be linked to terrorist threats. Since 9/11 such investigations had become routine.

It was possible she had unwittingly stumbled onto incriminating evidence or come close enough to frighten the perpetrators into action. The hypothetical suspects would have had no means of knowing she'd advocated that the home office close the case.

But there was absolutely no reason for Elliot to think she couldn't handle her assignments. "This isn't the first case I've run into danger on. Remember the year before last in Vienna? Even I was scared then and you didn't balk at the risk."

He paused at a signal light and grumbled about the traffic, yet she sensed he was annoyed with her. "We weren't dealing with terrorist threats."

"Point taken. Still, backing off hasn't removed any heat."

He reluctantly agreed.

"It's clear that I was stupid enough to get caught off guard and as a result got mugged." She knew she should resign herself to being more careful and forget the incident.

Elliot shot her a skeptical glance. "I've circled this block too often to believe in coincidences."

However much she'd like to, Gayle couldn't disagree. A pulsating sense of anxiety descended as he pulled up to the curb of her apartment building. She drew in a sharp lungful of air and let it go.

She missed her home, job and friends, but she'd changed. She was ready to let go of Dominic. That wouldn't stop her from making inquiries about him, but she would no longer live for the results.

Gayle wasn't sure when exactly she'd reached the decision. Perhaps it was while she'd sat alone at Dom's favorite restaurant, rehashing their time together. A part of her realized she couldn't live indefinitely on dreams, as she'd been doing since Dom's disappearance. She'd wanted to believe he cared for her, but the evidence refuted this. A trained investigator ignored the truth at his or her own peril.

Gayle shook off the past, prepared to move forward, resolved to focus her attention on her career. She turned to Elliott. "I can't thank you enough for coming to my rescue."

He smiled. "You'd have done the same for me."

"Yes, given the chance. Actually, I'd like to call in a favor."

He gave her a penetrating look. "Dominic?"

She nodded. "If you could find out for sure he's not hurt, it would make it easier to. . . ."

"Stop. Not another word. I'll do what I can."

"Thanks. Would you mind terribly if I go in alone? I need some downtime to sort this out."

"Let me run up with you and make sure everything is all right."

"That's not necessary."

"I insist. Let's not forget you were attacked. Until we know if it was a random act, you should be cautious." Elliott climbed out of the car.

Gayle followed suit and together they crossed the lawn and entered the building, taking the elevator to the third floor. She veered to the left and rang the bell. "I leave a spare key with my neighbor, in case of an emergency."

The neighbor opened the door and greeted Gayle stiffly. "Oui?" Her silver head was bowed slightly and her shoulders stooped with arthritic pain.

"Bonjour, I'm sorry to disturb you, but I've locked myself out."

She appeared bewildered. "But you're no longer residing here."

"Of course I live here."

Madame's rigidity faded to thoughtful concern. "Earlier this week, I watched as your furnishings were carried out and new tenants moved in. I was hurt because you neglected to say goodbye or even to stop and collect your key."

Shock rippled through Gayle. She and Elliott exchanged quick glances as he stepped farther back, out of view. Gayle struggled to reassure her neighbor. "There must be some mistake. I was in an accident and have just recovered enough to come home. Are you sure of this?"

"Unfortunately, yes. I saw the movers empty your place."

"Do you have any idea who took my belongings?"

"They were movers," she said helplessly.

Gayle didn't want to intrude on this kind lady's routine any more than she had. "Don't worry. I'll see the manager and get this straightened out."

"I sincerely hope so but wait . . ." Madame opened the door wider and reached over into the drawer of a small chest in the foyer. She drew out a key and handed it to Gayle. "Let me hear how it turns out."

Impulsively Gayle hugged her. "You've been a grand neighbor. I'll be back to visit after I get resettled."

"I'll hold you to that promise. God be with you, dear." Her door closed.

Gayle walked across to her apartment and with a shaky hand slipped the key into the lock. Nothing. A bone deep tremor rocked through her. Her tongue pressed against her teeth in distress. Who was sabotaging her life? She strove to clear her head. She had to think. This must be a misunderstanding. It had to be.

Elliot had been silent for the most part, for which she was grateful.

It was upsetting enough to learn everything she owned had apparently disappeared. She wasn't ready to verbally reason out the whys of it.

Gayle headed downstairs, Elliot beside her. On the ground floor he stopped. "Will you be okay here on your own? I can't afford to be overtly associated with your dilemma. Not until I get higher clearance. I may have already overstepped."

"You wouldn't dare desert me in the middle of a situation like this."

"You know the rules. And you do have resources." He squeezed her shoulder and handed her a wad of cash. "Here's some money in case you need it for cab fare. Take care of yourself, Red. I've grown rather fond of working with you."

A sense of doom overshadowed Gayle as she watched him leave. Yet the reality of finding a place to sleep before night forced her to move on. With a firmness that was pure bravado she rang the manager's bell.

Their chat brought minimal satisfaction. He told her he had received a phone call from a person whom he thought was Gayle, giving up the lease and asking him to allow movers in to pack her belongings to be shipped back to America. He said the woman told him she was quitting her job and returning home. Now, her place was already leased, and he could not undo it.

When she asked for descriptions of the movers and their truck, he shrugged. "Who notices these things? I had three other families leaving the same day."

"Isn't that unusual?"

"Perhaps, but times are not the best economically. So, it's understandable."

"Please, there must be some tidbit you recall."

That's when he admitted he'd not even been around when the movers arrived, but he had left a key under the mat.

In frustration Gayle said goodbye and departed, wondering what to do. Who wanted her to leave Paris enough to murder her and steal all she possessed? Was the department's covert investigation behind this? She considered Dom's parents. How much of an embarrassment was she to them?

Gayle sifted through her options. She was without a home or any identification. Her passport, credit cards and money had vanished with her purse when she had been attacked. What about her bank accounts and car? Had they been conveniently disposed of as well? Her Porsche might still be where she'd parked it on the Left-Bank.

Gayle sank onto the entrance steps, giving herself a few minutes to regroup. She could phone her office and have Helen or Kara pick her up but they'd ask questions.

She thought the Transway investigation had died a natural death. When no evidence of wrongdoing surfaced, she'd nearly decided to quit the service. Gayle had believed she would be marrying Dom. Even her recent red flag discoveries wouldn't have prevented her from filing a report and resigning, if Dom hadn't left.

No one outside of the CIA and Transway's CEO and CFO knew she was an agent. She'd never told her family or friends, not even Dom when they were engaged. She hadn't planned to keep it secret once they were married. Naturally, Gayle had dreaded confessing how early in their relationship she'd known he was being investigated as a suspect in the St. Abient affair.

With his desertion, she'd let her life slide. That had gotten her in trouble. It was time she started paying attention to what was going on around her.

Gayle decided to walk to her bank and make a withdrawal if her accounts hadn't already been emptied. Then she'd check into a hotel for the night. Gayle wanted to avoid contacting friends who would ask questions she couldn't answer.

She guessed Elliot wasn't returning. She rose wearily and walked out of the building, crashing into the man entering the place.

<h1 style="text-align:center">12</h1>

Gayle gaped at Mitch Carey and realized she was clutching his shoulders.

"I beg your pardon," he said, his southern drawl, reminding her of home and her brothers. "Are you all right?"

"Fine, thank you." What was the CEO of Carey International doing at her apartment building? She took a hasty step back, aware that she had been staring. "I'm surprised to see you."

He raked a lean tanned hand through his dark brown hair. "I wasn't able to contact you at the office."

"Sorry, I've been on vacation." Mitch wouldn't know that since they last spoke, she'd been on a chilling roller coaster ride. With regret she took in the old wrought-iron fence entwined with climbing roses and honeysuckle. For the most part she'd been happy there.

Gayle wrinkled her brow in sudden impatience at the direction of her thoughts and treaded around Mitch. "Unfortunately, now is not convenient either. If you'll excuse me, I'm extremely late. Nice seeing you again, Mitch."

He moved into the path, blocking her. "I've been trying to get an appointment with you for days."

Gayle exhaled sharply, feeling as if the landscape of her life had been transmuted into a war zone. Still, she made an effort to be kind. "I'm aware of your situation and despite it, you should have received the renewal contract I drew up last week."

He gave her a hard glance. "Yes, you told me to expect it that day by special messenger. It never arrived. Then I received a letter from you, stating it's scheduled to be canceled."

Gayle, surprised to hear that, recalled checking out CI's stats before her accident and drafting a renewal contract. When she got resettled, she'd have to figure out what had happened. Perhaps Clyde had reexamined CI's business viability, discovered new negatives and stopped Helen from posting the letter. But why had he sent the termination contract in her name?

Gayle summoned a diplomatic smile. "Mitch, I know zilch about the letter but will do my utmost to resolve this when I return to the office. If there's a rush, which is understandable given your circumstances, contact my assistant Clyde Mort or my PA who will arrange for someone else to handle this."

"I don't want to be handled. What I want is to sit down with you and discuss any issues Transway might have and negotiate a resolution."

"I assure you; my staff is quite competent."

"I'd rather not change agents midstream. I signed the initial contract with you."

"Then it will have to be later, because I'm on my way to the bank."

His no-nonsense expression declared disagreement. In an effort to appease him, she explained, "I've been in an accident and lost my purse. It's urgent I get to the bank to draw out funds before it closes. We can talk later." She finished with a wave and hurried off.

He sprinted down the entrance steps onto the sidewalk, catching up to her. "Let me drive you." Mitch crossed to the Renault by the curb and opened the passenger door.

As driving would be quicker, Gayle got into the vehicle and directed him the few blocks to the bank. He parked in front and she climbed out, her emotions on a seesaw. "I shouldn't be long."

"We'll talk afterward?"

"Sure, at some point. I still have to locate my car." She turned, amazed at how composed she sounded, and strolled into the bank. Dear Lord, let the funds be there.

She requested three withdrawal slips and filled them out. Thanks to her training she'd made it a point to memorize her savings, checking and money market account numbers. She handed the forms to the teller.

The middle-aged woman punched in several keys on her computer and gave Gayle a curious glance, before typing in a rapid succession of commands. Gayle's stomach roiled like butter in a churn, leaving her queasy.

The teller frowned, studying her carefully. "I'm sorry, these accounts have been closed. May I see some identification, please?"

Gayle gulped, feeling as if she were circling the borders of a foreign land, the language beyond her comprehension. Worse, there was no guidebook or code of conduct to which she could refer.

"Mademoiselle?" the clerk prompted.

Her conditioning kicked in and Gayle conjured up an embarrassed look. "Sorry. I was in a rush and left home without my purse. I'll come back later." She whirled to exit.

"Wait, Mademoiselle. I must call the manager. Stop! Please!"

Gayle rushed out of the bank, hoping its staff wouldn't call the gendarmerie. Somehow, her cover must have been blown. Her mind reeled at the implications. The bank suspected her of being an impostor and of stealing her own assets. Fate was catapulting her into a terrifying, alien world, one in which she had no experience to cope.

She crossed the street amid blaring horns. Gayle wasn't sure why she was running, but instinct warned her to get out of there and avoid everyone until she understood who was targeting her and why.

13

Mitch started the car when he saw Gayle race out of the bank, but in order to follow her he couldn't very well cross four lanes of traffic and make a U-turn going in the wrong direction. He glanced into his side mirror and pulled out, intent on circling the block. He didn't want to lose her now. His fledgling airline stood on the brink of bankruptcy unless he nailed the Transway contract.

When Mitch first met Gayle, she'd been as warm and open as Seth had said his little sister would be to any pal of his. In her sophisticated, downtown Paris office, she managed to be both welcoming and professional, which he knew from personal experience required a certain finesse.

Granted, their mutual business accommodation had been beneficial to both parties. His jets were vetted and Carey International (CI) was gaining on the exchange. But recently, the situation had gyrated into a downward spiral. One of his pilots, Frank Hassledorf, had died. Frank, allegedly intoxicated while flying a scheduled freight shipment, had crashed the plane, also killing the copilot. Hassledorf's family was suing the company for allowing the flight to take off, and CI's insurance provider was balking about paying.

From the start, Mitch had taken steps to ensure that CI security procedures were in place to prevent such incidents. Yet in this case, his every maneuver and inquiry to uncover the truth had hit wind shear, the subsequent fallout creating even more debris to sift through.

The crew on duty for the preflight external check had disappeared from CI's facility in Tulsa. One of those men, Ryan, was a close buddy Mitch had worked with for five years. An unreasonable anger on low burn stayed with him, sparking a vulnerability that was as unwanted as it was unfamiliar, especially when Mitch considered what might have happened to his friend.

Ryan's wife Laura had been both bewildered and scared. Their two-year-old twin sons had Ryan's same crooked grin, blond hair and keen green eyes. The boys needed a father. Laura needed her husband. And Mitch needed his buddy back.

The Feds got involved, intensifying CI's misfortune with their investigation. Not long ago, Mitch had been excited about the possibility of a renewal contract with Transway, contingent on his airline's performance review. He had planned to ship a larger percentage of Transway's surplus freight. Carey International had been slated for a two-year extension that Transway now seemed bent on withdrawing. Rumors about the crash were circulating. If his other clients got wind of his company's troubles, he feared even more contracts would be canceled.

Mitch hoped he might capture a break with Miss Priss but he'd lost her somewhere on the street. He would camp out at her old apartment. Eventually, she would have to return.

Seth arrived in Paris somewhat refreshed from the sleep he had caught on the flight from Houston. Despite the anxiety he couldn't shake, he wanted to believe Gayle was okay. He took a cab to her apartment, hoping her ankle had recovered enough for her to return home. When he rang the doorbell, she didn't answer, and he noticed that her name had been scratched through on the nameplate.

He located the manager's office and was told he'd barely missed Gayle. He gave the man a searching look. "Why is my sister's name marked out on her door?"

The manager frowned, sullenness creasing the worn furrows about his mouth. "She's moved, and it can't be undone. That's all there is to it."

Coldness settled in the pit of Seth's stomach. "Would you mind explaining?"

"It's like I told her. I received a phone call from her, informing me that she was moving out. We're not responsible for the loss of her apartment and belongings."

Seth was perplexed by the manager's disgruntled claim. "What exactly are you saying here?"

"Only that no one told me she had been in an accident and whoever called sounded like her. Otherwise, I would have never let the movers take her possessions."

Seth's gut clinched. He felt as if he'd walked into a *Looney Tunes* recital. He pressed for more information. After a few moments, he realized, however slipshod the man's management style might be, he was in earnest about Gayle's departure. "Are you telling me on the strength of a phone call you canceled my sister's lease and disposed of her personal property?"

"How could I have known it wasn't Mademoiselle Regan?" he whined.

Outrage, disgust and a burgeoning fear for his sister simmered in Seth. The manager's actions approached criminal negligence. "Legally, you should have requested proof of ID. I'm not sure we shouldn't sue you for damages." He held up a hand to halt the influx of objections pouring forth from the manager. "Tell me where she's gone."

The man shrugged with a martyred air. "Mademoiselle said she'd give me the address to forward her mail once she found a new place."

Seth realized that it would be futile to ask any more questions. He left the building, a sense of disquiet coloring his frustration and annoyance. What was happening to his sister?

First, there was the canceled wedding, preceded by her fiancé's desertion. Then she had an accident that put her in a place where no one seemed able to reach her. Finally, she had been forced out of her apartment and stripped of her possessions. Seth couldn't imagine why anyone would want to hurt a sweet, personable woman like her.

Where was she? Gayle must have friends in Paris who would support her in a crisis. He found it strange that she hadn't contacted anyone in the family. This was taking her desire for independence a bit too far. Their father's weak heart made calm rest imperative and worrying about his youngest wasn't improving his condition.

If Gayle had a fault, it was her stubborn tenacity in refusing to accept her brothers' help. He smiled faintly at how more often than not, Gayle had labeled their efforts on her behalf unwarranted interference. Seth only had one kid sister, and his brothers had designated him to unearth her. And find her he would.

Seth couldn't recall who her friends were, aside from the woman in Legal at Transway. What was her name? Kara something. He pulled out his mobile, rang Transway and asked for Kara in Legal. The receptionist put him through to her office.

Seth introduced himself. "I'm trying to find Gayle. She has spoken of you often. I wondered if you might know her whereabouts."

"I heard she hurt her ankle. I did try calling and stopping by her apartment but never found her at home. Then I learned she was staying with a friend in the suburbs. I'd be glad to check with the main office and get her exchange for you."

"Great. I was given a number the other day but no one ever answered. Frankly, I'm concerned. I'm not sure if you are aware of what's taken place." He filled her in on Gayle's loss of the apartment and her belongings.

"How awful. I can't believe this has happened. She's been through so much lately."

"Yes, she has," Seth agreed, his throat thick with emotion.

"I wonder why she hasn't phoned me. She must know I'm here for her."

"Kara, we're all wondering where she is."

"I'll see if I can locate her. I've got your mobile on caller ID and will get back to you as soon as I learn anything."

"Thanks, I appreciate the help." They hung up, and Seth phoned Transway again and asked for Clyde who wasn't in. Seth's attempt to strike up a passing acquaintance with the receptionist to gain any information regarding his sister's private life failed as well.

It occurred to him Mitch might have her address. Hadn't he been attempting to reach her when they last spoke? Seth dialed his number. "Hey Mitch! I'm here in Paris. Do you have any idea where Gayle is?"

"Seth?" Surprise edged his voice. "Yesterday you were in Houston."

"Yeah, well, when I couldn't reach Gayle, I decided to come and find out what's going on."

"Good luck with that."

They spoke for a few minutes. Seth realized his friend was preoccupied and worried about his company. Since Mitch was in the area, he offered to swing by and pick up Seth.

When Mitch arrived, Seth couldn't stop stressing about Gayle, and Mitch appeared anxious to see her too. They stood outside Gayle's former apartment building, trying to decide what to do.

Mitch told Seth, "She rode with me to the bank yesterday and then gave me the slip. I came back here to wait, but she never returned. I wanted to stop by today to see if I could catch her." Mitch said this with an air of frustration. "Believe me, she's hard to pin down."

Seth found it curious the two had such difficulty meeting up. But both his sister and Mitch were confronting extraordinary challenges. "Well, you've missed her again."

"It figures."

"That doesn't sound like Gayle."

"Maybe you don't know her as well as you think." Mitch told Seth about bumping into her as she was leaving the building the day before and the gist of their conversation. "Then after promising to talk later, she raced out of the bank and down the street like—"

"Yes?"

"Almost as if she were frightened."

Seth groaned and ran a jerky hand through his hair. At Mitch's look of inquiry, he revealed what he'd learned so far about her accident and her apartment. After some discussion they pooled their knowledge and decided to return to the bank, where Seth hoped to convince the bank manager to share her new address.

They climbed into Mitch's Renault and were there in minutes. Seth approached one of the tellers who immediately contacted the bank manager, then ushered them into his plush office.

"Please be seated," the banker said curtly.

They slid into two chairs placed across from the tall dark-haired manager's desk. Seth glanced at Mitch, who raised his eyebrows at the man's brusqueness.

The man began by ascertaining their identities and Seth's relationship to Gayle. "A woman who was impersonating Mademoiselle Regan ran out of here yesterday after discovering there were no more funds in her accounts."

"It may have been my sister." Seth explained the pertinent facts about Gayle's accident and subsequent loss of her apartment and belongings. "It's obvious she must have been under great duress when she arrived at the bank and learned her savings had disappeared as well."

"Perhaps what you say is true, still how can you explain the woman with Gayle Regan's ID who showed up at the bank last week to find her accounts had been illegally emptied?"

"Maybe, this person came by in an attempt to establish her false identity," Mitch said.

Seth was stunned, incensed and confused in turn. He learned Gayle's funds had been siphoned via wire transfer. The bank suspected his sister of not only being an impostor but of stealing her own money. It was ludicrous. Seth pointed again to the photo he kept in his wallet. "She's not an impostor. She is my sister. And we have proof. The real Gayle was with Mitch. He spoke with her at length and then drove her here yesterday."

"Monsieur Regan, obviously these two women are similar in appearance. If the woman yesterday had been Gayle Regan, she wouldn't have run. And you say she failed to return to Monsieur Carey's car. All of this points to her being the impostor."

"Normally, I'd agree with you. Recently, she had her home, possessions and accounts wiped out. She came to the bank to get money to live on. How could she prove who she was? I imagine she went straight to the authorities for help to try and get her purse and car back. Have you contacted the police?"

"Yes, we've reported the incident. The gendarmerie is searching for a woman matching your sister's description."

Seth didn't have any answers; what he had was a growing list of questions and a gut instinct that Gayle was in deep trouble. He should be the one contacting the police.

The banker continued. "Monsieur Carey, how well acquainted are you with Mademoiselle Regan? Isn't it possible you might have been mistaken in who she was?"

Mitch and Seth exchanged incredulous glances. The possibility was enough to make Seth's head pound yet he couldn't deny the supposition, because it made too much sense. If it were true, no one had seen his sister in more than a week, a scenario which left him nearly panicked.

He met the banker's gaze. "There's one way to find out. Introduce me to the woman you believe to be Gayle Regan. I'm her brother. She can't fool me."

"An excellent idea. Unfortunately, Mademoiselle told me she'd be out of town on business the rest of this week."

"May I ask where she works?"

"Naturally, she's immensely respectable and is general manager of marketing at Transway Airline."

"In that case, there you have it. My sister holds the exact same position. Let me have her number and I can settle this over the phone."

The banker threw him a suspicious look. "It is strange, oui, you do not have your own sister's telephone number?"

"I believe I alluded to her extreme situation earlier."

"Oui, however Mademoiselle Regan did not mention any such problems to me. Under the circumstances we will leave the matter with the authorities. I will naturally share this information with them."

Seth held in his anger. "In that case, we'll be going." He and Mitch rose stiffly and left.

Dominic returned to Switzerland reluctantly, choosing to stay at a remote lodge in the Alps. He needed to get Abby on board with Interpol's plans and hoped a weekend together in the plush resort would help accomplish this.

He crawled into bed and was reaching to switch off the light when the phone rang. "Hello."

Francois greeted him and said, "Gayle has disappeared. I tried to run interference but there was nothing I could do."

Dom squeezed his eyes shut in an effort to block the images burrowing through his mind. "What's happened?"

"A somewhat strange turn of events. I am not sure if it's related to you or our operation."

"Francois, give me specifics rather than the rumblings of an old woman. I'm not clairvoyant."

"You'll like the facts even less. Gayle's assistant at Transway and his accomplice, an al-Qaida operative, nearly killed your former fiancé."

"You mean Clyde and an al-Qaida operative are working together?"

"Yes. Fortunately, the CIA rescued Gayle in the aftermath. Interpol is buzzing, because absolutely zero adds up, and the CIA is denying any knowledge or involvement." Francois went on to relate Interpol's newest intel.

"It seems incredible, to say the least." Dom inhaled, striving to calm himself. Had the attention and notoriety he brought Gayle made her a person of interest?

Before his departure from Paris, he had asked Francois to check on her, fearing such a situation might arise. But neither the CIA nor al-Qaida had entered into the equation. Dom found it difficult to believe Gayle had enemies who wanted her dead. "Stay on it, will you? Find a motive and get back with me ASAP. And thank you."

"I'll do what I can."

Francois, a longstanding, trusted friend, was one of the few who knew of Dom's double life. An inheritance and a trust fund from the maternal grandfather for whom Dominic was named made it unnecessary for him to work. He managed his own trust and others he'd established for the causes he favored. With his father's retirement, Dominic became CEO of the Trudeau's extensive holdings as well. Still, much of his time was taken up with intelligence work and would remain thus until France's present threat alert lessened.

Gayle's disappearance was particularly disturbing, in light of Francois's failure to find her. Francois was an extremely competent agent, one of the best. Dom tried to make sense of the developments unfolding. Was he being lured down a false trail?

For five years Dominic and Ari had been searching for *the package*. Finally, Dom had stumbled onto what appeared to be a promising clue, when the agency assigned him lead in the taskforce to uncover al-Qaida's link to the US disappearance of a top German diplomat's wife. Pia Helmut had vanished on the night that terrorists shot her husband. Interpol had surveillance video of Walter Helmut's murder.

A trace on the terrorists the Helmuts had inadvertently bumped into in Copenhagen five years earlier failed to yield any concrete evidence. Dom began exploring the links between these terrorists and three Jakarta students in Paris who had purportedly carried out the Swiss diamond heist in Basel for Fahid. The agency suspected those stolen diamonds were the ones mixed up in CI's plane crash.

The agency tailed the students, hoping to link the jewel heist to Fahid, and had learned of the students' peripheral involvement in al-Qaida plans for its three-prong attack targeting Paris, London and New York. The students were now in custody and being interrogated.

Despite Dom's demanding job, memories of Gayle intruded. He felt lonely and lost, caught in the agency's web. Interpol needed him, and he would do whatever it took to keep France safe in spite of his feelings.

He phoned the front desk and reserved the suite adjoining his, then punched in Abby's number. After they exchanged greetings, he said, "I've booked us a suite for the weekend. Can you possibly meet me at that little spot in Switzerland we've always enjoyed?"

"Sounds delightful."

"I'll be counting the minutes, chéri." He detested the lie and wished there were another way. He didn't want to be involved with Abby, romantically or otherwise, especially not while his feelings for Gayle were still simmering.

Dom poured himself a drink and studied the files on his laptop. He couldn't seem to penetrate the fog obscuring the case. He gave up, switched off the lights and headed for bed. There was always tomorrow. If he was lucky, he'd still be alive and so would Gayle.

Monday afternoon in his Paris office, Dom studied the forensic reports he'd received from the lab. Ari's wife Sara, known as *the package* for security reasons, had disappeared about the same time as Pia Helmut. Walter Helmut and Ari were both foreigners, married to Americans. And their wives were former college roommates. On a hunch the two women were one and the same, Dom had ordered fingerprint comparisons. Their fingerprints, however, were not a match.

Dom was relieved for Ari's sake. Intel had also surfaced proving that the woman murdered on the outskirts of Moscow previously thought to be *the package* was not. Despite being knocked about with every bit of news, Ari was a survivor.

Dom sifted through the papers on his desk, anxiously scanning for the coordinates he'd requested. Jake in Syria had uncovered a link to Fahid through his brother Matrouk's wife, yet another American who had mysteriously vanished. That made three American women married to foreigners and three disappearances. The probability of any relation between these strange coincidences increased with every tie-in.

Dom studied a missive from one of Interpol's moles in France. It reiterated that Pia was the third cousin of Sequor, the French politician whom the Helmuts had seen with Fahid. The agency already knew this.

Francois maintained Sequor was as straight and sturdy as a palm tree, but Dom had seen palm trees wavering in the breezes and uprooted in storms.

14

Gayle had left the bank and Mitch Carey far behind. She regretted wearing the lime green pantsuit as she trekked through the streets, striving to keep a low profile. Emotionally it was as if she'd paused at a traffic light and blinked, and in that nanosecond the signals changed to a code, which made zero sense.

She crossed rue Saint-Jacques and walked rapidly to Rene Vivani square, the sight of Saint-Julien le Pauvre Gothic Cathedral reassuring. Aware of her strong evangelical leanings, Dom would have been amused that the Melkite Greek Catholic edifice brought her even fleeting comfort.

To deter anyone who might be following her, she circled to rue Saint-Jacques, past Saint-Severin, cut through to rue de la Parcheminerie on to boulevard Saint-Germain, then slowly traced a path to the outskirts of the Latin Quarter and beyond to Café la Maison.

Gayle glanced at the blackened windows, walked under the graying awning, went inside and sat at the bar. *"Bonjour. Café au lait, s'il vous plaît."*

The motherly barkeep raised a hand in greeting. *"Ça Va."* Several minutes later she set the coffee before Gayle, wiping the surrounding area with a damp rag. "How was your day, mademoiselle?"

Gayle tensed, praying the words wouldn't fail her. "The birds sang so prettily outside my window at work today."

With a sage nod of her head, the barkeep agreed. "Spring is early and the birds are happy."

Gayle lowered her voice, "I wish I had a bird book to help me identify them."

The barkeep fixed her with a hard stare. "I do. It'll be a few minutes before I can get to it."

Ten minutes later Gayle left, trying not to hug close the shopping bag she'd been given. She stopped at the nearest department store and took a detour into the ladies' room, opening the package in the privacy of a stall.

Quickly, she changed into the black dress, which made her look dumpy and washed-out. The nondescript purse she slipped onto her shoulder contained a new identity, bank card, Euro checks, cash and keys.

She rode the underground to the modest two-bedroom safe house, a black Mini Cooper parked in the attached garage. The brown and beige living quarters were equipped with adequate furnishings and supplies. By design, nothing stood out as memorable.

Gayle dropped onto the couch, feeling drained yet grateful she'd landed in a haven before nightfall. At moments like this, she wondered why she had ever agreed to work for the government. Her position at Transway as general manager of marketing offered more than sufficient salary and challenge. What draw had brought her to the agency?

Fresh out of college, eager and naive, she'd been impressed and flattered by the CIA operative who initially approached her. Her country needed a woman with her qualifications in the airline industry. An in-depth screening and interview process had followed. A subsequent year of training in Switzerland had preceded her first airline job.

Excitement was part of the pull. Gayle never knew when the agency would contact her or where the assignment might lead. With intelligence work, the cases were often formidable, taking unforeseen twists.

She'd had enough. Exhausted, Gayle closed her eyes and dozed.

When she awoke it was early evening. She stood and opened a window, letting the night spill into the room. The darkness seemed to encircle her, like the bleakness within, robbing her of happiness.

Into the silence, calm seemed to gather in advance of the storm she sensed was coming. It was almost as if the atmosphere and she were in collusion, each mirroring the other's turmoil. Gayle leaned into the window casement and watched the lightning-streaked sky. She loved the fresh smell of the rain as it poured to the ground. Wind whipped through the trees, tossing limbs across the yard. The storm stopped as abruptly as it began. Gayle stepped back and closed the window.

Her whirlwind relationship with Dom had been brief and dramatic. Would she ever be able to settle into a life of status quo with someone like Perry Langston? She smiled at the thought of her former boyfriend, now a doctor, and guessed many a pretty nurse had tried to snare him.

When their college romance had withered, Perry accused her of an unwillingness to deepen their relationship. His hazel eyes warming hers with tender concern, he'd said, "You're too reserved with me. Someday you'll meet the man who's going to knock you off your feet and you won't stand a chance. Unfortunately, I'm not him."

Yet they had remained friends. She groaned. How could she have forgotten? Perry had moved to Paris two months ago, and she'd promised to have dinner with him soon. He'd never believe her reasons for forgetting. She picked up the phone. No one would suspect her association with him, and he could be trusted to help.

Gayle knew his hotel number as she often arranged for clients to stay there. "Perry, how are you?"

He said in a rush of excitement, "I was beginning to wonder if we'd ever connect."

"Sorry. I've been busy. Are you free for lunch tomorrow?"

"Name the place."

"It's a rather remote café, I think you'll like."

"Sounds great."

They arranged to meet and rang off.

Her thoughts turned inward and Perry's image faded. Had she recognized in Dom a reserve matching her own? She had felt safe with him—an apparent illusion. Yet, Gayle still found his desertion hard to accept, which proved how deluded she was. She needed to get a grip. Think like the trained agent she was. Start with the obvious.

Was there any connection between her recent difficulties and Dom's vanishing? She couldn't think of any, so she focused on her investigation of the accounting fraud at Transway. It had initially appeared to fizzle. Then, she had uncovered what appeared to be an unusual volume of buying and selling after hours, which was illegal. No one besides Transway's CEO and CFO, and the CIA knew of her investigation or discoveries.

Gayle went into the kitchen and opened the pantry, pressing the wall until it slid back, revealing the department's standard issue laptop stashed in the hidden compartment.

She set it up on the table, switched on the power and entered her password. On the off chance she was wrong, she ran a security check on Dom's financials but as expected, he was in the clear.

What about Mitch Carey? In retrospect, she realized it was odd how he'd arrived at her apartment building and then coerced her to accompany him. Was it possible he was somehow tangled up in what was happening? He seemed like a decent man, and she sympathized with his frustration at his company's recent problems.

A message from Elliot popped up on the screen, and she clicked to open it:

Sorry to have run out on you, but protocol must be followed. Study the encrypted dossiers and report back.

You owe me. E.

Gayle scanned the report on Dominic and read with relief, there was no indication he worked in intelligence. The report placed him in the Swiss Alps with an unidentified woman. Shock lanced her. A detailed description of the relationship followed. How could Dominic have fooled her so completely? Gayle hated him in that moment.

She pulled herself together enough to read Elliot's note tagged at the bottom of the page:

Sorry about this. Wish I could take him out for you.
Keep your chin up.
E.

In a skirmish of emotions, Gayle rose. She walked into the living room, physically distancing herself from the data, and flicked on the radio, letting the soft jazz wash through her.

She swayed, swirled and stepped to the soulful beat, trying to clear her mind of all but the music. The thought of Dominic's trysts with another woman shadowed her moves, as she adapted to a semi-classical style, mixing *plies, temps liés, pirouettes* and variations of the *arabesque* into the jazz steps.

God, why? Tears mingled with sweat as she pushed herself harder and harder, losing herself in the sounds of the horns and the piano. It was best to face the truth and vanquish the uncertainty. She didn't understand Dominic, maybe she never had. Yet, she'd have to let him go. In essence, he'd already left.

Gayle switched off the music and went into the bedroom. She lay down on the bed and wept. Then she knelt and prayed. "God give me strength. Guide me. I'm so lost." After a bit, she rose. It was time she read the other documents.

Barefoot, she padded into the kitchen, sat at the table and deleted Dominic's file, surprised at the depth of her anger.

Interestingly, the remaining docs centered on her assistant Clyde and Mitch Carey. Clyde had a history of questionable associations. Her instincts not to trust him were more than vindicated.

Mitch had either stumbled into a smuggling ring or he was on the take. She hoped it was the former, but either way he was in deep trouble. Maybe she could help him sort it out. That was presupposing she resolved the issues plaguing her.

15

Gayle rose early, feeling fragile emotionally yet steadier than the previous evening. She phoned Clyde to explain she'd recovered from the accident but was in the process of moving and gave him the number of her new throwaway phone.

"Take whatever time you need," he said. "Don't worry about the office. I've got it covered."

"Plan on me being there later in the week." It was impractical to leave her responsibilities hanging indefinitely, especially given Clyde's seedy associations. Besides, she craved normalcy and her old routine could provide it up to a point. If Clyde was her enemy, she'd discover it sooner working with him.

"There's no urgency. We're getting along fine without you," he reiterated, a thread of disquiet stealing into his voice.

Obviously, Clyde couldn't be trusted. She knew he would try to undermine her position. "You're doing a good job," she said in an effort to soothe any suspicions he might have. "While I have you on the line, bring me up to speed on the situation with CI. I was surprised to learn that a letter went out with my signature canceling their contract."

He was silent for a moment, then said, "I'm here taking care of business, and decisions have to be made while you're out managing your personal problems."

"Still, I'd appreciate being consulted when you're signing my name to cancel a pending contract. I want a report on my desk explaining why you thought it necessary to act without prior authorization."

"It'll be there, if and when you're well enough to come in."

It hadn't taken much for Clyde to unveil the side of him she'd long suspected lay beneath the surface of his oozing charm. She'd have to go into Transway soon . . . before he stole her position entirely. The CIA expected her to remain on the job.

First, she wanted to set her affairs in order. Fortunately, Gayle had received enough funds from the agency to do so. A few blocks from her new home, she hailed a passing cab and headed to Thea's. She slipped an envelope, thick with a wad of Euros and a thank you note, through the letter slot on the front door. To meet with Thea would expose her new friend to danger.

Gayle caught the métro to the suburbs for her lunch date with Perry. They chose a table on the café veranda. She looked around with interest, aware that she remained a moving target. Her tension eased once she ascertained she hadn't been followed.

They ordered.

"You should slow down," Perry said, with a warm smile. "You seem tired." He rushed to add, "though as attractive as ever."

"It's great to see you, too." They talked casually about the latest plays and books, then brought each other up to date on their mutual chums. His carefree conversation was doing her a universe of good, allowing her to unwind as they discussed friends and family back in the States, a reality apart from her current crisis. Gayle had forgotten how much they enjoyed the same sense of the ridiculous. It seemed ages since she had let go and laughed.

"Now, tell me why you're in Paris. What kind of lunacy are you specializing in these days?" she asked.

"The criminal kind. I've taken a position with the Cremont Sanatorium. Confidentially, the cases are fascinating, classic examples of how the human mind reacts in instances of crises." He suddenly appeared troubled.

"Is anything wrong?"

"Not really."

"Are you enjoying Paris in the spring?" *The season for lovers, the unspoken thought hanging between them.*

His gaze narrowed, his sandy hair ruffling in the dancing breeze. I t was a shade longer than she remembered, and it suited him. Dressed in jeans and sweatshirt, he looked wonderfully American.

"Enough about me." He covered her hand with his. "Tell me what's keeping you busy."

She shrugged, thoughts of Dominic and the wedding that wasn't to be almost choking her. "I suppose you were surprised by the cancellation of my wedding," she managed.

"A bit. You've got to take care of yourself, Princess," he said, his old nickname for her slipping out. "Don't repine too much about Trudeau. There are a few good men left out there."

"Yes, but you see, that's the problem: They're not him. Besides, I don't want Dom or anyone else."

"Ouch!" A trace of a shadow crossed his face, vanishing so quickly she wondered if she imagined it.

"I'm being moody," she apologized.

"Have dinner with me tomorrow to make up for that crack."

She chuckled as he intended. "Sounds delightful, but I'd better not," she said, regretfully. Gayle couldn't chance putting Perry in danger.

"I'd hoped we could catch a ballet together after we ate."

Tempted as she was to accept his invitation, she declined. Gayle possessed an inborn love of dance. Her petite mother, also enamored of the ballet, had dragged her to classes and every performance possible. To her mom's delight, Gayle took to dancing like peaches to cream.

She supposed her mother had harbored a secret ambition of Gayle becoming a classical ballerina star. However, a growth spurt in junior high precluded that from ever happening. With her many interests, Gayle was far from disappointed. She loved to dance and until recently had belonged to an amateur modern jazz dance troupe, which performed semiannually. Perry, like most of her friends, knew of her avocation.

"Another date?"

"No. Merely a demanding deal I'm handling."

"I understood you weren't working."

"Perhaps not in the office, but I'm still on the payroll."

"Working from your apartment, then?"

"Not exactly," she said with the awkwardness of evasion. "What is this, the third degree?"

He grinned, a playful glint in his eyes. "Call it concern, though why I bother with anyone as uncooperative as you is beyond me."

They soon parted. Gayle headed to her temporary abode, ensuring she wasn't followed. She'd failed to ask for Perry's help, which raised more questions. Was there a reason not to trust him? Probably not. Her usual training had simply kicked in. She'd kept secrets far too long to let them go easily.

Back at the safe house, Gayle slipped off her shoes and wandered into the kitchen for some crackers and cheese to nibble. She'd have an early night. There was no reason to bring Perry into this. He couldn't be connected.

Yet, her inner radar had homed in on his niggling interest in her work. A check would have to be run before she could let it go. She flipped open her laptop and ran the search, coming up with zilch. Perry was in the clear.

If she was ever going to identify her antagonists, they must be drawn out of their deep cover. Gayle had to get back into circulation regardless of the risks. Let her adversaries realize she wasn't running scared.

With that end in mind, Gayle ignored her instinct to stay hidden and dialed Perry's number. "Perry, it's Gayle. I've freed up my schedule and would love to attend the ballet. Though I'll have to take a rain check on dinner."

"Wonderful. I'll pick you up at seven."

"I'll be downtown already. Let's meet in front of the Opéra de Paris at seven-thirty. Perhaps you know it as Palais Garnier."

Perry agreed, and Gayle rang off with the sudden recollection she had nothing suitable to wear to the ballet. And no money she could call her own. What was she going to do about a dress? And more important, was she placing Perry as well as herself in danger?

Langston glanced up as Leah entered the office with a distracted air. It was impossible to get a read on her expression. Perry sensed she was near the edge. From there a patient could either spiral into an oblivion from which there was no return or start on an upward path to recovery.

That Leah was stepping off the plateau she'd lived on for several years was significant. If only he knew more of her background. Perry had obtained the notes from Leah's prior psychiatrist. Those records verified Leah had failed to make any appreciable progress under his care. About the time the doctor started to inquire more deeply into the causes of her psychosis, he was terminated.

Strangely, it was as if she hadn't existed before her arrival at Cremont. Perry's search through newspaper archives for clues as to her identity came up empty as well. Wouldn't any wife who had heinously murdered her husband have made the headlines?

He watched Leah sink into the chair. She kept her head down. Was she sick or avoiding him? "Tell me about your day," he invited in an encouraging tone. When she failed to respond, he repeated the same words in a louder voice.

She shrugged, without looking up.

He feared time was against Leah. Perry had arranged for an experienced colleague who had no connections with the sanatorium to meet with Leah in the next week.

Perry's frustration regarding her case was natural, yet its depth surprised him. He wasn't certain why she touched him, even challenged him to unravel the mystery of her terrible psyche. Was poetry the sole medium to reach her? Last night he'd memorized one of Dickinson's poems that he sensed Leah might identify with. The text was a metaphor on acceptance and growth amid darkness and tragedy. Perry cleared his throat and spoke:

'We grow accustomed to the Dark —
When Light is put away —
As when the Neighbor holds the Lamp
To witness her Goodbye —

A moment — We uncertain step
For newness of the night —
Then fit our Vision to the Dark —
And meet the Road — erect —

And so of Larger — Darknesses —
Those Evenings of the Brain —
When not a Moon disclose a sign —
Or star — come out — within —

The Bravest — grope a little —
And sometimes hit a Tree
Directly in the Forehead —
But as they learn to see —

Either the Darkness alters —

Or something in the sight
Adjusts itself to Midnight —
And life steps almost straight’

Leah lifted her gaze, and he saw a reflection in the murky hazel of her eyes, much like a shaded stagnant pond caught by a ray of sunlight flickering through the trees. Then as if she could read his mind, she said in a younger breathless voice he had not yet heard, “Have you found out who I am?”

“Not yet. I was hoping you might help me.”

She said with an agonizing sadness, the bare glint of sunshine now past, “What would be the use? It’s all there.” She gestured to the recorder. “There’s nothing new. No one believes I could be true.”

“Leah, you mustn’t give up. I’m examining your case from a fresh perspective. Any snippet you share might assist us.”

She seemed to understand. She embraced the thread of promise in his words, and with them, the courage to reveal more of herself. “I have a poem for you too. In its stanzas, rest my life before.” Leah recited in a rushed singsong voice:

She spoke, but
He never understood,
She couldn’t find the window out.

Nights of quiet.
Rattled nerves.
Questions unanswered.

Must she wait?
Cheated and beaten,
Lies her only truth.

She finished the poem, her pale-tapered-artistic hands folded in her lap. Perry thought perhaps Leah had been a painter or a musician or a writer. Her mouth held the faint trace of an untried smile as her front teeth pressed her lower lip. She appeared to wait in nervous expectation of his response to the simple verses.

He gave her a reassuring smile. "Thank you for that insightful poem. Will you interpret it for me?"

"I can't." Her furtive gaze avoided his.

He decided to try a different tactic to reach her. "Tell me about your parents." Silence met his query. "What were they like?"

"You ask too much of me." Leah rose, ending the session.

He hesitated, not wanting to yield to defeat. "Our time is not up yet. Sit down."

She looked startled, and it was the fear in her eyes that stopped him.

In resignation, Perry rang for the attendant, unable to fathom how to crack her reserve without fatally damaging her.

Dominic checked into the Munich hotel and took the elevator to his room on the third floor. Inside, he crossed to the window and stared intently down at the crowded street near Marienplatz. Then he relaxed, sank into a chair and phoned Francois. "Has Gayle surfaced?"

"Steady, old boy. I've traced her to a CIA safe house."

"Are you sure?"

"Undoubtedly."

"Have her followed. See what else you can discover. I don't want her endangered. Understood?"

"It couldn't be clearer."

How was Gayle involved with the CIA? Dom was missing something vital and in his experience that could be deadly.

Besides keeping tabs on Gayle, Dominic was knee-deep in counter espionage. The Jakarta students had confessed to the Swiss diamond heist but denied any direct contact with Fahid. They allegedly were working for a woman who fit the description of Ari's wife Sara and they admitted to meeting with her on three occasions at the Paris San Régis, a hotel frequented by the discreet wealthy. Unfortunately, there was no video surveillance to back up the students' story.

16

Seth placed his bags on the king-sized bed and sank into a chair. Unsure how to locate Gayle, he had accompanied Mitch to his hotel and arranged for a room. After some discussion they agreed to split up. Mitch would call the gendarmerie and Seth the hospitals.

He picked up the directory on the desk and prayed. "God, You know where Gayle is. Please let her be safe and help me find her." A sense of comfort and assurance engulfed him as he flipped to the H listings in the directory and began dialing.

An hour later, Seth hung up the receiver. He'd phoned every hospital in Paris. His sister wasn't in any of them. Where was she? Had anyone even seen or spoken to her in the last week? Or had they met her mirror image, the woman set on destroying Gayle? The motivation behind such a travesty was a disturbing mystery.

Finally, Seth realized his mother would have kept up with Gayle's friends. His parents were like that, always there for their grown-up children. Why hadn't he thought of asking her sooner? He phoned his mother and hearing her voice pushed the nightmare of his missing sister back to manageable levels.

"Mom, I'm in Paris and before you imagine the worst, everything's okay. I haven't seen Gayle yet and thought I'd drop in on her."

"I'm glad you're there, Seth. I've been a bit concerned because she hasn't been in touch lately."

"I think she might be staying with one of her friends while she's looking for a new apartment. I figured you'd know who's close to her."

"Is something wrong?"

"Nah. Her lease was up, and she wanted to find a place closer to work." It wasn't an out-and-out lie. Besides, it could be true. Moreover, he hoped his thoughts would soon become fact.

He could hear her thumbing through the address book she kept on the desk. "Let's see," she said. "There's Kara, and also Abby. I'm sure they would be the ones she'd stay with." She gave him their information.

"Thanks, Mom. Talk to you later."

Seth had spoken with Kara when he first arrived in Paris but she'd never gotten back with him. Now he could reach her at home. Seth rang both women, leaving messages in their voice-mail boxes.

He wondered how Mitch had fared checking in with the police stations. There was a rap at the door and his friend entered. The frustration on his face meant he'd struck out as well.

It was time Seth started asking some tough questions. He grappled for the right words, but in the end came straight to the point. "What are the chances this situation with Gayle is somehow connected with the crash at CI?"

Mitch seemed to draw into himself, throwing up a shield between them. "I haven't been threatened. Why should Gayle be in danger? She isn't connected with this."

"Isn't she?" The jetlag snaked in and settled over a skin of worry, heating his temper. "You've been anxious to see her about nothing? With all CI's problems in Houston, I find it strange the company CEO is camping out in Paris hunting for my sister. Your intentions might be good, but don't tell me I don't have reason to be concerned. One of your staff has disappeared and the flight crew are dead. It doesn't smell right."

Mitch looked as if he wanted to punch him. "I wasn't aware your interest in CI ran so high."

"I own a sizable number of CI shares. You better believe I care about the company."

The news seemed to unsettle Mitch. "Why am I just finding this out?"

"I didn't see any reason to add to your worries. Besides, I don't have enough stock that anyone would take notice, but it's big to me. I'm asking seriously, could there be a connection?"

Mitch shrugged. "Maybe, but I don't see any from where I'm sitting." He held up a hand as Seth started to interrupt. "Frankly, I'm more than glad to fill you in. I could use a sounding board."

Seth stared out the window at the exclusive hotels, clubs and boutiques lining the Champs-Élysées. He felt alienated from the glittering life below. Had Gayle been pulled into the seedier side of Paris and swallowed into its dark night? One heard stories of Americans disappearing in foreign countries. The fear of where his sister might be was gnawing at him. He needed to know she was okay. With a sigh, he turned his gaze from the traffic swirling around the Arc de Triomphe and said to Mitch, "Go on. I'm listening."

"The truth is, CI is on the verge of bankruptcy and the renewal of the Transway contract is a major part of our survival strategy."

"Yet we're staying at one of the most expensive hotels in town."

"I can't let anyone get a whiff of our financial woes. It could signal the death of the company," Mitch said.

"Okay. Tell me more."

"The family of the deceased pilot, Frank Hazzledorf, is suing CI for allowing him to fly while intoxicated. Despite what I believed was the finest security system available, all the men who worked on that preflight external check detail have disappeared. One of those men is a close friend who left behind a wife and twin toddlers." Mitch faltered, then continued in a gruff voice. "The Feds are giving me nothing but heartburn. Well, you wanted the list and there it is. Not a pretty story, is it?"

Seth was embarrassed for doubting Mitch and wished he had read him better. "CI's got troubles but if you're on the up and up, the

Feds will find the thugs behind this, and the airline will be exonerated. If you're involved in any shenanigans, your baby's going to fall and me along with it."

Agitated, Mitch rose and paced around the room before facing Seth. "Name one advantage I would gain from dragging my company through the mud like this."

"I haven't sold any shares because I still believe in you. It's my gut feeling, and I'm counting on you to prove me right."

Mitch appeared cheered by the vote of confidence. "Thanks. Any ideas?"

"I'd guess the cargo is key. What was the pilot hauling and for whom?"

"Our records show it was a routine flight booked for Malone Exports. We were flying some of their personnel and semiprecious gemstones. Nothing fishy there. The Malone Export employees and jewels were dropped off in Oklahoma. On the flight crew's return flight to Houston, the aircraft crashed shortly before landing."

"There has to be some link. You must have thought this out."

Mitch dropped into the chair. "And come up with zilch."

Seth frowned. "What about the FBI? They didn't find any trace of drugs?"

"How about we locate your sister first? Trust me. The two are unrelated."

Seth wasn't sure. "What did you tell the police about her when you called?"

"That she was late and the family was anxious. I asked if they'd received any reports of her being in any difficulty."

"Nothing, right?"

Mitch concurred. "Have you considered she might not want to be found? She could be involved in illegal activities."

"Not a chance. I know my sister too well. This is Gayle we're talking about. It's simply not possible."

"I think it's time to notify your family. This is getting weird."

Seth ran his hands through his hair distractedly. "There are a few more items I should check before calling in the cavalry. You can go. I want to sit here and consider this from a different perspective. See if I can come up with a plan of some sort."

"You're sure?"

"Positive. Mitch, thanks for your help. I'll contact you later tonight or in the morning."

"I wouldn't blame you for selling your CI shares. Regardless, I'm here if you need me." He left.

Seth stared at the closing door, registering the enormity of what had occurred. He dialed the eldest of his siblings, hoping J.O. could shed some light on what was happening.

J.O. answered. "Seth, what's up? Have you found her?"

So much for how's Paris, he reflected. The transatlantic vibes must be aligned. "No. I need you here pronto. Sis is in deep trouble. Can you get away?"

"It depends. What degree of difficulty are we talking about and should I phone Jason?"

Seth considered how best to explain what amounted to gut feelings and theories. "For starters, I need a background check run on Mitch Carey and CI. Can you handle that from your end?"

"Sure, I don't have security clearance, but I have friends who do. Now, what's this about Gayle?"

He filled J.O. in, beginning with Gayle's accident, the takeover of her apartment, the theft of her possessions and the funds in her accounts, followed by her subsequent disappearance and replacement by a lookalike.

J.O. was silent. Seth gave him time, sympathetic of how hard it was to wrap one's mind around the news. Finally, Seth said, "Gayle's tough. She'll be okay."

"I hope so, Bro."

"I have one more request. Find out if Mitch has been selling his CI stock." Seth pondered the reasons he'd hesitated this long to ask.

Gayle worried the ballet excursion might be a violation of the rules of safe protocol, placing herself and others in danger. Yet on another level, she believed smoking out the antagonist was her most viable option. Thus far, she'd been fumbling in the shadows, straining to counter an invisible opponent. She wanted to reverse the situation and put her unknown nemesis on the defensive. It was time she enacted some offensive maneuvers of her own.

She recalled that Kara also wore a size six. As it was Saturday, her friend would likely be home. Gayle phoned and arranged to drop by.

"I heard about the loss of your apartment and belongings. I am sorry. Anything I can do to help, let me know. Why haven't you called sooner?"

"Kara, please don't be offended because I haven't phoned. I've been unconscious for most of the week." At her friend's gasp, Gayle rushed to say, "There's no reason to get excited. I'm fine now." She briefly explained how she'd been mugged, about her date for the ballet and wanting to borrow a dress.

"Sure, I have the perfect gown. But you'd better call and reassure your brother. Seth is frantic."

"You talked to my brother?"

"Yes. He's been combing Paris for you."

Gayle closed her eyes in an attempt to stay calm. The thought of him naively blundering into a trap set to catch her almost had her hyperventilating. That settled it. She was going to put a stop to this. She drew in a deep bracing breath. "I wonder why Clyde didn't tell me. We talked this morning."

"As if we'd confide in him. He told us a friend had left your number with the receptionist, but we couldn't get any response."

"Clyde is such a pain."

"No argument here."

"Would you let Seth know I'm okay? Tell him I'll be in touch soon." She didn't want her family involved. It was too dangerous.

"He said he might ask your brothers to fly over and help find you."

"Then hurry and make that call. I'll be there shortly."

Gayle dressed in baggy jeans and a navy sweater and stuffed her hair inside a matching beret. Contacts changed her eyes to walnut and a cranberry lipstick modified the shape of her mouth. She locked the house and got into the black Mini, then drove a circular route to Kara's, watching her rearview mirror for a tail. Satisfied no one had followed her, she parked a few blocks away and entered through the back entrance.

She caught the lift to the seventh floor, then climbed the stairs to the ninth and rang the bell. Kara opened the door and Gayle dashed inside.

Kara moved back in surprise. "Well, please do come in. Wow. I almost didn't recognize you."

Gayle slipped off the beret, finger-combing her hair. "Any better?"

"You could stand to lose some of the makeup, too."

"What have I done to deserve such honesty?"

Kara chuckled and led the way into the living room. They settled on the couch. A pot of coffee with cups and saucers sat on a nearby table. "*Un Café?*" Gayle nodded and Kara served them.

They sipped in companionable silence, Beethoven's Fifth playing in the background. Kara reached to turn the music up. "My favorite part," she said, raising her voice, then softer as if she didn't want anyone to hear, "Are you going to tell me what's going on?"

Her friend was too sharp not to pick up on the various nuances in Gayle's situation, yet Kara acted as if the apartment might be bugged, which was strange considering Gayle had never confided in her. She came to a hard-fought decision to level with Kara. "Get me that dress and brace yourself. I've got a lot to say and for both our sakes I can't stay any longer than is absolutely necessary."

"It's ready." She motioned to a dress bag draped across the sofa.

Gayle made to rise and Kara stayed her with a gesture. "There's no need. I think it will suit you nicely . . . if you're positive you want to go through with this, considering the risk involved."

Gayle instinctively drew back, a chill creeping up her spine. "I don't know what you mean."

Kara dug into her right jean pocket and flashed a CIA badge. "I'm your handler."

Gayle's head spun, the cells and axons of gray and white matter connecting the data, marinating at the edges of her brain. "You're Crazy Charlie?"

"Guilty."

"I never even suspected. You always acted so natural." She laughed.

Kara's eyes twinkled. "Thank you."

Gayle sobered. "What happens now?"

"Fill me in on everything, and then we'll decide."

Gayle started with the research she'd done her last afternoon at the office, then the decision to have dinner at Louis's Bistro, the ensuing attack and her recuperation at Thea's. She bemoaned the disappearance of her belongings and funds. "I've hunkered down in the safe house until I figure this out."

Kara grinned. "It sounds as if you've stirred up a hornet's nest."

"Yes, but whose?" Kara was treating Gayle's position too lightly, but then she wasn't the one running for her life. "I sensed from Elliot the agency had thrown me over."

Kara held her gaze. "His involvement strikes me as curious. How did Elliot happen on the scene and what does he have to do with this case?"

The weight of going it alone lifted a notch from her shoulders. The agency hadn't burned her as Elliot led her to believe. She needed to find out if any of her associates from Transway were involved and if the danger came from them, or elsewhere. She asked, "Do you think Clyde is involved or merely a petty annoyance?"

Kara warned, "The situation is complex. Let's see how the ballet unfolds tonight and take it from there. For now, you'd better get going and cover your tracks leaving."

"When will I see you again?"

"I'll be at the ballet. In fact, your brother can be my escort."

"I don't want him involved. It's too dangerous."

"He's been implicated since the day he invested in Mitch Carey's company and referred his friend to you. Sorry, but no one's in the clear, not even Seth, until this plays out and every last card is on the board."

"I know my brother. He would never get mixed up in any shady business dealings."

"Your job is to be objective, not Seth's sister. It's impossible to be both. If you can't handle it, tell me and I'll have you replaced."

"At this stage?"

"Yes. I never operate without contingency plans. No one is irreplaceable, not even me."

Gayle thought for a moment. "I'm in for the long haul."

"You're a good agent."

"Thanks." Gayle hugged her. "I'm glad it's you." She stuffed her hair back into the beret, picked up the dress bag and departed.

Abby left the office at 10 p.m., which was much later than usual for her. She was vexed about Elliot involving her in his underhanded maneuvers, especially those that put her at risk. Abby had enough to deal with, trying to distract Perry from his investigation into Leah's background.

The longer Abby worked with the doctor, the harder it became to pull off her deception. His growing interest in his patient's history threatened her plans. Abby hoped her subtle attempts to steer him from the case might negate any further action.

With a grimace, she started the ignition and drove to the rendezvous. Near the intersection of rue des Ecoles and boulevard Saint-Michel, she slowed, allowing faster traffic to pass. She needed a red light. About a block from the crossroad, Abby braked for the signal and Francois Rodiet climbed into the car.

"Chéri, you look more beautiful each time we meet."

"Cut the crap, we haven't long, maybe once around the block."

"I had hoped for an entire evening with you. If you will pass the folder bulging from your jacket, however, I will endeavor to pass the night on my own."

"Here." Abby slipped him the information. "You could at least have the decency to be grateful."

"So I am, if you would only let me show you how much."

Abby slowed the car and stopped on a side street. "All right, Casanova, this is where you and I part. Don't forget, you owe me big time."

"Au revoir, my sweet. I'll let you know what we decide. That should more than pay my debt."

She nodded and watched him slide into the darkness. They'd managed nicely without using any names. Twenty minutes later she parked Clyde's car and stepped into the camouflage of night, stuffing the wig she'd worn into her bag. What a long day's work it had been. She felt like a quadruple agent, if such a position existed. Sometimes her dual roles became confusing as to whom she was playing against to whom. With a sigh, she stared up at the moon and wondered if any of it mattered.

17

Gayle and Perry met in front of the Opéra de Paris as arranged. No longer the largest theater in the world, the marble Palais Garnier remained a worthy epitaph to the Second Empire's architectural achievements.

"Wow! You look fabulous," Perry said, admiringly.

She felt elegant and feminine in the burnished gold satin gown. "Thanks. You dress up nicely too."

They entered the magnificent baroque foyer and ascended the gilt staircase to their seats. She glanced at the ceiling created by Chagall and sighed. *Sleeping Beauty* was one of her favorite ballets, and Tchaikovsky's accompanying musical score was superb. Gayle spotted Kara and Seth crossing the aisle to meet her and waved.

Seth gave her a crushing bear hug. "Where have you been? The entire family has been worried."

"I'm sorry. I lost touch."

His eyes narrowed. "Lost touch? I've been trying to reach you since— I've been worried, but you look great. I guess that means you've recovered. We've got to talk."

She murmured, "Yes, but not here. We can talk later, after the ballet."

"All right. The most important thing for now is that you're okay." He turned to say hello to Perry, and Gayle greeted Kara.

They settled into their seats. Then, as she relaxed her guard, she caught sight of Clyde and Chantal seated a few rows back. Gayle worried at her lower lip. She had nothing but conjecture to go on.

Besides what danger could either of them pose with hundreds of witnesses around? The ballet began and she relaxed, enjoying the performance.

Toward the end of *Sleeping Beauty's* opening prologue, the king and queen and their guests were gathered on stage for Princess Aurora's christening. The music swelled to exciting crescendos as the evil fairy Carabosse arrived and cast a curse on the baby.

Suddenly, shots rang out near Gayle. She ducked instinctively and, grabbing Perry's arm, shoved him to the floor. When he tried to rise, she hissed, "Stay down."

Fear crowded the pounding in her chest, as she searched for Clyde. There. He was staring straight at her. He raised his arm, and without blinking she fired the pistol hidden beneath the jacket she carried, striking his hand. Clyde's shot went amiss, and Seth crumpled. He'd been hit. Gayle's heart constricted as she urged Perry up and pulled him alongside her. She should never have come to the ballet. This was her fault for placing her family and friends in danger.

Perry leaned over Seth, assessing the damage. Perry quickly slipped out of his jacket, rolled it into a bandage and held it against the wound in Seth's chest to slow the bleeding.

Kara whispered, "I've called emergency services. They'll be here any moment. Let's get out of here."

"I can't leave my brother."

"This is not a request. It's an order. Now get moving." Kara addressed Perry. "We'll meet you at the hospital. Can you keep our names out of this?"

He seemed surprised but nodded.

Gayle knelt beside Seth, frantic at the amount of blood spreading across his chest. "Perry, is he going to be okay?"

"I can't be sure but the bullet seems to have missed any vital organs."

"You'll stay with him?"

"Of course."

"Please don't ask me to explain, but I won't be coming to the hospital. My very presence places him in danger. Watch over him. Someone may try to hurt him because of me."

"Gayle, what's this about?"

She kissed Seth's cheek, then said to Perry. "I've got to go."

She and Kara left the theater, going their separate ways. Gayle caught a cab, then a train and finally the métro to ensure she wasn't followed to the safe house.

The attack at the theater had shaken her. *Please God, let Seth be all right.* Gayle hadn't prayed much lately. There were no words for the ice and pain within, only tears. Where else could she turn but to God?

Gayle feared the new orders she'd been awaiting weren't coming. The agency probably considered her a liability and wanted her off the case. Kara had hinted as much, as they left the theater. Aside from Kara, no one had contacted her except for Elliot, unofficially.

"Lord, help me let go of the past and get back to you," she murmured. "To fight this. I am so tired. So sorry."

Sometime during the night she heard Him, light as air, calling to her. "Gayle, I haven't deserted you. Believe in me and everything will come right."

She felt conflicted and angry. Her weakness confused her. She'd led her brother into an ambush. How would she bear it if he died? Her relationship with Dom had failed. Her job with the airlines and her undercover operations with the CIA were out of control. Life taunted her with its circle of failure.

Gayle bowed her head in despair, and despite everything, Dom's image rose before her. After Elliot's report she should have had the strength to let Dom go, yet the past still haunted her.

How could she give him up? Why must she lose him? Was chance never true? She had to think! What was this about? *Dom, speak to my heart, wherever you are and I'll find you.*

No. She had to stop imagining the best in him. He was the past she could no longer trust. She was through with him.

On an island in the Pacific, Dom paced the floor of his hotel room, brooding about Gayle. He sensed her nearness, impossible as it might seem, and was puzzled by it. How long before he could locate *the package* and move on? It had started ages ago. He settled into a chair and thought through the night.

At seven a.m. he heard knocking at the door. He grabbed his gun, rushed to the window and crawled out on the ledge, creeping along until he reached his prearranged safety net, a vacant room a few doors from his. He raised the window and climbed inside.

Quietly waiting in the darkened hotel room, he sat on the edge of the bed, his pistol drawn. Several minutes later, he heard a whistle and the key in the lock as Francois walked in.

"You scared the daylights out of me," Dom said. "Was that you knocking? What was the idea?"

Francois dropped down beside him. "Sorry. I was about to give the signal, when the person across the hall opened his door and simply stood there watching me like he was at the theater. Under the circumstances I thought it better to knock and then retreat, leaving the impression you weren't in." He scowled. "I'm getting too old for these games."

Dom sighed his agreement. They returned to his room. "Any news?"

"Elliot tipped us off that the CIA suspects Abby has turned."

Dom quipped, "*Mettre son grain de sel.*"

"Yes, Elliot likes to add his grain of salt."

"Maybe we can use Abby's defection to our advantage, and have Ari drop the news in Fahid's ears."

Francois said, "Ari hasn't given us any worthwhile intel in a while. Are you positive he's not working against us?"

"Absolutely."

"Interpol is shadowing Abby now as are the CIA and probably every agency in Europe. Perhaps she'll lead us to Sara."

Dom worried how Ari would handle the news about Sara, if it turned out she was involved with the Swiss diamond heist. "Once we've located her a lot will change."

Francois agreed and they discussed plans for their next foray.

And there would be another and another. It would never stop until they found the stolen jewels and other sources of revenue helping to fund the terrorism in Paris and stopped the threat of imminent attacks from the Middle East.

After Francois left, Dom stared glumly out at the stormy sky. His clandestine work with French Intelligence had started in his first year of college. The agency suspected Ari, his Syrian roommate, of spying and planning terrorist activities. Dominic, as the son of a high-placed government official, had managed to uncover the classified documents to help clear his friend.

Dominic loved his family yet deplored their beastly attitude toward Gayle and those who weren't part of the aristocracy. His home life had offered far more than surface glamour. From an early age he was taught the importance of nobility and the responsibility it brought. His parents and sister had been warm and loving.

Yvette had asked him once, "Dom, do you believe we're truly better than others?"

"No, chéri, never better. Just blessed with much. The Bible teaches, 'To whom much is given, much is expected.' We've been given such riches, wonderful homes, schools and connections, advantages most will never experience."

She nodded reflectively. "Yes, I suppose we have. Does it matter?" she asked with a catch in her voice.

He gave her a reassuring smile. "I like to think of it as a trust to be shared and managed. Perhaps we are the beggars, impoverished because we've seen only one side of life. Don't you wonder at the passion and depth we see around us?"

Yvette rose and hugged him. "You are absolutely marvelous. Then you think it's okay for me to see Pierre?"

"Naturally."

But their parents objected. They distanced themselves, refusing their blessings when Yvette and Pierre, her music instructor, announced their engagement. The two ran off to America. There, Pierre made a name for himself as a concert pianist, and Yvette completed a law degree specializing in child protection cases. Dominic was proud of them both.

Then he had met Gayle and known exactly how Yvette felt. His parents were disappointed about his engagement but with the rift between them and Yvette as a forerunner, they had kept their feelings private until after he'd left. Now his mother and father had forsaken Gayle, leaving her exposed to the whims of the media. Dom wasn't surprised, having lived with them most of his life. Besides, who was he to criticize his parents? He'd deserted her too.

"Dom, stand tall, shoulders back. You are a Trudeau," his mother would say when he was three. And at four, when his parents were off to some house party, travels or duties, they would bid him and Yvette good-bye, forcing Dom to swallow his tears and stand straight, promising to be the little man of the house and take care of his baby sister.

His mother would hug him. "Don't look so serious, darling. The servants will see to everything. You'll both be fine. Now give maman a kiss." The scent of Christian Dior that was his mother enveloped him as he kissed her and shook his father's hand.

In college, after helping Ari escape prosecution, Dom's interest in the study of the law had broadened to international law, and he had pursed a doctorate in that field. One week after he completed his studies at the university, he'd received the call from Interpol.

18

Disguised as an old woman, Gayle visited Seth in the hospital. Her brother remained unconscious, but his doctor's prognosis of a swift recovery was encouraging. She scooted a chair next to the bed and placed her hand on his. "I'm sorry," she prayed softly. "God, please, let Seth regain consciousness."

She left him at about noon and caught a taxi to a modest café on the Left-Bank where she had arranged to meet Abby, the Interpol associate with whom she had worked her first case on the Riviera. Gayle spotted the dainty brunette, who had the good fortune to be an Audrey Hepburn look-alike, sitting at an outdoor table. Gayle hugged her. "It seems like ages."

Abby smiled. "Long enough for you to land in hot water?"

The waiter brought coffee and they chatted leisurely. The perfumed breeze smelled of rain and roses. Nimbus clouds scudded across the pewter sky. "Looks like we might be in for a drenching."

"Perhaps we should move inside, but I'd rather not," Abby said.

"Then it's settled. I'm content to sit here and watch the storm roll in." Gayle's thoughts centered on more pressing matters. Abby was a veteran in the intelligence community, and her contacts were myriad. Gayle decided to be direct. "I need to know, is Dominic an agent?"

Abby's dark eyes widened. "I assumed you knew Dominic worked with Interpol. You seemed deeply in love. I imagined he'd told you."

Gayle was stunned to discover Abby and Dominic had colluded on cases through the years. And yet Abby had obtained his phone records for her without mentioning it. Why hadn't the CIA briefed her on Dom's connections? She'd been working blindly to defend him from drug allegations during the St. Abient case. Gayle was mortified. Had her colleagues all known the truth? "I suppose I made a nice cover for him," she said bitterly.

"Don't be too hard on yourself. I've never said anything to you before now, and technically I still haven't because I simply don't discuss cases except on a need-to-know basis."

"Well, you've confirmed what I suspected," Gayle said. True, her suspicions had resided more in her subconscious. After Dom's strange disappearance, then Francois's reaction and the letter that followed, she'd sensed she was dealing with an entirely different man than the fiancé she'd known and loved. What kind of man was Dominic?

On the surface, she had been clueless. Ironic, wasn't it? Both of them being undercover agents, while neither trusted the other enough to confide the truth. Gayle sighed. "Everything makes more sense to me now. I don't think either of us knew what love was. All we shared was based on a lie."

Abby said gently, "It's tough to maintain relationships in our line. Did you ever tell him about your work?"

"No. I guess we're even on that score." Gayle divulged some information about what had been happening. "My next question should be, is he somehow involved in my present situation? Could he be on a case that's somehow affecting me? Maybe it's why he left."

"Gayle, I haven't a clue what he's working on, but I hear it's big. Would you like me to see whether I can reach Dominic for you?"

"No. There's never been any doubt Dom knows where I am. He's chosen his path. I won't interfere, with the proviso, his case has nothing to do with my predicament."

"I'll see what I can unearth. Otherwise, you're probably better off letting it rest, however hard that may be," Abby said, an understanding glint in her eyes.

Gayle swallowed. "Is he aware of my affiliations?"

"I've never mentioned you to him. I wouldn't reveal your cover unless a case depended on it." She dug into her purse. "Oops. I almost forgot. Here's the info on the Houston number you asked me to trace."

Gayle scanned the page and saw the number belonged to Guy Williams, an Interpol agent. "Hmm. The Houston connection is interesting. I don't suppose you've met him?"

"Sorry, no, but Elliot might have. Check with him."

"Thanks. I owe you." Gayle hugged Abby and left.

Gayle phoned Elliot from the safe house. "What can you tell me about Guy Williams?"

"Let's see. He's an Interpol agent based out of Houston."

"Could he be working with Dominic?"

"It's highly possible, but I haven't heard of anything other than a jewel heist Williams has been working to solve."

Her courage crumbled at the realization Elliot had been less than truthful with her. "Curious. I thought you weren't aware Dominic was an agent."

"So, I lied. It wasn't my place to tell you."

"Yet you made it your responsibility to inform me about the other woman? How will I ever know when you're telling the truth?"

"Red, you're overreacting. I don't have time for these games. Grow up."

"Fine. Thanks for the info."

Gayle hung up and wondered what else she was missing. She tried a mental run-through of every incident. First, there was her transfer to Paris to investigate the two unidentified security brokers suspected of embezzling. About to close the case, she'd noted an abnormal volume of buying and selling, then irregular activity in accounts that were usually dormant popped up. Even more of a red flag, most of the transactions occurred after hours. Still, she had nothing concrete to incriminate the culprits.

What if they were taking advantage of the market's different closing times around the world, buying when specific mutual funds had blocked clients from trading? And what if they were using false identities to make the fraudulent trades? How would they circumvent the legalities? Maybe by changing random account numbers to execute preset purchases. If only she could link the embezzlers solidly to the fraudulent numbers.

If they were skimming profits from long-term shareholders, she should have found proof. Had she been sidetracked by Dom's disappearance and entirely missed the trail? She couldn't shake the sense that there was some elusive and important fact right in front of her.

It was late when Gayle climbed into bed and tried to sleep. In her mind, she saw Seth lying there bleeding. Her chest tightened. He went to the ballet to see her. She swallowed past the thickness at the back of her throat and rolled over but couldn't escape her thoughts. Last night kept replaying in her mind. Through half-opened lids, she eyed the slowly ticking clock. She was floating on a river of guilt and needed rest.

With a groan, Gayle sat up and reviewed the previous evening's events again, along with her visits with Seth and Abby. If her other brothers arrived in Paris, how was she supposed to keep them safe?

Dreams haunted Gayle's sleep.

She stumbled into a rose garden and inhaled the sweet fragrance of velvet-red petals sparkling with morning dew. To her astonishment Mitch walked through the side entrance and gathered her close. She savored his nearness in wonder, until a whirlwind whisked her from his arms.

On an island in the Pacific, Dom held her hand as the gilded dawn washed across the sandy beach and faded into day.

Dominic left to join Abby in the Swiss Alps. Alone, Gayle watched the sun set over Switzerland.

All at once she was biking in Belgium through a rainstorm, tasting the rain as it sloshed down her face. The tame rumble of thunder was at her back, the lightning far enough to the north to enjoy without fear. The tangled roadside greenery reminded her nostalgically of Houston and in a wink she was there, happily curled up in her favorite club chair, reading a novel.

Gayle awoke and lay there, a symphony of melodies from the past singing through her mind. She was a child again, playing in her grandmother's antique rose garden, helping to squash the bugs and pulling off the yellow leaves diseased with black spot.

As payment, her grandmother would relate the history of each rose. "This is the Duchesse de Brabant tea rose. It was Teddy Roosevelt's favorite. He often wore one on his jacket lapel. Smell how sweet."

Gayle breathed in the delicate scent of the cupped pink rose, regretting the passage of years and her lost innocence. For a moment, the veil dropped and with embarrassed confusion she recalled Mitch cradling her in his arms and something about Dom and Abby in her dream.

The phone rang, breaking into her reverie. She sat up with a jerk. Why was the agency contacting her now? She rushed into the bathroom, closing and locking the door before making a sweep of the soundproof room. In one fluid motion, Gayle opened the medicine cabinet, locating and pressing the lever that slid the false wall aside. She grabbed the phone on the third ring. "Oui."

Elliot spoke in French as well. "Red, this is an unofficial warning which could cost me my head. Go home. I can't go into details but—"

A flutter of unease assailed her. "I've already arranged to return to work next week. Besides, you know I can't leave without orders."

"Haven't you figured it out yet? Someone has assumed your identity, which is impossible without the agency's approval. Call Transway and ask to speak with Miss Regan. Then please, go home."

The pieces fell together too conveniently for her peace of mind. Fear scalded her, simmering up her spine until it burned in her. Terrified of his answer, she managed to ask with a semblance of calm, "Are you inferring the agency wants to take me out?"

"I'm telling you point blank; there's a contract on your head."

Her sensibilities balked, while her mind raced ahead, assessing her position. She was hiding in a CIA safe house. If the agency wanted to finish her off, they could have—unless the department ordering the hit hadn't received access yet to the pertinent info. There were certain protections in place in the organization to prevent such overlapping of powers.

"No. I don't believe it," she said. "Not the United States government. This isn't some spy movie. It's my life. I haven't uncovered anything worth murdering me for."

"Call Transway. Don't trust anyone, not even me. I have my orders as well."

"Elliot, what are you saying?" she sputtered as the phone went dead. Had he just warned her that he had been ordered to eliminate her? This couldn't be happening. Could it?

With her hand trembling slightly, she rang Transway and asked to speak with Miss Regan.

"Whom may I say is calling?"

She scrambled for a name, any name but hers: Dom's mother. "Madame Trudeau."

"A moment, please," her PA said.

A voice came on the line as familiar as her own. "Good morning, Madame Trudeau. How may I assist you?"

"Is this Miss Regan?" Gayle asked hesitantly,

"Yes. You wished to speak with me?"

How could the woman mimic her voice so perfectly? Gayle struggled to recover from the shock. In a husky voice edged with the arrogance typical of her almost mother-in-law, she said, "Have you heard from my son?"

An intake of breath was followed by a stretched silence. Gayle found some satisfaction in having fleetingly discomfited the impostor.

There was a clearing of the throat. "Yes, I received his post card from Switzerland only last week."

"When you reply, please ask him to write his mother," Gayle said stiffly, in what she considered a fair imitation of Madame's haughtiness. She then ended the call quickly before unwisely drawing attention to herself.

Instinctively, she knew she ought to run as far and as fast as possible to sort out the details and the inherent complications from a safer vantage point. "Wherever that might be," she muttered. The few clothes she'd purchased were tossed into a bag with her ID and cash. A few moments were spent retrieving the laptop as well. Gayle ran out to the garage, threw her bag on the passenger side and scooted into the driver's seat.

She turned the key as a chilling thought sent her scrambling out of the car. She barely made it outside before the vehicle exploded, taking part of the house with it. Hunched low, she sprinted through the backyard into the alley. Dirty, disheveled and trembling, she dug a tissue from her pants pocket to wipe her face and hands, before running unsteady fingers though her hair to smooth it.

She was thankful to be alive. For the second time in a matter of weeks someone had attempted to kill her and had managed to strip her of her belongings.

She walked as casually as possible down the alley to the wooded park on the corner. There was a good chance, at least initially, the agency would believe she'd died in the explosion. "God, are you trying to send me a message? I need some help here," Gayle prayed.

19

Once her terror had subsided somewhat Gayle caught the train to Laval, fleeing Paris. The clank of the wheels on steel tracked her thoughts as they spun out of control and into the past.

The week after her graduation from college, Gayle had been approached by the CIA. Elliot had stopped at her table in a crowded Starbucks. "Do you mind if I join you?"

She hesitated, glancing about for a free seat and seeing none, nodded. She remembered thinking how handsome and continental he appeared.

Elliot introduced himself and drew out his ID. Puzzled, she studied it. "Look up the CIA's number, then call them on your cell phone. Ask to be connected to the CIA Recruitment Department, extension one-zero-two."

There was a sense of authority about him that had her obeying his instructions implicitly. Gayle dialed the number, was transferred to the proper department, and was promptly assured that Elliot was indeed a government agent.

She put her mobile down thoughtfully. Was someone she knew in trouble? "What's this about?"

"The CIA is interested in you, Miss Regan."

"Me?" she asked, astonished, a rush of exhilaration crowding in. "I don't understand. What brought me to your attention?"

He smiled faintly. "Actually, a former acquaintance working in special operations."

She mentally ran through several possibilities. "I have no idea who you're talking about."

"Sorry, there's no point in guessing. Our sources are confidential."

As if the secrecy wasn't enough to pique her interest, he launched into a tantalizing, concise summary of the position the agency had in mind for her and the training required. Elliot touched on the challenges and risks before plunging into the special qualities required to serve one's country.

That summer, when her family and friends believed she had left to spend a year with a college roommate abroad, Gayle was steeped in counterintelligence discipline. Afterward, she had stepped into a starting position at the Houston hub of Transway Airlines, embarking on the career she had imagined prior to her recruitment. Two years passed without any CIA contact until orders for a transfer to the Munich branch of Transway and her first assignment arrived simultaneously.

As it happened, FBI and CIA cooperation set in motion the workings of an international drug bust. Gayle was instrumental behind the scenes, baiting a trap for an airline executive suspected of cooperating with foreign drug lords. The experience was unnerving and challenging.

Another year passed before she was approached while on vacation in southern France. As directed, Gayle put in a request for an extended holiday. The agency supplied her with German identity papers, a traveling companion, a private suite at a deluxe hotel on the French Riviera, and a new wardrobe and driver.

The CIA was testing her, and she relished the experiment, especially as it netted a war time criminal, in part thanks to her. After that, she was sent on annual assignments with the department initiating contact during her vacations.

The case level was sufficient to keep her alert and prepared when needed. In between, there had been a few instances of counterintelligence involving the airlines, an area in which she particularly excelled.

Gayle had never imagined the path she'd chosen would lead her to this dangerous precipice. Still, she refused to believe the US government was responsible for the attempts on her life or the complicated situation she was currently ensnared in. She suspected a rogue element was on the move. Her temper flared at the gross injustice that had been perpetrated on her. Eventually, whoever was behind the attacks would be caught and prosecuted.

With that thought, Gayle rose and made her way to the conductor. "How long until the next stop?"

He pulled out his watch. "Another fifteen minutes to le Mans."

"Thank you. I'll be getting off there."

Gayle walked to her seat. She had never backed down from a fight and she wouldn't start now. She would return to Paris and face this with God's help.

Gayle caught the train to Paris and proceeded to the safe house she'd maintained without the agency's knowledge—insurance she'd purchased on a whim in her great-grandmother's maiden name. Gayle had not used the house before, because she was saving it as a last resort in case her job with the CIA ever went south. She had hoped never to reside there, yet considered it a shrewd investment, if nothing else.

Since Plan A had failed, she would set Plan B into play. Her forethought in developing alternate strategies was a Godsend, especially as the agency's car had been destroyed. *Thank God for the whisper within moments before the explosion, Run for your life.* Those words had sent her flying out of the car seconds before it blew up.

It was night before Gayle reached the modest residence on the outskirts of 15 ème. She'd chosen the house because of its relatively safe and affordable locality. Paris, she'd learned early on, was divided into twenty neighborhoods called *arrondissements*, each numbered according to the last two digits of their postal code. The convoluted path she had taken to the area left her reasonably certain no one was following her.

Glad of the dark, she skirted through the rear gate, to the porch, punched in the backdoor code with trembling hands and then stepped inside. The simplicity of the gray stucco three-bedroom home embraced her. Rounded arches led her through the small entryway to the living room. Exhausted, she dropped onto the shabby uphol-stered couch and fell asleep while contemplating her next move.

The following morning when Gayle awoke, her mind was set. She phoned Kara to put Plan B into motion. Fortunately, she had made it a practice to keep various supplies for disguises on hand. She secured her shoulder length curls up on her head and set a cropped black wig over them.

New contacts modified her eyes to chocolate brown. An application of tanning lotion, makeup and a change of wardrobe completed her metamorphosis. Satisfied, she glanced at the clock and realized it had taken a while to effect the transformation.

That evening, dressed in somber pants and a shirt, Gayle climbed out of a taxi several blocks from her destination. She walked down the street, turned at the corner, then darted into Transway's shadowy entry and pushed *Send* on the text message, alerting Kara. As pre-arranged, Kara would disable the alarm and cameras briefly, giving Gayle enough time to rush into the elevator and reach her office.

Flashlight and key in hand, Gayle unlocked her office door and stepped inside, shining the light around the room. A picture of herself wearing a dress she'd never seen was on the desk. Gayle realized she was staring at the pretender.

How could she prove this woman wasn't her? There must

be something aside from the clothing and pose that was off. The impostor wore the earrings Gayle's mother had given her on her last birthday. Dominic's engagement ring to Gayle sparkled on the third finger and left hand of this stranger. The jewelry that was stolen when Gayle was attacked was a painful reminder of all she'd lost.

Questions bubbled and boiled in her mind, and her heart. Did this woman know Dom? If so, how well? Were they working together? Gayle began searching her desk for evidence to expose her nemesis. Tears wet her face as she closed the last drawer.

She pulled the thumb drive with the remote access software from her purse, booted up the desktop PC, installed the program, and then removed the disk. This would enable her to view the files from anywhere and study them at her leisure.

Gayle quickly moved on to Clyde's office and hunted through his desk for a list of his associates. Somehow, she would find a way to prove the woman impersonating her was the real criminal. Gayle doubted that Clyde had the intelligence to mastermind the attacks on her, but she could be mistaken.

At the sound of approaching steps, she whirled, dropping her flashlight. "What are you doing here?" she exclaimed, hoping Mitch wouldn't see through her disguise.

He took in her crouched position, the flashlight on the floor and the gun pointed at him. "I might ask you the same."

Gayle scrambled to her feet. "How did you get in?" She had used her key to enter and was certain he didn't have one.

He studied her for a long moment. "Mind telling me what this is about?"

"I'm holding the gun. How did you get in?"

He moved forward. "Let me have the pistol. You won't be needing it."

Gayle's training kicked in. "One step nearer and I'll shoot."

"You wouldn't dare advertise to security you're here." He lunged for the weapon as she grabbed his wrist and flipped him onto his back.

Mitch groaned and struggled to a sitting position, then stood. "Was that necessary?"

She refused to be sidetracked. "I'll ask again, how did you get in?"

"I bribed the security guy, Gayle."

"Oh." He'd said her name. How had he seen through her disguise?

He grinned as if reading her thoughts. "It's the stubborn look in your eyes, much like Seth's. He underestimates your ability to take care of number one."

"Exactly what my parents have always said."

His mouth quirked in amusement. "Are you dressed for a masquerade?"

"Don't be ridiculous."

"Hey, I'm not the one gussied up like—"

"Don't say it. I have perfectly sound reasons for not wanting to be recognized."

"So, I've heard," he said, concern edging his voice.

She blinked in surprise. "From whom?"

"Seth."

"You've seen him?" When he nodded, she said, "Then you know he was shot."

"Yes, but he's recovered."

Gayle realized how much she wanted to trust Mitch. It was a relief someone outside the agency knew who she was. She placed the gun in her purse. "Why were you following me?"

"Certainly not intentionally. I received an anonymous text message that you were at Transway HQ and in danger."

"It sounds like we've been set up. Let's get out of here ASAP." Although Gayle had every right to be there, she had no desire to put Clyde on the alert or herself in the awkward position of proving who she was and explaining to company security why she was in her office at three in the morning. She didn't dare let her defenses drop until they were out of the building and any evidence of her entry erased. "Let's go."

"Wait a minute." He picked up the CI file on Clyde's desk and leafed through several pages, then slipped it into his jacket and grabbed hold of her arm. "Come on." He urged her through the door and into the elevator.

A security guard met them on the ground floor and Mitch thanked him for his help. "Let's keep this between us."

The man nodded and led them down the hall, hastening to unlock the outside door.

Mitch waved and they stepped outside. "Let's take my car," he said. "It's time we had a talk."

She had a few questions for him as well. Suspicions flew through her mind like arrows. Mitch hadn't shown any qualms about paying off the guard or copping that file. They walked up the street to his car, and Mitch drove to his hotel.

Gayle stifled an urge to reach over and straighten his dark windblown hair. He was attractive. Strangely Mitch left her feeling vulnerable and yet protected. Maybe it was that male-Texan-take-charge attitude; all the men in her family possessed it in varying degrees. She'd grown up wrapped in the cocoon of their caring.

It would be nice to work with someone like Mitch. Someone she could lean on. But it was too soon to trust anyone after everything that had happened. The animosity aimed at disarming her constituted a dangerous conundrum. The motivations eluded her. She'd only dug herself in deeper, trying to resolve the case on her own. Her controller appeared to have conveniently left her to manage alone. Elliot or Kara could have identified Gayle and stopped her impersonator. Abby could have as well. They had all refused for reasons of their own. And no one else knew Gayle was working for the CIA.

Mitch stopped in the hotel parking garage. They clambered out of the vehicle and rode the elevator up to his floor. His room was as good a place as any for them to talk. If only she didn't fear the outcome.

20

Gayle stepped into Mitch's room and sank into the nearest chair. She kicked off her shoes and leaned back, glad to be off her feet.

Mitch gave her a sympathetic glance and handed her a bottle of water. "I hate to pile it on, but you owe me a conversation."

She wrinkled her nose. "I promised we'd talk, but I never said when."

"A mere matter of semantics."

"Okay. Before we begin though, mind if I take a look at your phone? I'd like to know who sent that text warning you I was in danger."

Mitch detached the mobile from its pouch on his belt, scrolled to the message and handed it to her. "I've already tried to trace it and couldn't. The call probably came from a throwaway cell."

She punched in the number, discovered it was no longer in service and gave Mitch his phone back. "So, let's talk."

Mitch frowned. "Carey International may appear to be in a more precarious position than when we first signed with Transway, but our company is as capable of fulfilling its commitments today as then. For you to withdraw that contract, however, puts our credibility at stake."

Gayle had considered the worst-case scenario: What if Mitch were criminally charged and sentenced to prison? Certainly, this was a possibility, but she'd play nice rather than go there. Since he wanted to discuss his options there was no sense in hedging. "What if the government shuts you down?"

"It's unlikely, but should it occur, we have partner airlines lined up to handle any slack."

She raised her brow. "That's exactly why I renegotiated CI's contract and ordered it to be posted to you express."

"But I–"

She held up a hand. "I'm aware you received notice of cancellation. I'm not sure why my orders were countermanded. Rest assured, I made it my business to investigate before offering to renew."

"That's welcome news. Thank you," he said warmly.

"Mitch, it seems to me if you're innocent, someone's going to a great deal of trouble to ruin you. Has it occurred to you I find myself similarly situated?"

"You mean there's a connection?"

"Not necessarily, only we are both being targeted. Beyond that I haven't the slightest idea what it's all about."

Mitch frowned. "What if there is a link?"

"We're associated professionally, but not closely. The two of us barely know one another."

"I wonder," he said. "We're two Texans from Houston, both in the airlines business. Our respective companies deal with freight, aircraft, pilots and customers. We're bound to have common clients."

Gayle groaned. He was beginning to make sense, but he had no idea of her double life as a CIA agent and how that played into events. "All right, for the sake of conjecture, get me a printout of CI's customer base and I'll cross-match it with Transway's."

Mitch crossed to the corner desk, sat, and then typed in several commands on his laptop. "Done. Now it's your turn."

"Move over. You'll have to share the computer. Remember. I'm homeless and broke." Her fail-safe home in her great-grandmother's name and the agency laptop were secrets she wasn't ready to share.

He vacated his seat. "Anything for a fellow Texan."

Gayle set to work, opening their clients' rosters onto a split screen for easy comparison. "Keep in mind, our corporate model is much larger than CI's," she cautioned.

"Naturally." He leaned over her shoulder scanning the data.

"The only viable reason for any of our patrons to deal with CI directly would be to get a cheaper rate."

"Mm, I see where this is going. My contract strictly prohibits poaching Transway's clients, but what if CI was duped into doing that?"

She blinked. "It's a possibility. The client would have used a different name, one not easily recognizable. If that's true, we're searching for a subsidiary or a privately held concern with the same owner on both lists." Gayle expanded the search to include directors and related enterprises, scrolling through them.

"Bingo," Mitch said. "Look here in Transway's column. Harri Malone is the CEO of Arab Imports and its subsidiary Malone Exports. The same company chartered the CI plane that went down."

"Hmm. We might be on to something. Let's see what else we can find."

Mitch looked at his watch. "Excuse me. I have to make a call." He stepped into the bathroom and closed the door.

She exited Transway's files and logged onto Malone Exports' site to study their business profile. The information was sketchy, but the business specialized in high-end diamonds and gemstones. A study of the associates' roster and financial statements revealed nothing out of the ordinary. Next, she visited the mother company, Arab Imports' website and learned they held widely varied interests. There wasn't much to go on.

Gayle glanced up as Mitch returned. She closed the laptop, deciding to continue the investigation at home where she could examine Transway's records on Arab Imports in depth. Her energy was winding down, and it was time for her to vacate the premises. Mitch sat sprawled in a large wing-back chair.

Perhaps, she should alert her brothers to her covert status. Gayle hadn't encountered the fix they couldn't get her out of, and that was the crux of why she'd neglected to call them. She was a federal agent, no longer the adventurous child her siblings rescued from trees and the class bully's taunts.

She needed her dad's calm reasoning and her mother's reassurance more than her brothers leaping wildly to her defense. Yet with her dad's weak heart, she didn't dare trouble him.

Who would have imagined her sojourn in Paris could become so twisted? The thought that Elliot and others had been using her all along hurt. Why hadn't she seen the truth sooner? Agents were taught how to manipulate and maneuver. Wasn't deception a part of her job description? Gayle was tired of secrets and wandering in the dark. She wanted out.

As if he were there and could read her mind, she pictured Elliot shaking his head. "It won't work. You can't walk away. The agency will never let that happen."

Was she finally losing it? Holding discussions with people who weren't even there, rather than concentrating on her present predicament. "Sufficient to the day is the evil therein." What a fitting Bible verse.

Someone knocked abruptly on Mitch's door. All at once her hands turned clammy as Mitch got up and opened the door. "You got here fast."

"I'm right down the hall," Seth said as he entered.

At the sight of him relief filled Gayle. She had no idea where he had sprung from. What mattered was he was there.

"Gayle," he said in a voice thick with emotion as he rushed to her side. "What's going on here?"

Tears gathered in her eyes. "When did you get out of the hospital? You have no idea how happy I am to see you."

"I might." He hugged her close. "The doctor released me yesterday. Before you ask, luckily it was a minor wound, and I'm fine now."

"I'd say you were blessed," Mitch said.

Seth grinned. "This is my sister, the real Gayle! I'd recognize her anywhere despite the weird hair and clothes. I can't believe you're here."

"So, you don't like my disguise?" Gayle didn't mind his scolding in the least. He was obviously worried and must have been frantic to find her. She had been concerned about him too. It was nice to see him looking well. Thankfully, the rest of her family had been spared the anxiety.

"How about explaining what's been going on?" Seth asked.

"Let's go to your room. Mitch must be exhausted."

"I'm not tired, and I'd like to continue."

Before Gayle could respond, Seth intervened. "Let me get her settled in my room tonight. We need some time. You two can meet tomorrow. Okay?"

She nodded.

"Mitch?" Seth queried.

"I don't suppose it'll hurt to wait until morning."

They said their goodbyes and she followed Seth down the hall. Gayle had much to consider, but she was beat.

They trudged into Seth's room, and he motioned her to a chair. The decor was much like Mitch's, expensive with a view people paid handsomely to enjoy. The Hotel le Burgundy was located near the Champs-Élysées. "Nice place." She bolted the door and then walked about, unobtrusively searching for bugging devices.

"Mitch was settled here, and it seemed easier to join forces. I'm glad he found you."

"Me too. Did he tell you where?"

"He did when he phoned."

"So, it was you he called. Strange how he showed up at Transway headquarters in the middle of the night. How well do you really know him?"

Seth dropped into the chair across from her. "There are a lot of unanswered questions, but I still trust Mitch."

She smiled, misty-eyed. "Hey, thanks for the rescue from him."

"A piece of cake," he bragged, a teasing glint in his eyes, "but you owe me."

"Somehow, I thought I might. Put it on the tab," she shot back with a wink. They understood each other perfectly. They weren't going to let circumstances dictate their attitudes and actions. *Thank you, Lord, for sending Seth to remind me of the good in my life.*

He picked up a menu lying on the table between them. "Are you hungry?"

"No, and there's no need for me to stay here. Why don't you come home with me?"

He frowned. "Then you do have a place and you haven't been destitute on the street?"

She shrank at the pain she had caused him by not staying in touch. "Guilty."

Seth looked hurt and disappointed. "I assume there's a reason you didn't phone. What were we supposed to think when you simply disappeared? This isn't like you, Sis."

Gayle considered how to answer and, in the end, decided to confide the truth. Someone outside of the agency should understand what was happening to her.

She drew her identification from her breast pocket and handed it to him.

He gave her a quizzical look. "What's this?"

"My ID."

He seemed embarrassed. "Don't be ridiculous. I was there when you were born or at least right after."

"Check it out, okay? If you had a nanosecond of doubt, it means you're a rational being. I forgive you." Thankfully, Gayle had kept her badge and ID in the safe at her fail-safe house and it hadn't been lost with all her other belongings.

His brow puckered. Clearly, she'd made him uncomfortable. "If this is an attempt to change the subject . . ."

"It's not. Please." Gayle hated breaking her pledge to the agency, but they'd faltered in keeping their commitment to her.

Seth gave in and opened the small leather case, his stunned gaze swung from the badge to her. He shook his head in disbelief, then seemed to gather his composure, digesting this new image of his baby sister. And as usual, wanting to get the facts up-front, he asked, "How long?"

"I started right after college."

"Those trips. They were never vacations, were they?"

"No. Now you know why I could never hook up with you and your friends."

He dropped his face into his hands. "What have you got yourself mixed up in?" Seth straightened. "No, don't take offense. I'm merely flabbergasted and scared senseless for you. All these years and we never knew. I wonder, did you tell Dominic? Could this be the reason you two broke up?"

"You're the first to know. I haven't even told Mom and Dad."

He shuddered. "Especially not them."

They stared at each other in understanding.

Then he grew thoughtful. "I didn't think agents carried IDs with them on assignments."

"They don't usually. But someone out there is pretending to be me. I'm not even sure I can trust my handler. If I got caught at Transway tonight, I wanted to be able to prove who I am."

"Are you swearing me to secrecy?"

"For now, but if anything should happen or you don't hear from me for a while—then you can shout it from the roof tops, though a subtle approach might be more effective."

"Gayle, we've danced around your present situation long enough. Give me the story unabridged."

She told him how she'd been mugged, then injured and had recovered only to find her apartment leased, her belongings stolen and her accounts wiped out. "Someone is not only impersonating me but trying to kill me as well."

Seth's lips tightened, and his blue eyes seemed to pale with feelings he kept on a tight rein. "I had figured that much out. Do you have any idea why you're a target?"

"There's the agency investigation I've been on, but I haven't uncovered enough to warrant that kind of attention." Gayle briefed him on Elliot's phone call, followed by the car bomb explosion she'd barely escaped, and went on to talk about her private safe house and money stash.

She watched him make a concerted effort to draw back from the situation and put the best spin on it. The move was so Seth-like she almost grinned despite the gravitational force threatening to extinguish her at every bend.

With a wry twist of his mouth, he managed, "I see you've been twiddling your thumbs in Paris. Not much excitement, huh."

She knew Seth was interjecting a light note for her sake and wanted to hug him for it. "Very funny. I've realized I can't let you come home with me. It's too dangerous."

His eyes held a warning glint. "It's amazing you're alive. Don't even think I'm going to let you out of my sight. That's expecting too much."

Before she could respond the phone rang and he answered it. "Yes, we've found her." He paused, then exclaimed, "In Paris. Come on up." He ended the call. "Reinforcements have arrived."

"J.O. and Jason?"

"You got it."

She shivered, the black rain cutting deeper within at the thought of placing not one but three of her brothers in danger. Gayle held Seth's gaze. "I need your promise now."

He gave her a pained look. "No."

"I'm trusting you not to involve them, maybe even save their lives. I may be your kid sister but I'm also a trained, qualified agent. I do this for a living. You three haven't a clue."

"Fine. I don't like it, but I have enough respect for you to back off. However, if I see you in another scrape that might get you murdered, the deal's off."

She tried to reassure him, explaining several of the dynamics governing her existence.

He shook his head. "I feel like I don't even recognize you when you talk like this."

"I'm still me, despite my work with the government."

Before Seth could respond there was a knock at the door. Gayle braced herself for the inquisition to come.

21

Gayle stared at her brothers, uncertain how she felt about their presence. Her joy at seeing them fizzled as panic set in. They might have already placed themselves in danger by being near her. *God, please, don't let anyone harm them because of me.*

Thank you Lord for being with us through the good times and bad. And there had been plenty *schlecht* lately, she acknowledged as she smiled at her siblings, listening to them throw verbal punches at one another. It was their form of a love fest. "Will you three cut it out?"

Seth quirked an eyebrow in amusement but nodded to J.O. "Fill us in on what you learned about Mitch."

Gayle shot Seth an accusing look. How much had he told them? The more they knew the deeper their entanglement. Her brothers would never back down if they knew she was in danger.

In an obvious attempt to dissolve the tension, J.O. said with an exaggerated southern drawl, "Sis, thank your lucky stars, we're here to get you out of this mess." He winked. "Just kidding."

She laughed. "I appreciate your efforts but really—"

His thick Texas twang was more pronounced than the other's as Jason said, "By all accounts you need our help. Let's hear what J.O. has to say." The men grunted in agreement.

J.O. ran a hand through sandy hair, his hazel eyes intent and sympathetic. "Seth, as you suspected, major insider selling has been going on at CI. But Mitch is clean. It's his CFO. The CFO of CI ran up gambling debts and couldn't pay. By the time he'd raised the cash from his company shares, an Arab group had bought his debts. Mitch's CFO has been suspiciously thick with them ever since."

"This is one time I'm sorry to be right," Seth said. "Mitch must have known about this. Yet he failed to warn me."

Gayle said, "Maybe he's not the friend you thought he was, but how does this tie in with what's happening with me?"

Jason leaned against the wall next to Seth, the two blue-eyed blonds a study in contrasts, one a breath of summer against the other's autumn coloring. "Seth has some investments riding at CI."

"You never mentioned this when you referred Mitch to me."

"I didn't want to influence your decision."

"You placed me in a compromising position."

Seth shrugged. "Hardly, as long as you had no knowledge of my interest."

"Is the loss going to break you?"

"My finances won't be crushed if I get a sell order in before CI's shares drop precipitously."

"I'm sorry, Seth. I'm guilty of being too focused on my own problems."

"With good cause. If I lose the money it will be a blow, but mostly, I'm disappointed in Mitch."

If J.O.'s conclusions were on the mark, CI was in worse shape than she imagined. Clyde must have discovered the truth and canceled the renewal contract she'd set in motion. Maybe she had misjudged him. Strange how when she'd checked CI's financials there wasn't a trace of any illegal activity.

She mused aloud, "I'd like to know how Mitch has the run of Transway's offices."

"I think he was making an honest attempt to find you," Seth said. "Or he could have been aiming to catch the woman impersonating you. Bottom line—he needs the Transway contract. His company is at stake."

"Mitch said he received a text informing him that I was at the office and in danger. What kind of contacts does he have that would give him access to security there? It doesn't make sense."

"He probably paid the night watchman to let him in," J.O. said. "It doesn't have to be complicated."

She grimaced. "So, he says."

Seth opened his laptop. "Hopefully, I can place a sell order before CI's shares plummet. Again, I'm disappointed Mitch didn't even try to warn me."

Gayle queried, "Are you sure he knows? I can't believe he'd condone trading any stock now. It would undermine his efforts to bolster the company." She grabbed the laptop from Seth to check CI's recent stock activity. Sure enough, there had been excessive selling. "You'd better phone him and find out if he's aware of his CFO's actions."

Seth dialed Mitch and talked for a few minutes, then plopped down next to Gayle. "He didn't have a clue. Now scoot over and let me use the computer to check on dumping my shares."

"Wait! You and Mitch should be buying more shares, instead of selling. It's the only way to gain control of the company and stop the bleeding."

Everyone seemed dumbfounded, and then they quickly began to weigh the pros and cons. "Sis, you're positively brilliant," Seth exclaimed.

Several minutes later Mitch joined them, and he and her brothers bought up shares until they saw the price start to rise. Gayle wished she could have fallen in with them, but it would have been an obvious conflict of interest even though she no longer appeared to be working for Transway. They discussed the situation at length, trying to figure out what was happening and why. The ongoing crisis at CI seemed almost as bizarre as her circumstances.

Jason yawned. "We can't solve this tonight. Let's sleep on it and talk again in the morning."

Everyone agreed. Jason and J.O., who had booked rooms on the same floor, left with Mitch. Seth insisted Gayle use the extra bed in his room. From years of experience, she knew it would be useless to argue. She thanked him nicely, comforted by her brothers' presence and care.

In bed, Gayle closed her eyes, only to imagine Dom's voice calling to her. Frustrated, she covered her head with a pillow in an attempt to shut him out. She fell into a deep sleep and dreamed.

The moon shone in the stormy sky as machine gun fire struck the building she hid in. "Help! Someone's trying to kill me," Gayle screamed.

"Come child, and I will lighten your burdens."

"Please, God, don't let them find me." Her heart raced wildly. She tried to steady her breathing, lest the enemy hear and find her.

Abby slowed the car, unable to see through the fog. She'd read about mists like this in Scotland but she was forty kilometers outside of Paris. Tension tore through her. She clung to the wheel, willing the fog to lift. Too frightened of being struck by another car to stop, she plowed forward, the sick feeling spreading with each painstaking mile.

How long before the CIA or Interpol discovered her dirty secret? Were they even now preparing to hurl her into the abyss where she'd sent others? "God, it has been years since I've prayed or believed. If you're there, please give me a sign."

The jolt struck from behind and sent her car careening forward into another vehicle. In a daze, Abby looked around, unable to see through the gray mist. Then she screamed as a van crashed into her side. Her door caved in, her auto spinning out of control.

❧ ❧ ❧

Chantal and her husband Troy sat at an outdoor table on Café Drouant's patio. She leaned back and fanned herself. It was hotter than she remembered it ever being in Paris. They sipped coffees, making desultory conversation. The city sounds swelled in a crescendo of honking horns, announcements and chatter buoyed by a wind of gaiety. Her gaze fell on the nearby opera house.

"What?" Chantal realized her husband was speaking to her.

He studied her, as if she were one of his patients. "Are you feeling all right, dear?"

She forced a smile. "Never better. What were you saying?"

"I was pointing out Veronica over there. We need to have her and Daniel for dinner. It's been a while since we've visited with them."

Chantal's disinterested gaze located Veronica, a plump woman of no consequence on the opposite side of the patio. She seemed to have quit living years ago. How could people let themselves go like that?

Chantal suppressed a sigh. Until recently, she'd allowed her selfish jealousy of Dominic's fiancé to dominate her existence. Before her marriage to Troy, she'd tried for two years to catch Dom's attention and had failed miserably. It would have ended there if Clyde hadn't taunted and challenged her. What began as a thrill was now quite the reverse. Chantal realized he had been using her to help get rid of Gayle. He coveted her position, and he wanted her gone before she discovered what he was up to. Chantal had overheard enough to guess Clyde was guilty of embezzlement and maybe treason. If he were caught and her association with Clyde and his friends became known, the bad publicity could affect the grants Troy had received to work with the underprivileged. Too late, Chantal realized she might lose Troy because of her selfish actions, and was surprised at how much she cared.

If only Troy had insisted that she travel to Milan and on to

Africa with him. She wouldn't have been bored and wouldn't have pretended to be more than she was. Though she couldn't suppress a delicate shudder at the thought of being there while her husband treated starving and dying children.

Troy was too good for her. He lived to help others while she demanded his attention and wealth and gave little in return. What would he say if he knew how she'd chased after Dominic and tried to hurt Gayle? One day he would discover Chantal was just a pretty package. What if Troy learned the truth and decided to divorce her? He might be happier married to one of his nurses. No. She wouldn't allow it. She'd find a way out of the maze she was caught in. As for Gayle and Dom, she'd lost all interest.

22

Harri Bustani walked quietly down the streets of Riyadh, the flowing white cotton *thobe* he wore brushing against his ankles. The Saudi capital was a modern marvel of architecture, roads and gardens. The city's name Riyadh rightly meant a place of gardens and trees. He infinitely preferred it to Paris, London and New York where he'd been until yesterday, straightening out the mess Fahid had created.

Harri looked to the cloudless sky for inspiration. Throughout the day he'd reflected on the unexpected changes to his plan. His orders had been pushed aside when Fahid hired the American pilot to help smuggle the hot diamonds. Then to ensure his silence, Fahid had him killed. The pilot meant nothing to Harri, but the recent interest in his death and the plane crash meant trouble. And that led to the necessity of Harri eliminating Fahid.

Once the cell members accumulated the funds to attack Paris, London and New York, they would purchase and conceal the explosives until the appropriate signal. When the sleeper cells were activated, the West would learn how deadly this business was. Harri would tolerate no mistakes. He wouldn't stop until he avenged his daughter, and the West paid for what they had done to her and to him.

Harri entered the furnished stucco house he leased covertly. His brothers, Matrouk and Rafiq, and his two brothers-in-law, Ibn and Ariaziz, were there to receive their instructions. The only one missing was Fahid.

To Harri's consternation, the others had failed to anticipate the necessity of Fahid's demise. Harri raised his voice over the din of speculation. "There was no other way. Fahid had to atone for his carelessness."

Ibn gave a reluctant nod as if regretting he had ever become involved. "When you took me into your confidence, I agreed to one attack on one person to avenge your daughter, no more. Now we're killing each other."

Harri's anger kindled. Ibn had no choice but to see this through. He'd signed on to their plan and wouldn't be permitted to live unless he committed to completing it. That hadn't changed.

Ibn foolishly continued sermonizing. "I'm older than the rest of you, old enough to see the pitfalls ahead. I'm sick to death of vengeance. Why keep stirring the coals of hate? We have gathered enough wealth to sit by our firesides contented, enjoying our children and grandchildren."

Harri said, "I believed thus before the West dishonored my daughter."

Ariaziz spoke, "When the infidel American raped our niece, our family was shamed. We vowed to make him pay. But the infidel is dead now. We never intended to reach out and wrap our hate around all Westerners."

Harri saw that his brothers smelled of fear, ensnared like rats between the Saudi government and the terrorists who employed them. In their hearts they said, see what has happened to Fahid. We may be next to die.

At least, he needn't worry about Matrouk. He had always followed Harri. They were all educated in the West, but unlike them Matrouk had married a non-Muslim.

Rafiq, the unmarried one, was somewhat of a Don Juan. Still, he supported the cause. He viewed it as a chance for the family to become wealthier, and he had the contacts to further the Bustani family's al-Qaida connections. Rafiq mistakenly believed he was the master puppeteer, cleverly pulling Harri's strings.

Yes, his brothers would be surprised to learn the truth. Sadly, they might not live long enough to hear it.

23

Dominic awoke to the ringing of the phone. He grabbed his mobile and glanced at the clock. It was three in the morning. "Hello."

Ari's Middle Eastern accent came across the line, "Harri ordered a hit on Fahid. He's dead."

"What?" Dom listened intently to the report from his colleague. "Good work. But we're desperate for more intel."

"Understood, although I must move carefully. My position in Syria is precarious."

"I realize that and don't want you to take any unnecessary risks."

They spoke briefly, and then said goodbye.

Dominic walked to the window and gazed out at the skyline. From his hotel he could see the Vienna State Opera brilliantly lit against the lingering night. Ari's intelligence brought the agency nearer to catching the terrorists. Still, there was work to do. Dom settled into a chair and phoned Francois to give him the news. "Fahid's dead. His brother Harri Bustani murdered him."

"Hmm. An interesting twist. I can't say I'm sorry or surprised. You heard it from Ari?"

"Yes, a few minutes ago." Dom filled him in. "The investigation into the plane crash and the deaths of the pilot and copilot alarmed Harri, who blamed Fahid for disobeying orders. Fahid had brought in Hassledorf, the American pilot, to smuggle the stolen diamonds, and then, suspecting the pilot might be working with the law, Fahid terminated him and the copilot in the plane crash."

"That makes Harri our lead suspect in the planned bombings. Check with US Intelligence and find out if Hassledorf was working undercover with them."

Dominic ran his hand through his hair in frustration. "If Interpol knew the names of Harri's people in Paris, London and New York, we could end this."

"We know that Harri uses the surname Malone in the West. It's a start. We'll locate him. Patience and diligence will prevail."

"Meanwhile, we are sitting on a keg of dynamite, wondering when and where it will explode."

"True enough. I need to go report this. Au revoir."

Dominic hung up and left for the office. It was early, but he couldn't sleep, and it was a suitable time to work his contacts on the other side of the world. He called Guy, his Interpol contact in Houston, and tasked him with discovering if Frank Hassledorf had been working undercover. It wasn't long before Guy called back with an unofficial yes, meaning if asked, the bureau would deny it. Interpol did not want to alert the terrorists to how much they now knew. Dom was pleased to know Hassledorf hadn't sold out his country and appeared to have stayed true to his inner moral compass. Next, Dom scheduled a meeting with one of Interpol's special task units involved in identifying and locating the enemy agents.

Doctor Perry Langston stood at his hotel window and stared unseeing at the view below. In his mind, the note, worn from repeated readings, loomed large. Who could have sent it? Who wanted his patient dead and why?

He couldn't bring himself to abandon Leah. Yet the threat was clear: *Cease immediate treatment of Leah. Her death will appear natural. Keep it low profile or else.*

The implication was that someone would murder Leah, making her death look natural. As attending physician, Perry was expected to sign the death certificate, c o nfirming hi s pa tient ha d di ed of natural causes.

When weeks passed and nothing happened, he'd assumed it was a hoax as he had initially thought. Then this morning he'd found another warning slipped under his door in the form of a newspaper, the circled letters spelling out the words.

Stop all inquiries if you want to live.

His instincts were sounding alarms, though it seemed incredulous. Someone didn't want him delving into Leah's background. Conversely, his assistant and patient had both expressed dismay at his attempts to learn more about Leah in order to better help her. Maybe it was because so much mystery already surrounded Leah. She was defenseless and yet, Perry was the one scared. Not particularly admirable, but he could afford to be honest with himself. After a struggle, he'd decided to be truthful with the authorities as well. Whether they believed him was another matter.

For that reason, he'd decided to have his friend Susan contact Francois Rodiet on his behalf. The Interpol agent was her former fiancé. Perry figured he stood a reasonable chance of appearing more credible with Susan to vouch for him.

He picked up the disposal phone he'd bought and punched in her number. They exchanged brief greetings. "Susan, a situation has cropped up here in Paris. Could you get hold of Francois Rodiet for me?"

"Has something happened to Gayle?"

"She's fine. This is a professional matter, in which I don't wish to involve the police. I need some advice."

"Perry, you're okay, aren't you?"

He reassured her. "I'm reluctant to go into details, but will you contact Francois and have him call me?"

"When?"

"Now, if it's convenient?" He gave her the burn phone number. "Susan, please, don't mention this to anyone. That point is critical."

"This is sounding very mysterious, but okay."

He hung up with relief and paced nervously, waiting. He grabbed for the mobile when it rang. "Yes?"

"Doctor Langston?"

Perry introduced himself to Francois and hurried to explain his position at Cremont, as well as the threatening note he'd received shortly after he began working there and today's warning.

"Most interesting," Francois said. "I would like to visit the patient and make an evaluation. Perhaps you could introduce me as a consulting physician. I must insist you tell no one about this, not even your superiors, until we know who is behind the threats. Is that clear?"

"Certainly, and I heartily agree." He made arrangements to meet Francois at the sanatorium in an hour and thanked him for his help. Perry didn't feel any safer, yet he'd done his duty. What if whoever wrote the note was watching him now?

He shook off the thought and hailed a cab to Cremont. He was in his office when Francois arrived. Perry rose to shake the man's hand. "I can't tell you how much I appreciate your being here. The attendant is bringing Leah in now."

"Do you want me to be a neutral observer or interact?"

"Let's see how she is today and take it from there."

Leah entered, orderlies on either side of her. At a nod from Perry, they left. He motioned her to a seat. "This is my colleague Doctor Rodiet."

Her gaze stabbed Perry, and she seemed to visibly withdraw.

"You don't mind if I stay, do you?" Francois asked.

Green eyes flashed. "What I think never matters, does it, doctors?"

There was a strange wildness about her that gave Perry pause.

He wondered what Francois made of her straggly appearance. Perry thought she cultivated it as a protective camouflage. He knew so little about her. "Leah, if I wasn't interested in what you have to say I wouldn't be here. Paris is miles from my home in Houston."

Unresponsive, she stared at the floor, her back rigid.

Francois said in an obvious attempt to reach her, "I've heard you like poetry."

She looked up at Perry accusingly.

He spread his arms in a gesture that included the three of them. "A love of literature is a gift to cherish and share."

"Personally, I'm more addicted to action-adventure in my reading leisure," Francois said. "I seem to recall a poem by Rodenbaugh from my college days. I wonder if you're familiar with it. Let's see, how does it go?" He spoke softly:

> *'When trees are bare*
> *And golden leaves scatter and turn brown*
> *I will fly*
> *To a tropical paradise*
> *Where bottle brush grows red*
> *And tides roll in*
> *Far from somber clouds of loss'*

She chimed in, reciting the rest with a heartrending wistfulness.

> *'And yet my heart*
> *Will always*
> *Remember you'*

"That was beautifully spoken, as if you were a professional teacher or writer." Francois smiled at her. "I'm curious, which was it?"

She frowned. "Don't act as if you aren't already aware of everything about me."

"I'm sorry. I don't know much," Francois said.

Perry nodded. "The file reveals little about your past aside from the crime you were alleged to have committed."

"Alleged?" A mix of wonder and fear flitted across her face. Her gaze darted to the vent in the room and hastily away, fear winning. "I have nothing more to say. Please, let me leave now."

He rang for the attendants. "You may go but consider how the future could be if you allowed us to help you get well."

Her nostrils flared. "You understand nothing," she said, as the orderlies led her out.

The two men heaved a collective sigh. "She's certainly difficult," Francois said.

Perry agreed. "My next case is even more urgent. The patient refuses to eat or leave his room. There may be nothing I can do, but I have to try. Let's talk over dinner tonight, my treat."

"Why not? Give me those notes we spoke of, and I'll have them analyzed."

"Yes, I almost forgot." Perry handed them to Francois and both men left.

24

Gayle felt renewed hope now that her brothers were involved. She awoke feeling she could surmount any obstacle with their support. Family spelled solidarity, a quality she had sorely missed of late. Her life resembled a spy thriller—the heroine attacked on every side, deserted by her comrades, stripped of her assets and declared persona non grata by the agency that left her in the lurch, much like in the movies. Yet there was no advantage in imagining what the heroes in classics like *The Bourne Identity* would do. Gayle didn't have fictionalized prowess and she wasn't a trained assassin. Nor did she possess the tech savvy superiority of the heroine in *Network*.

She was plain and ordinary Gayle Regan. Still, she had the greatest backup in history. Nobody could beat God. She trusted Him to ensure justice prevailed and Gayle would do everything in her power to assist.

Gayle showered and dressed, then padded out to start the coffee.

Buried beneath the covers, Seth opened one eye and closed it with a groan.

"Hey Sleepy Head, time to wake up."

"Call me when the coffee's ready," he mumbled.

"In your dreams, bro. You might as well rise and shine before the force descends. You know how J.O. gets . . ."

"Ugh, how could I forget." Seth stood and stretched. "Good morning."

"Back at you and I'm glad you're here," she admitted.

"Hmm. Had to meditate on it, did you?" His probing glance wasn't in the least bit sleepy.

"I don't want to put any of you in danger, and I can't promise you'll be safe."

Seth gave her a long look. "I've been thinking."

"Oh, no, not again."

"Very funny."

She grinned. "Okay. I'll behave. What's this about?"

"Come clean with the others." He held up a hand. "Hear me out. The CIA isn't riding to the rescue. You stand a greater chance of succeeding with our help. It may be a cliché, but more heads are better than one. Let us do the leg work, following your directives. And more important, you can trust us. Mitch too."

"Seth, you've already been shot once. I couldn't bear it if one of you were hurt again because of me."

"We're not going anywhere. Wouldn't it be better to collaborate instead of us proceeding alone in the dark? At least then we would have a far better idea of what's at stake."

"Let me think about this."

Seth finished his coffee. "I'll get dressed while you do." He crossed to the bathroom.

Gayle realized her siblings were as determined to protect her as she was them. Could she let her siblings risk their lives? Even more to the point, could she stop them? Maybe Seth was right. It made more sense to work together and to protect each other.

Before she could decide, her brothers arrived with a box of Danish and Cappuccinos. "Mm." She bit into a cheese pastry, washing it down with the delicious brew.

Seth raised an eyebrow in question, and she nodded her acquiescence. He raised his Styrofoam cup in a silent toast, praising her decision.

Thanks, she mouthed the word with a sigh, not looking forward to the next few moments.

In typical man fashion, he whistled to gain everyone's attention, the shrill sound resonating above the general melee of conversation. "Gayle, the floor is yours."

She squared her shoulders. "Some secrets are not ours to share. When I went to work for Transway, they required me to sign a confidentiality contract. You must have had to deal with similar issues in your jobs."

A murmur of agreement went through the group. She nodded at Mitch, who had just entered and joined them.

"What I am trying to say is there are positions with certain branches of the government that are sensitive enough to require oaths of silence."

J.O. quipped, "Spit it out, Sis. We can guess the rest. You're working undercover with the FAA."

Mitch paled. "You're investigating me?"

The others looked concerned.

"Mitch, first I am not with the Federal Aviation Agency. Second, what I'm about to share should make it clear that if I didn't trust you, you wouldn't be privy to this conversation."

"Thanks for the vote of confidence."

"Before I continue, I want each of you to pledge that what I am about to say will never be repeated without my explicit permission."

Jason said, "Gayle, you're starting to scare us."

"You should be scared because knowing what I am about to reveal places each of you in danger. So, if anyone wants to leave and come back later, this is the time."

J.O. looked uneasy. "This is starting to sound like the last stand at the Alamo when Travis drew a line in the sand."

"It's not my intention to overdramatize, but there are some

parallels. Travis warned his men they might die and gave them the opportunity to leave. I'm doing the same."

"Gayle, quit kidding. This isn't funny," Jason said.

She frowned. "I'm serious. My car exploded a few days ago and destroyed part of the safe house where I was living. I escaped by mere seconds."

They gaped in shocked anger and vocally threatened to kill whoever had tried to harm her.

J.O. stood, his fists tightened and his jaw set. "As for leaving, it's like the 'Ballad of the Alamo' said, 'not a soldier crossed the line' and neither will I."

The others quickly spoke up in agreement.

Gayle blinked away the mist clouding her sight. "Come here all of you." She spread her arms and indulged in a group hug as they held her close.

Her brothers stepped back, almost in unison, demanding to know everything at once.

Whether they liked it or not, they were playing by her rules for their own safety. "I'm more than glad to tell all, but I want your oaths of silence before I begin."

Jason said hotly, "You can trust us."

"I do, to ride roughshod over me whenever it suits the male ego."

"Ouch. There's no sense in trampling on us," Seth complained. "We're on your side." He turned to the others. "But hey, I already gave her my word on this. And when you hear more, you'll understand her caution a bit better."

"I'm willing," Mitch said.

"Me too," J.O. echoed.

Jason groaned. "All right I'm in as well."

She sagged in relief and had them repeat after her, pledging their silence. Afterward, Gayle revealed she was an agent and again stressed the importance of their silence. "If any of you so much as says a word, it could land me in major trouble."

Everyone's shock was apparent except for J.O. who seemed to be taking the situation in stride. She sensed he knew more than he was letting on, which set her to wondering about some of his connections through the years. With the others clamoring for answers, she shelved the thought until later. Gayle addressed her brothers' questions and went on to relate the pertinent details of her present crisis.

Jason and Mitch found it as difficult to believe her story as Seth had initially.

In spite of her protests, the siblings' hierarchy of old emerged as J.O. took charge firing out directives. "Seth, take the lead in tracing the external flight check crew that disappeared around the time of the CI plane crash. Jason, he's going to need your help."

"Good luck," Mitch said. "I've certainly failed."

Seth threw him a sympathetic glance. "Perhaps with good reason. People in the industry know you. It will be easier for Jason and me to get past their defenses."

Mitch drew out a pen and paper, listed the flight team's names and passed it to Seth. "I'll have my secretary forward you whatever we have on them."

Seth scanned the page. "Great. This will save us some time."

J.O. ran a hand through his sandy hair. "Gayle, you and Mitch continue following the money trail. It sounds as if last night you made some headway working together. Keep it up."

"What exactly will you be doing?" she asked, mock sarcasm lining her voice.

A smug smile lit his hazel eyes. "I'm going to find out who wants you dead and stop them cold."

"I let you give out orders, however, this is my investigation. You're to take orders from me. Is that understood?" Gayle asked.

"Naturally, what is it you want me to do?"

"Stay alive!"

"I've every intention of doing so."

"I don't think you realize how ruthless these people are."

"I promise we'll run any plans by you first. For now, we're only investigating."

"Fine. Let's get started." She couldn't seem to make them understand a little snooping on her part had set this entire disaster into motion. She turned to Mitch. "Are you ready?"

"Sure. Let's work out of my hotel room and meet your brothers back here before dinner. Does that suit everyone?"

The men agreed and J.O. walked Mitch and Gayle out as he made his way to his room.

Abby slowly regained consciousness. She heard voices but couldn't make out the words. Her head ached as she forced one eye open and saw the fog was lifting.

A *gendarme* opened the smashed car door with some difficulty. "Mademoiselle, are you all right?" She started to nod and stopped, wincing in pain. "I think so."

He studied her in concern. "Are you sure? An ambulance should be here any moment."

"No thank you. I'm fine." She moved to get out of the car, and the officer supported her arm until she was steady on her feet. She glanced about. "What about everyone else? Was anyone hurt?"

"Fortunately, it appears no one was seriously injured."

"I'm glad. The fog was terrifying to drive in."

"Yes, it was." He walked around her car examining it. "Looks as if you were struck from behind and on the driver's side."

"In this weather it's no surprise, and I'm not even sure who all hit me. My insurance will take care of it."

"Good. Then if you will pardon me. I must clear a path for the doctor. I believe I see him coming down the road."

Abby watched the gendarme leave, wondering how long before the traffic started moving again. She scooted behind the wheel and gingerly leaned against the head rest.

Somehow the accident had helped solidify her thoughts. She needed to deal with Gayle and Dominic as well as Sara and Pia while she could. There was no doubt as to what must be done, Abby's personal feelings aside.

In the beginning it had seemed simple, some innocuous information in exchange for a sizable deposit into her Swiss account. Only later, she'd learned there was no quitting and no way out.

Unlike Sara, Abby hadn't acted out of confused loyalties. It was all about the money and power, the challenge of moving pawns on a global board until she won. Now the stakes were higher than ever and the cost wrenching. Soon Abby expected to be reviled by those she'd worked with in the West. Before those doors shut new hunting grounds were a necessity.

Like a ticking bomb set in motion, she would stay the course. Abby had run out of options long ago. The anticipated implosion must be faced by her and her alone. There was no one else to pin the blame on.

25

Gayle met her brothers and Mitch in Seth's room before dinner for updates and to plan their next moves. She and Mitch had spent the day following the money trail. Their in-depth examination of Transway's records on Arab Imports uncovered considerable freight traffic going to and from the Middle East, which was not surprising. The large number of shipments directed from Russia and Iran to Paris, London and New York was curious. Deeper research revealed it was Clyde who had signed off on those cargo flights.

Gayle knew France had reduced its economic cooperation with Iran, going beyond the UN Security Council sanction requirements. And despite US pressure, France had resisted scaling back bilateral trade with the rebel country.

England's policy in many areas mirrored those of the United States. US imports from Iran consisted mostly of artwork and antiques, and these had dropped substantially in volume. This was mainly due to the 2010 Comprehensive Iran Sanction, Accountability, and Divestment Act, which limited commercial imports from Iran. America, however, shipped tons of wheat and other products to the Iranians.

When Mitch checked his company records, consignments flown for Malone Exports revealed a similar pattern. Also, Mitch's CFO, whom they already considered suspect, had signed off on the CI routes and freight in question. More was at stake than she and Mitch had imagined. Yet they remained in the dark as to motive.

J.O. broke into her introspection. "Did you two have any luck today?"

"Luck." Mitch peered down his nose at them. "Remember, I was with a professional whose skill gave us the needed edge." He gestured to Gayle. "Go ahead and fill them in."

She grinned at his teasing and briefly brought everyone up to date, often deferring to Mitch. She had enjoyed working with him. They made a good team. His astuteness had challenged her and he was quick to treat her ideas with the same consideration he would his own.

Together they answered her siblings' questions. They seemed to regard her with a novel deference. Gayle concluded, "That a b out sums it up. We're eager to hear what the rest of you found out. Who's next?"

Seth jumped right in. "We contacted the deceased pilot's wife, Lauren Hassledorf, and she consented to a Skype interview, which Jason recorded on video. Go ahead, Bro, and play it."

The clip rolled and they watched with interest. At its fi ni sh, Jason spoke. "Mrs. Hassledorf never thought to tell the FBI that her husband had started bowling on Thursday nights. She has terminal cancer and a friend stayed with her on those evenings to give him a bit of R and R. In our follow-up with the bowling alley there was no record of his ever having been there, which we were able to verify with surveillance video footage."

Seth continued. "What we did find was a series of hefty deposits to his bank account beyond his pay grade."

"How did you manage to access his financial records?" Gayle asked.

Jason ran a hand through his thick unruly blond hair. "We were fortunate. His wife gave us the access codes after we talked. She's dying and would like to know what happened to her husband before she passes."

"How tragic," Gayle said.

"I agree." Mitch frowned. "I'm surprised she was willing to cooperate with her family suing CI."

"We didn't divulge we were acting for CI," Seth said.

J.O. cleared his throat. "Did you find out where Hassledorf's funds came from?"

Seth's blue eyes twinkled. "Patience, Big Bro. The money was in cashier's checks, which suggests a cover-up."

After a period of discussion, the group's attention switched to J.O. to hear what he'd discovered. "Sis, I'm sorry, what I have to share isn't going to be easy for you. I learned from a friend and reliable source at Central Intelligence that your friend Abby has turned. This has caused a certain amount of suspicion to fall on you."

Gayle drew in a deep breath, as her universe shifted. How was it possible? Abby a double agent? She gazed at J.O. in astonishment. And how could he know this? Unless. . . . No. It couldn't be.

Everyone seemed to be talking at once, asking who Abby was and what exactly J.O. meant when he said she'd turned.

He looked at Gayle intently. "It's not what you're thinking. I'm not and never have been an agent."

"Then how?"

"I have an old army buddy whom I won't name for the sake of security. He owes me his life. When I ran into him last summer in Europe, I happened to discover by chance that he was working as a covert operative. He was in the middle of what he called deep cover. To prevent me from exposing his disguise, he entrusted me with the truth, which I've never told anyone until today."

Her thoughts churning, Gayle said, "He must work in my division. How else could he have access to that level of operational information? What a strange coincidence."

"You're becoming suspicious. You've been undercover too long, Sis."

"You're probably right."

"It does feel like we're making progress," Mitch said.

"If we could figure out the motivation angle, it would reveal a lot and make the job easier," Gayle added.

J.O. looked sheepish. "Did I neglect to mention my friend told me the authorities are anticipating possible terrorist attacks on New York, London and Paris?"

They glared at him in unison, threatening him with annihilation unless he stopped playing games and leveled with them.

"Is anyone else starving?" Mitch asked, lightening the tension. "We could have dinner downstairs in the restaurant."

Everybody agreed and they filed out, sibling rivalry in full play. Mitch walked alongside Gayle. "Are you okay?"

"I think so. It's hard to believe Abby's a traitor. She might be helping terrorists attack the West."

"That makes her doubly dangerous. What a tough break."

Gayle needed time alone to digest the news.

They stepped inside the elevator with the others.

Gayle knew it was useless to feel depressed, but it didn't stop the pity party building within. What kind of agent was she? Her siblings were capable of eliciting more answers than she could, despite her training. She would resign if she didn't need to clear her name and help protect her brothers. She sighed. In reality, the session went well. The group had gathered a lot of new intel.

Mitch pressed her hand in empathy. He had reasons to feel chagrined as well. Jason and Seth had found answers when he couldn't. Perhaps she and Mitch were too close to view the circumstances objectively.

The lift opened and the group strolled out to the restaurant. The hostess seated them at a window table overlooking the street. Gayle peered out at the bleak sky and pouring rain, glad to be cozy and in good company.

"Geez," Jason complained. "We might as well be back in Houston from the looks of this weather."

"That's heresy with food and atmosphere like this," Seth quipped. "Let's hope the chef didn't hear you."

After several minutes of debate regarding what dishes on the menu were the best, they ordered. Gayle leaned back and relaxed, sipping a delicious French roast coffee. As her gaze fell on her brothers and Mitch, she experienced a floating sensation, like a weight had suddenly lifted. In that moment, a calm willingness to believe everything would be fine wrapped around her, enticing her to drop her guard.

Soon Seth had them laughing at his ridiculous imitations of the fictitious pompous Monsieur Finch and his recalcitrant lover Madame Beale, who were representative of the couple at the next table. They couldn't quite come to terms. She insisted upon a house and no children, while he wanted an apartment and four boys. Eventually, the couple compromised on a townhouse with a daughter and son. Rings were exchanged with ardent kisses demonstrated by Seth's smacking in the air and the wedding was on.

They laughed hilariously, drawing curious but not unfriendly attention. Their enjoyment was a sweet fragrance Gayle yearned to bottle like perfume, keeping the aroma always near. How blissful to be with family and friends she held dear. She whispered a prayer of thanks just as gun shots blasted through the window, shattering the glass where they sat.

Gayle grabbed hold of Mitch and Seth, who were seated on either side of her and dove under the table as screams rang out in the restaurant. Frantically, she searched for Jason and J.O. but was momentarily blinded by the tablecloth.

Mitch held her in place. "It's okay. They weren't hurt."

"Let me go!" She struggled to free herself from his hold, but he clasped her tighter, as if fearing what might happen if he released her.

"Wait." He freed one hand and lifted the cloth so she could see her brothers were unharmed.

She sagged against him in relief and realized they had to get out of there before the gendarmes arrived. She looked around and saw most of the people were on the floor, and uninjured, hiding under the tables amid the chaos. Gayle signaled Mitch and her brothers to follow her, and they crawled their way clear of the windows and on to the elevators in the hall. When they finally stood, Gayle hugged her brothers.

Seth patted her shoulder. "We're fine. Come on, the lift is here."

They rode the lift to Seth's floor and walked to his room, too stunned by what had occurred to speak of it yet. She couldn't stop praying and sensed the Lord's whispered reassurance. Sometimes she prayed and felt empty. Perhaps that was what the Apostle Paul meant when he said to pray without ceasing, in season and out of season.

Mitch sat beside her. "Are you all right?"

"Yes, but when I think of what could have happened. You and my brothers could have been killed."

"Thank God everyone's okay." He squeezed her hand briefly. "Do you think this was a random coincidence?"

"I might, except it keeps happening. The venues and props may differ, but the effect is equally devastating. I'm afraid I've placed all of you in danger. Perhaps if I left, these assaults might stop."

"Nonsense. We're in this together."

The others must have been listening because they each nodded. "Don't go noble on us," Seth said.

J.O. dropped an arm around her shoulders. "We'll get through this together, but maybe we should relocate to your safe house."

"Good idea. Let's travel by twos, taking different routes and modes of transportation." She shivered, still reacting to the senseless shooting.

The men nodded their approval and she continued. "Since I live here and know the city better, I suggest that Mitch and J.O. travel by train." She grabbed a pen and paper and wrote out directions. "Seth and Jason can ride the métro." She took a city map from the drawer and marked their route. "Don't forget to burn these directions. I don't want them falling into the wrong person's hands."

"You got it," they all agreed.

"How will you get there?" Mitch asked.

"I'll take the tram."

"Not alone, you won't," J.O. said, his jaw set in stiff disapproval.

How could she have failed to remember there were two sides to having family near, especially when they continued to treat her as their baby sister? She strained to hold on to her temper. "I'll disguise myself. No one will even recognize me."

J.O. threw up his hands in frustration. "Let's see you in camouflage first."

"In case you missed it, I'm adult enough to decide for myself."

"True, but we're a team and that means everyone remains in harness together." He gave her a hug. "Am I being unreasonable?"

"Yes, because you're always right." She exchanged knowing looks with her grinning siblings.

"It's the BBS," Jason said.

She groaned. "How could I have forgotten?"

"What's that?" Mitch asked.

"It's the big brother syndrome, a case of he's older and wiser and usually on the mark," Seth said.

"Strangely, it's true in J.O.'s case," Jason added.

"Thank you. I try my humble best." J.O. bowed to the room at large.

She laughed. "Humility has nothing to do with it. In the spirit of cooperation, I'll go effect my change."

Gayle stepped into the bathroom and closed the door, glad they could smile after what had happened. She realized that being together made an enormous difference. No one was left to struggle through the devastating chaos alone.

She grabbed Seth's jeans and flannel shirt hanging on the back of the door and slipped them on, then set to work on her face. Last, she pulled a man's short-brown wig from her purse and placed it on her head, tucking her hair beneath it, out of sight.

With a man's stride she walked out and introduced herself. "Excuse me for interrupting. Name's Larry Wenter. Happy to meet you all." Her brothers' expressions of astonishment made her chuckle. "Well, J.O., do I pass muster?"

He surveyed her carefully, before giving his approval. "Good job."

"It's uncanny," Jason said. "How did you do it?"

"A mere trick of the trade, one of the many things I learned while training to be an agent." Gayle turned aside, embarrassed. Would the little girl buried within ever stop trying to impress her three elder brothers and prove to them she was an adult? Maybe when they quit treating her like an adolescent . . .

Thus, the cycle went round and round until one day, you wished there were someone near who knew you and cared enough to be protective. She smiled at the men. "I appreciate what you're doing. I was lost here without you." She blinked back tears. "We better scoot before it's too late. J.O. and Mitch, you go first. We'll wait ten minutes, then the next two will leave. I'll bring up the rear."

"Aye, Aye, Captain." J.O. saluted. "Might I suggest you depart when we do, but in a different direction. If there's a tail, the pursuer will have a much harder time following us."

"Good idea," Gayle said, and with a wave to the others, she left.

26

At Interpol's Paris headquarters, Dominic ran a tired hand through his hair as he scanned the reports on his desk. It had been a grueling night and the week showed no promise of improving. Through the window, he could almost smell the sultry summer's day. From the looks of the darkening sky, the light rain threatened to turn stormy. His mood dour, he reflected on the future forecast for himself and this city he loved.

Dom had learned about Leah from Francois who had managed to get her fingerprints from her doctor at Cremont Sanatorium. Astonishingly, her prints were a match for Pia Helmut, the missing German ambassador's wife. Upon further investigation, Interpol had discovered the prints in Cremont's file on Leah a.k.a. Pia belonged to a patient who had died shortly before Pia's arrival there.

Fortunately, Doctor Langston was quietly cooperating with the authorities. Behind the scenes, everyone connected with Cremont was being vetted. The agency's inquiry had already revealed the sanatorium's chair of the board, Doctor Madeleine Dubois, allegedly a widow, was in fact Ari's wife Sara, *the missing package*. At this rate, Dominic mused, the patient roster might turn out to be a list of Who's Who from *Le Monde*.

Interpol was reluctant to make any sudden moves that might undermine the operation to recover Pia and bring her husband's murderers to justice. The agency must determine Pia's role. Was she guilty, mentally ill or simply a victim?

If she was innocent, what possible incentive could her assailants have for keeping her alive? There was her connection to Sara. Th e two former college roommates had vanished at about the same time five years before. Could they have chosen the sanatorium as a place to hide from their enemies?

Doctor Langston's link to Gayle appeared to be another of those bizarre coincidences that kept popping up. Like the discovery that Langton's assistant was none other than Abby, whom Interpol now knew to be a double agent working against the CIA.

Was she at Cremont to keep tabs on Pia? Could Abby be responsible for the threatening note Langston received? Or might she be there to ensure Pia's permanent silence? What if Abby and Sara a.k.a. Doctor Dubois were coconspirators? According to Langston, Abby had warned him not to become too involved in Leah's case if he wanted to avoid trouble.

Dom's instincts told him a devious plot was in the making and speed was of the essence. He still didn't believe in coincidences. And in this case, they were stacking up like anchovies packed with olive oil in a tin can.

The agency had placed wire taps on Abby's and Sara's phones, and the two had been placed under surveillance. Meanwhile, IT experts were remotely analyzing the personal laptops of the two women, as well as the sanatorium's computers.

Dom's long-term on and off relationship with Abby threatened to submerge him in the sludge oozing out of the Middle East. He was swiftly running out of options and worried his cover might force him to go so deep he would never resurface. Meanwhile, he was glad his parents were not in Paris, while the city was in danger of attack.

Somewhat shaken from her accident, Abby drove to Paris and checked into a small, obscure hotel instead of going to her apartment. It might be nerves, but she sensed the CIA was on to her. Better to run afoul of them than the Iranians. There were moments when she considered making a clean breast of the treason in the wind, before it was too late to prevent the disasters about to unfold. But to be branded a traitor and spend the rest of her life in prison was unthinkable.

With a heavy heart, she phoned Sara. "The three belles are set for the party." The die was cast. There would be no going back from what she had begun to imagine as Armageddon. Was Sara as torn and tortured about the path they'd chosen?

Sara's assurance terminated any foolish visions Abby might have entertained of Sara's relenting. "The king is ready to marry here too. Keep me posted." Sara hung up with a decisive click, leaving Abby dazed and frightened.

The attacks were going to happen and she should be prepared to leave. Abby's mobile rang and her mother's name flashed. "Hi Mom. I was thinking of you. How are you?"

Her mother sounded excited. "Your dad and I are coming for a visit. We'll be in New York next week."

"Oh dear, I'm in Paris. I meant to tell you but it happened so suddenly." Her family believed she was a corporate medical secretary and nurse. "The doctors were having a problem with the clinic here and I'm sorting it out for them."

"I understand," her mother said, her voice faltering, her dashed hopes clear. "Your father will be disappointed to miss you. It's unfortunate our tickets are non-refundable, and the dates can't be changed."

Her mother was a beautiful, impulsive blonde. She had probably bought the tickets on the spur of the moment and then informed her husband. Abby sighed. "I wish you'd checked with me first."

"Yes, it would have been best. Don't worry, dear. We'll visit with you another time."

Abby hated to hurt her parents, and she'd feel worse once they learned the truth about her, but at least they wouldn't be in New York when and if the attack occurred. She had spared them that much. Generosity of spirit wasn't a luxury she could afford.

This might be her last week working with Doctor Langston, and maybe her final weekend with Dominic, unless he chose to accompany her. He was a valuable asset she didn't want to lose. Poor Gayle was clueless and fortunate that Sara had no idea she was an agent. Abby's silence had protected Gayle from certain death, thus far.

<h1 style="text-align:center">27</h1>

Gayle set out in the opposite direction from Mitch and J.O., going several blocks out of her way before boarding a tram traveling east, then switching to one westward bound. Reassured no one was tailing her, she boarded the métro and got off at a station near her home.

She walked to her house and crept from the back to the side yard and hid in the shadowed shrubbery. If her brothers were being followed, she needed to know. To date their resourcefulness had surprised her, and more than likely, they were staying alert to their surroundings as well.

Their arrival had changed her situation immensely for the better. Her siblings had sprinkled their love and prayers, guiding her into a sweet spot of brotherly care. Their support, as well as Mitch's, made her feel worthwhile again because as much as it vexed her to admit it, her spirits had been at a low.

Strange how her thoughts on Mitch had reversed. Last week she had viewed him as an annoyance. Now she saw him as a staunch friend and ally. She liked how his smile started slow, his mouth curling slightly until he was grinning like a kid who'd won his first baseball game. She wished they had met before. Before Dom. And before her universe had become the disaster it was.

Most of her life had been blessed and calm, but lately, Gayle led such a crazy mixed-up existence. She wanted off this track to destruction. To reside on Normal Street. *Hey Mister, can you direct me to this side of Graveyard Avenue where the people are still living? Send me a*

Gayle swiped at the tears smearing her vision and realized she
must be experiencing post-traumatic stress. She needed to lighten up
and quit being melodramatic.

Thankfully, she heard the distracting sound of feet shuffling
along the street and saw J.O. and Mitch. Her brother punched in
the door code and they went inside. Ten minutes later, the other two
joined them. She delayed a bit longer, but observing no signs they
were followed, left her hiding place and let herself in through the
back entrance. "Where have you been?" Seth asked. "We thought
you would be the first one here."

"I've been outside hiding in the shrubs. I wanted to be sure no
one was tailing any of you."

"And were they?" J.O. asked, his brow raised eloquently. "I had
assumed we were reasonably savvy. After all, we are related to you."
There was no mistaking the twinkle in his eyes.

She laughed at his absurdity, realizing he wanted her to unwind,
and yet his smile appeared forced. What wasn't he telling them?
She pretended not to notice. "Point taken. The area is clear for the
present. How about a brief tour of the place?"

Everyone agreed. They exclaimed over the house, giving it a
cursory inspection and dropping their gear in the rooms where they
would sleep.

As they trooped into the den, Gayle observed J.O.'s pensive expression and asked, "What are you worrying about? I mean besides
the obvious."

He shifted uncomfortably. "Dad has had a heart attack. He's in
the hospital but stable. Mom called me on my way here. She said for
us not to worry or bother about coming. Dad's well cared for."

A haze of fear and uncertainty lodged in her throat and she urged the words around it. "You'll have to go back. We can't leave Mom alone at a time like this."

The men exchanged glances of concern.

"We can't desert you either," Jason said, his rigid posture betraying his anxiety.

"Gayle, you're going to have to suck it up," J.O. said. "The folks would be more distressed if we left without you. Mom says it's taken a massive load off Dad's shoulders to know we're with you."

Her dad wouldn't be able to relax and recuperate as he should if he were disturbed about her. "Okay. I get it. Fine."

The men heaved sighs of relief, and J.O. suggested they call Houston. They were able to reach their mother and each of them spoke with her in turn.

Their father's prognosis was good. Their mom possessed a positive nature that would do much toward helping him recover. They talked and eventually phoned his cardiologist who personally assured them the worst was past. Though recovery might take several weeks, the doctor expected her dad would have no problems if he convalesced as prescribed.

Afterward, Gayle wandered into the kitchen and sliced some fruit and popped corn, then grabbed several bottles of lemonade from the fridge as Mitch entered. "You're just in time. Mind carrying these?" she asked.

"Glad to. The food smells great." He moved closer. "Are you okay?"

"Yeah. It took me a few minutes to process it. Dad will come through this. He's got to."

Mitch's arms slipped around her. She rested her head on his shoulder and cried into his shirt. "Sorry." She drew back, and he released her. "I'm not usually such a baby."

He touched her hair lightly in a gesture of understanding. "I know, but it's good for you to let go for a bit."

"Thanks." He seemed to have the uncanny ability to read her, seeing more than she wanted him to. She placed the popcorn and bowls on a tray with the fruit and napkins and slid a large basket with the drinks across to him. "Ready to go feed the lions in there?"

In the living room Gayle passed the snacks around and the conversation drifted to plans for the morning. It was decided that she and Mitch would continue to follow the money trail. Jason and Seth would extend the search for the missing crew, while J.O. concentrated on finding out who was trying to get rid of Gayle.

Gayle slipped out early while the others still slept. She wanted to speak with Kara before drawing any conclusions about J.O.'s latest revelations. She arrived at her friend's apartment unannounced, wearing her gangly, awkward teenager disguise, and rang the bell.

Kara opened the door cautiously and dragged her inside, raising the volume on the background music before speaking. "I thought I told you it would be better if we avoided meeting."

"I had to speak with you."

"I figured you might after everything that's happened. I was sorry to hear about the safe house explosion and the hotel shooting. I'm glad no one was hurt."

Gayle said, "I need to know if you trust me."

Kara reached across and took her hand. "Of course, I trust you. That's not the issue. The CIA has ordered me to cut you loose until this is resolved."

"Because of my friendship with Abby?"

"I suppose Elliot couldn't resist filling you in?" Kara gave her a quizzical look.

"No, I haven't even spoken with him."

"Then how?"

"Let's say I have my own sources."

"Don't make me think my trust in you has been misplaced. It sounds suspiciously as if you've been listening to Abby."

Gayle shook her head. "No. It's not like that at all." She had to set the record straight. "When Dominic disappeared, I asked her to get me copies of his phone records. She gave them to me about a week ago. We had lunch and I asked her about Dominic. She told me he was with Interpol. I didn't even know that, but I bet you did."

Kara ran a hand through her pomegranate tresses in exasperation. "Are you ever going to forget about him? Hasn't he caused enough problems?"

"Stop avoiding the question."

"All right, I knew. You weren't even aware I was your handler. How was I supposed to explain my knowledge of Dom's activities?"

"I see. And later, after I learned who you were?"

"You were finally getting over him. I was afraid if I brought it up you might become obsessed again."

"I understand. You were thinking of how to save the operation and keep everyone alive in the process."

Kara's eyes twinkled. "Yes, that too, now that you mention it."

Gayle sniffed. "I've missed you."

"Me too."

They hugged.

"Kara, someone is trying to frame me."

"I'm aware of what's going down. I'm working with your double at Transway."

"How can you allow that impostor to get away with pretending to be me, while I'm fighting for my life and reputation?" Gayle struggled for control. She was losing it.

Kara sighed. "We're trying to catch the bad guys here. If terrorists knew Interpol was on to them they'd regroup and the agency would have to find them all over again."

"I understand, but what I can't comprehend is why the agency has left me hanging." She stopped herself from saying more. They stared at each other a moment, both saddened by the twist of events. Gayle knew what a difficult position she was urging her friend into, but how else could they figure out what was happening?

Kara said, "I realize how hard this is. Still, if you simply disappeared, they might conclude we're on to them. This is big. It could impact the safety of millions of people."

Gayle immediately thought of what J.O. had heard from his acquaintance and decided to probe deeper. "Yes, I heard a rumor about some attacks."

"Where did you hear this?" She crossed her arms tightly against herself.

Gayle's hand crept to the locket around her neck. The one her mother gave her years earlier had been lost with the rest of her possessions, but J.O. had surprised her with a new one he'd bought for her. As a child she'd often slept clutching the necklace from her mother. That her brother had remembered and bothered replacing it touched her, especially as he'd added recent photos of their parents.

"Well?" Kara asked.

"It's not my secret to tell. Besides, I've told you what my friend said. He has absolutely no connections to government agencies. He asked an old schoolmate who's now in intelligence to find out what's going on . . . for my sake."

"That's almost scarier. To think Joe Smith on the street is hearing confidential data like this."

Gayle gripped the edge of the sofa, stifling her anger. "Forgive me for failing to concern myself with the details. I have more pressing issues at stake."

"You wouldn't be so blasé if you knew the entire truth."

"I refuse to deal in the hypothetical when I'm battling to survive."

"You signed on because you believed in helping others."

"I didn't count on the agency disking me. I believed there was commitment on both our sides." Unable to bear the hurt, Gayle rose and paced around the couch as if the action could somehow distance her from the pain.

"So, you don't like how the game is played and you want to pack up and go home." Kara pointed an accusing finger at Gayle.

"I wish I could," Gayle wailed.

"I'm on your side," Kara said gently.

"Prove it. For every morsel of information I give up, you do the same."

"I took an oath."

"So did I, and I remember the section about protecting one's team members when they're under attack. Have you gone to bat for me even once?" Gayle swallowed back a sob.

Kara fidgeted with the volume knob on the radio until the music entirely drowned out their voices. She whispered. "Understand, this has to remain strictly confidential. You cannot confide in your brothers."

Relief whooshed through Gayle. "Deal."

"Let's go someplace where we can talk freely."

Gayle agreed, whispering over the music was too exhausting. They trooped downstairs to Kara's car and drove to the southern edge of the city. She stopped at a small park, sparsely populated by children and their mothers. The two women strolled over and sat on one of the benches. "You've been here before?"

Kara nodded. "It has come in handy. Let's go ahead and say the words that must be spoken. I'll start. Intelligence has picked up chatter of a three-prong attack but nothing has been confirmed."

Gayle hugged her. It must have cost Kara to share the info against orders. "Thanks for trusting me."

"I always have."

"For proving it, then," Gayle said, absurdly encouraged.

"Fine. You're up, now shoot."

She considered her choice of words carefully. Whatever she revealed was akin to spending precious capital needed to buy herself out of this imbroglio. "I'll let you in on the fact Arab Imports is a Transway client. Malone Imports is a subsidiary of Arab Imports and both are owned by Harri Malone."

"You're supposed to trade me new information. Have you forgotten I'm legal counsel for said firm? To clear the record, Malone Imports was created to allow Arab Imports to ship with Transway's competition without breaking their contract."

"Wow. It took me weeks to figure it out. How's this? Malone Imports chartered the CI plane that crashed."

Kara blinked, the single indication that she might have been surprised. She said, "The agency suspects the terrorists are using diamonds to fund subversive activities."

"It makes sense. There were some heists recently in Amsterdam." Gayle floated the piece of undocumented information with the secure knowledge frequent diamond robberies occurred there.

"I've gone as far as I can," Kara said. "My advice is to lay low and try to weather this. Leave it to the department to catch the perpetrators. We'll get them and then your ordeal will be finished."

"Sure. It's been fun." Gayle tossed her a wry look. They strolled to the car, silent for the most part on the drive back. She considered what had been said, weighing the words and their meanings in light of recent events.

Kara dropped her off downtown at a random métro stop. Gayle left her without a backward glance. They both had to assume surveillance might be ongoing and react accordingly. This was the life they'd chosen.

28

Despite her brothers' objections and warnings of disaster, Gayle limped into Transway's lobby. Disguised as a plump gray-headed woman in the janitorial crew, she was pushing a cleaning cart. She went straight to the ladies' room and started scrubbing the sinks while surveying the area. If only she knew the motive behind someone stealing her position and identity. She wanted to make sure the pretender wasn't using Transway to steal money or gain access to information that could facilitate an attack on Paris. Kara was right. Much more than her brothers' safety was at stake.

Her ruminations were interrupted when the bathroom door opened and her assistant Helen entered. Gayle stopped herself from calling out a greeting and dashed into one of the compartments, wheeling the cleaning supplies with her. She squirted disinfectant and used a brush to slosh it about in the toilet bowl, then wiped the seat and flushed the commode in an effort to sound industrious.

Several minutes after Helen left, Gayle ventured outside the ladies' room, scooting the cleaning apparatus and supplies alongside her. She began mopping the floor, working a path toward the elevator. The plan was to gain access to her office and ferret out what her double was up to. When the lift opened and the pretender strolled out surrounded by a bevy of staff, Gayle gritted her teeth and backed away, stunned anew by the resemblance.

Employees from the downstairs offices poured into the lobby. Her double greeted the staff in a gracious lady of the manner style. "I want to assure you, everyone here is important to Transway." Then, she launched into a condescending pep talk, which was bound to make her unpopular.

It was uncanny how much she sounded like the real Gayle Regan and disheartening to see the woman taking over her identity. Gayle left the building, disquieted and discouraged. The idea of penetrating Transway and exposing her nemesis was more difficult than she had imagined. How could Gayle prove her false?

Yesterday, she had been sure her situation was reversing for the better. Then she and her brothers had been shot at in the restaurant and she later learned of her dad's heart attack. She knew it wasn't her fault. The criminals were the ones who had fired the bullets in a crowded eating place. Yet her heart said different. She brought danger to those around her.

She caught the bus home, praying silently. *God, my brothers are vulnerable, because they're trying to help me. Please, don't let them be hurt. I'm also asking you to heal Dad. He worries about me and that can't be good for him or Mom.*

Her despondency began to lift. So what if she failed again? She'd keep trying. The case wasn't going to solve itself.

She arrived at the safe house, determined to be upbeat. "Hey, hope I didn't worry anyone, but I got held up at the office."

"They didn't recognize you, did they?" Jason groaned.

"No." Gayle dropped her gaze, then shrugged. "I hate to admit it, but I never got beyond the first floor."

"Oh. Why not?" J.O. gave her his I told you so look.

"Because the impostor showed up to chat with the downstairs staff. Very gracious of her. J.O. called this right from the start. He said I would never get into my office during working hours."

Mitch said, "Tough break. It sounds as if your double is overplaying her hand."

She threw him a grateful glance. "My thought exactly. She has to be an associate of Clyde. Her manner was as obsequious."

"How did you avoid being seen?" Seth asked.

"I hid behind the potted trees. Stop laughing. It wasn't funny. I could have easily been caught."

"As I was saying before you left," J.O. said with a raised eyebrow.

Mitch asked, "How about helping me go through the reports I pulled this morning?"

"Sure. Any progress?"

"You tell me. Come on, I'm set up in the dining room."

She followed him into the next room and took a seat at the table, across from Mitch. Gayle thumbed through the reports, scanning for the most relevant details. An hour later, she cast them aside and rose. "I've found absolutely nothing to incriminate Malone. Everything's circumstantial."

Tears gathered in her eyes, the pressure of her dad's illness at the top of her worries, bubbling dangerously near the surface.

"Gayle." Mitch stood and came around the table. He opened his arms.

She welcomed the comfort, her head resting on his shoulder. After weeks of struggling alone to stay alive and find answers, having the support she craved left her emotions spilling over and puddling at her feet.

"Better?" As if uncomfortable with their closeness, he stepped back.

She nodded. "Thanks for the sympathy." Awareness settled in her, and she returned to business. "Let's take a crack at tracing the money through Malone's bank accounts."

"Neither of us has the kind of access required."

"Then we hack our way in."

"Isn't that illegal without a federal warrant?"

"Mitch, in case you haven't noticed our enemies are not playing by any rule book. They're trying to kill us."

"Point taken."

"But before we resort to hacking, I've got an idea. The other night at Transway before you arrived, I loaded software onto Clyde's PC to give me remote access." It seemed ages ago to her now. She stared into Mitch's eyes, and a wall seemed to crumble. The next moment his arms were around her and he was kissing her hesitantly, tenderly. He drew back, looking as surprised as she felt.

"Gayle."

"Shh." She placed her fingers against his lips. "Don't say a word."

His arms fell to his sides. "We can't pretend this never happened."

"No. I don't think we could. Still, let's not blow it out of proportion. It happened. Let's move on."

He gave her a tight smile.

"Mitch, someone wants to terminate us. Not only are these people capable of murder they're in the process of committing other monstrous crimes that we've inadvertently stumbled onto. Try to understand. My life is complicated. I can't handle diversions."

"I see." His gaze avoided hers. "You're right. Let's start on the business at hand."

Contrarily, her spirits sank as he conceded to her wishes. Gayle flipped open her laptop and remoted into Clyde's PC. She skimmed through his program files. "I may have found what we've been searching for, but it's password protected." She made several attempts, using various combinations of words, numbers and letters to no avail.

"How about Catherine Deneuve?" Mitch said. "Clyde had photos of the French film star hanging in his office. She might be his dream girl, the key to his getaway account."

"Wow. You are observant." She typed in the name. Bingo! They were in. She maneuvered through several directories and files and soon located his personal account information hidden in an unlikely folder.

"Yes." Mitch slapped his hand to hers in the high-five sign.

She clicked on the file and did a double take. "His Swiss online bank account! We may have hit the jackpot."

Mitch frowned. "His deposits were made in cash. He's not an imbecile."

"Close enough. I can't believe he's very clever. I'll check out these other documents and see what's there." Gayle flicked through them and then stopped. "Unbelievable. A list of his passwords. One must be connected to Malone."

She cautioned herself not to raise her expectations too high. The Malone question could transmute into zilch. Strange, all at once the pressures of the last few weeks were pressing in.

"Gayle, are you okay?"

Her hands clenched at her sides. She rose. "You do this."

"Fine." He took her place.

She paced, something niggling at the back of her mind. Then it hit her. Harri Malone seemed familiar, but where had she seen him? Could it have been in a newscast? She sat at Mitch's PC as he was on hers and googled Harri Malone. There he was on multiple occasions escorting a string of beautiful film stars. She kept searching to discover if there was one woman in particular whom he was seen with more often.

"Gayle, come see this."

She moved to peer over Mitch's shoulder. "Nice work. This is what we've been after."

"You bet." He scanned through the listings in the online Swiss account. "There are several deposits from Arab Imports as well as Malone Imports. Though I doubt these entries would ever hold up in court."

"At least we're certain there's a link."

They shared a smile and Mitch whirled her around the room. "Let's go tell the others and see if they've made any progress."

They strolled into the den, and Mitch related their success at ferreting out Clyde's links to both Arab and Malone Exports. Her brothers looked excited.

"We're beginning to think the preflight external check crew was kidnapped," Seth said.

Mitch tilted his head to the side, pursing his lips. "How is that possible? No one has ever received any ransom notes."

"You're right," Jason said. "However, as we are not there on the scene, we hired a detective in Houston to help with our investigation. He has questioned several witnesses who reported what might have been an abduction in Tulsa before the plane took off for its return flight to Houston. He also located a security cam that seems to verify it. The license plates on the car in question are being traced at this moment." He turned to J.O. "How about you, any luck?"

"Nothing to report yet, but I hope to get a breakthrough soon."

"You're more secretive than Gayle. If we weren't brothers, I'd think you were the spy," Seth said.

J.O. arched a brow in rebuttal. "I've always played my hand close to my chest. Why should this time be any different?"

"The difference is we're all in this together and all our lives are at stake," Seth said.

"Got it. Let's break and grab a bite to eat," J.O. suggested. "Is there any food left in the house?"

"Funny. Not much chance of food lasting with you guys around." Gayle grinned. "Except I did happen to bring more groceries home with me today. I'll go see what I can rustle up."

"You have our sincere appreciation," J.O. said sardonically.

Gayle ambled into the kitchen, humming under her breath, and enjoyed rummaging about while deciding what to cook. She opened a box of fettuccine noodles and set a pot of water to boil, then sliced the chicken breast left over from the night before. In another pan she placed a stick of butter to melt, added a cup of cream and grated a generous amount of Parmesan cheese, stirring it into the Alfredo sauce, then tossed it with the chicken. They could afford the extra wallop of fat calories this once.

There were enough greens for a salad. She rinsed the lettuce and tomatoes and set them to drain, then mixed up a vinaigrette for the dressing. She washed and snipped the grapes into small bunches and arranged them on a tray with Camembert for dessert. After all, they were in Paris.

She sliced a loaf of French bread, reflecting on how much she had changed during her stint as an agent. Her naivete and idealism had both suffered severe blows.

Mitch wandered into the kitchen and offered to set the table. Jason trailed in and began filling the water glasses.

The others soon followed. "Smells good. Yum. Chicken Alfredo, my favorite," Seth exclaimed.

They gathered around the table and J.O. said grace. Before long, the conversation gravitated to their dad.

"Remember when he caught the huge trout on that camping trip in the Colorado mountains," Jason said. "He was proud of reeling in that fish."

Gayle glared at Jason. "It was the day you dared me to jump in the creek with you. I dove in and cut my knees on rocks, and you never even budged from the bank. Dad had to carry me to the car."

"Can I help it if you're gullible enough to fall for every trick?" He grimaced. "I got a scolding for that. Dad said you could have broken your neck diving into water with rocks. He was right too. Sorry, Sis. I was fairly young myself."

"Surviving living with you three has prepared me to confront any challenge." Gayle chuckled. "How could I ever forget when the Simms came to visit and their youngest boy asked, 'How are those wild Indians of yours doing, Mrs. Regan?' His parents were embarrassed because it was obvious, he'd overheard them calling us wild Indians. But mom graciously said, 'They do play a bit wild on occasion.'"

The rest of the evening was spent recalling various comical

and somber episodes from their childhood. At some point they phoned and checked on their father's progress, glad to hear he was holding his own.

Gayle sank onto the sofa next to Mitch. "You've been patient listening to our stories tonight."

"I enjoyed myself. It makes me realize how much I missed as an only child."

"Believe me, there were moments when each of us wished our siblings didn't exist."

"Yes, I'm sure, but never truly."

"No, never truly," she said with a wistful sigh for those bygone days of youth.

"You must have been a bright child and a handful."

"I tumbled from one escapade to the next, striving to keep up with my brothers and prove to the family I could take care of myself."

He studied her with approval. "I'm glad there's still a smidgen of that little girl left."

"Thanks. I thought I had lost her entirely." She liked the laugh lines at the corners of his eyes, blue as a Texas sky. When Mitch was disturbed though, she'd watched them darken and turn stormy.

29

Dominic returned to France and settled into the family's Paris estate. His parents were staying at their summer residence in Monte Carlo, and the servants, except for a skeleton staff, had accompanied them. Those who remained in the city with Dom were under strict orders that he was at home to no one. His days, and much too often his nights, were spent toiling with his team at Interpol headquarters. The work was arduous.

He let himself into the house at about three in the morning. Weariness seeped into his bones as he trudged up the long arching staircase to his room. He sank into the gray leather club chair by the phone and pressed his fingers to his aching head in an attempt to relieve the pain. The Trudeau's motto resounded through his mind as strength for the tasks ahead seemed to fail him.

He murmured the memorized verse in his native French. "For unto whomsoever much is given, of him shall much be required; and to whom men have committed much, of him they will ask the more." Dominic found comfort in the words of Luke 12:48. He smiled at the memories of his father and his grandfather repeatedly explaining its significance.

The act of reciting the scripture that had become his mantra at an early age seemed an affirmation of everything good and worthy, a welcome contrast to the evil he confronted.

He remembered, ironically, it was Gayle's air of fresh innocence that first attracted him. Her artlessness, gilded with a charming elegance, had caused him to imagine he was in love.

Yet, he had obviously never grasped the essence of the woman he'd planned to marry. Dom realized this when he learned she was a CIA agent. The news had astounded him. How could she have kept an item of such magnitude secret?

True he had committed a similar faux pax, but he was after all a man, destined to be the head of the family. Some might label him a chauvinist for considering her omission a betrayal, while believing his silence understandable and entirely necessary. He was old fashioned in this regard, but not a martinet about it.

He lifted the glass of water on the side table in a silent toast to his ancestors. "To a lost generation." The women had adored their men and knew their place and in return the men supported and protected them.

Well, he would do his duty, although he doubted his parents would be happy if his plans ever came to their attention.

Tired, he rose, took a quick shower and tumbled into bed.

The next morning Dominic rubbed his eyes and sat up in bed. He stared sleepily at his valet.

"It is seven, monsieur." Jarvis served him breakfast on an ornate silver William and Mary tray presented to the Trudeaus in the seventeenth century for services rendered to a cousin who had married an English duke. He poured the coffee from an exquisite Toulouse silver pot that had survived Louis XIV's edict that all silver must be melted to finance the treasury. Jarvis added a dollop of heavy cream.

Dom inhaled the delicious brew. "Splendid." He buttered a croissant, spread cook's cherry jam on it and took a bite. He glanced at his valet fondly.

Jarvis was a prodigious snob and considered his knowledge of items in the Trudeau estate a source of immense pride. He opened the drapes. "Will there be anything else?"

"Thank you, no." Dominic swallowed a sip of the hot coffee. "Wait. Have there been any calls?"

In anticipation of the question, Jarvis slid the list of messages onto the tray and left.

Dominic smiled his appreciation and scanned the notes. He finished breakfast, rose and dressed, then phoned Francois and arranged to meet later.

Dom deliberated over what he'd learned. The wiretapped conversations between Sara and Abby confirmed they were collaborating. The problem was deciphering the cryptic language in the code the women used. Despite his careful reading of their communication transcripts nothing struck him as unusual.

He dreaded breaking the news to Ari of his wife's betrayal. But Ari, being an undercover Interpol operative in Syria, had a right to hear they'd found Sara. Dom made the call. "How's it going over there?" he asked.

Ari's cheery baritone came across the line. "What a question. I'm in Syria. The rebels are fighting and the government's bombing them. Meanwhile, I'm walking a tight rope with Harri and his men in Saudi."

"What you need is a vacation from the Middle East. Ari, I need you at Paris headquarters tomorrow. You can brief me then."

He grunted. "Rather short notice."

"It's about *the package* you lost a while back."

Ari's sharp indrawn breath was audible, followed by a moment of what appeared to be shocked silence. "I'll be there," he said in a tight voice and rang off.

Dom set the receiver down, his shoulders drooping. Optimists alleged life was what you made it. If it brought limes, they made limeade. Dominic's taste for limeade had soured.

He rubbed the back of his neck with a sigh and ordered his car.

He had his chauffeur drop him midtown because it was less

conspicuous. From there he caught a cab to the airport and boarded a jet to Geneva. He had plenty to consider during the flight. With a grim twist to his mouth, he mentally ran through the facts.

How would his old friend react to the agency's request? Should Interpol have waited for more conclusive intel? Time, however, was of the essence. He had to stop second guessing every decision.

As the plane circled to land in Geneva, thoughts of Abby and the promises he had made to lure her circled him like a vulture after prey. She had resisted giving up any substantial information. Would she ever willingly come to some sort of binding agreement? Abby might be playing a triple game, reeling him in. If so, the lady was in for a surprise.

The harsh thump as the wheels hit the tarmac jolted him back to the present. Soon the seat belt lights went off and Dom picked up his case, exiting the small craft. He made his way out of the airport to the taxi area and climbed into the cab at the head of the line. "Take me to rue Rodolphe-Toepffer fifteen."

His first stop was the Banque Genevoise de Gestion where he had arranged to meet Jean Voumard, both friend and the exchequer's VP.

Contrary to the hyperbole many believed, banks in most places were prohibited from sharing clients' data. Swiss law was exceptionally severe on any breach of confidentiality, whether in banking or other commerce. The country had enacted laws in 1934 to protect the accounts of Germans, especially Jews, from Nazi confiscation, making it a criminal offense for the institution, its employees or agents to improperly divulge information.

Thus it was interpreted, both in practice and by the courts, as a serious infraction to disclose a customer's info to any third party, unless extremely specific criteria were met. This included official requests from foreign governments. Too often current laws had stalled Interpol's ongoing operations. Dominic believed his petition met the prescribed conditions.

In Swiss banks, a constant awareness of the obligation to maintain sub rosa was reinforced. Employees were required to sign the secrecy portion of the banking act. Still, Swiss legal authorities routinely worked with their foreign counterparts in investigative matters. The general rule was both parties must consider the activity a crime prior to cooperation.

Dominic hoped to convince the Swiss banker, Jean Voumard that Madame Dubois's affairs qualified as such a case and thus provide Interpol access to her safe deposit box and accounts.

The belief that Swiss bank secrecy could still be used to hide illegal acts was a myth. Prior to the '80s, a number of transactions that some nations considered reprehensible were permitted.

Switzerland's fiscal legislation had since evolved and was similar to that of most OECD (Organization for Economic Cooperation and Development) members. Financial crimes committed in other jurisdictions were likely to be just as illegal in Switzerland. This was good news. Interpol's difficulty lay in obtaining the required evidence to support their requests.

Despite the evolvement of internal and international practices, investigators remained frustrated. Dom mused this was due to specific differences in criminal laws, occurring because legal definitions varied between borders.

As a significant participant in the global community, the Swiss had tax treaties, which provided automatic exchange of financial and tax information about Swiss account holders. Dominic considered this trend of cooperating likely to continue. The days of being able to use the quirks of Swiss jurisprudence to avoid taxes were rapidly ending. Terrorists and criminals prone to launder money to avoid reporting questionable income were more in Interpol's reach.

The truth was, he reflected, as the world became more connected, Swiss banking secrecy provided about the same protection as bank confidentiality legislation in most OECD countries.

The taxi halted. Dominic paid the driver and entered the impressive granite and glass building of the Banque Genevoise de Gestion. The receptionist verified his appointment and Jean's secretary came and escorted him to his office.

With a cry of welcome, Jean rose and kissed Dom's cheeks in rapid succession while shaking his hand. "How are you, my friend? You never seem to grow older like the rest of us."

Dominic laughed. "It's the children who mature you, but you have the beautiful Madeleine as compensation."

Though Swiss by birth, Jean had been raised in Belgium. His inquiring eyes, round face and sophisticated, biting wit reminded Dom of Agatha Christie's character Hercule Poirot.

Dominic quickly began presenting the case for investigating Madame Dubois's accounts. "There is a situation and frankly, Interpol needs your help."

Jean's smile wavered. "I'm entirely of your persuasion in these matters. The bank, however, must abide by the law. Show me just cause, and then perhaps I can be of service."

Dom leaned forward, his hand on one knee. "Do you remember when the German ambassador was assassinated in the United States and his wife disappeared?"

"Yes, I recall the circumstances were particularly horrific." He looked questioningly at Dominic. "I vaguely recollect the case was never solved?"

"Right. Few knew that when Pia Helmut dropped out of sight, her former college roommate, Sara, vanished at about the same time. Sara had married a Syrian, Ari Mslam. Perhaps you knew him back when we were all in college together?"

Jean nodded. "Not well. Wasn't he a particular friend of yours?"

"I helped him out of a scrape once. He approached me five years ago and asked if I could assist in locating his wife."

"This is all very interesting." He cleared his throat a bit nervously.

"But I have several more appointments to get through. Let's talk over dinner. Maddy will be delighted to see you."

"I wish I could," Dom said regretfully. "I'm expected in Paris tonight. Ari's flying in from Syria to meet me. I've found his wife."

"You're as tenacious as ever. He's lucky to have you on his side."

Dom hesitated, realizing he'd have to level with Jean in order to gain the access they required. "Sara's operating under an alias as the acting director of Cremont Sanatorium in Paris. There's a lot we don't understand as yet, but everything we've learned smells. Sara, alias Doctor Dubois, is also using false credentials."

"I'm sorry for Ari. I suppose the fool loves her?"

"Yes. Her story only worsens. She's working with a group of terrorists who are intent on blowing up Paris, London and New York. I need your help to stop her."

Jean gasped, his eyes bulging in shock.

"I apologize for breaking it to you abruptly."

"I take it Madame has an account with us."

"It's my understanding she does."

Jean pulled on his ear thoughtfully. "I still have to see some documentation to prove this isn't a fishing expedition. Do you have any proof of international criminal activity?"

The fact that Sara had assumed an alias as Dr. Madelaine Dubois and the directorship to which she clearly lacked the credentials to hold, and was in contact with terrorists, seemed to weigh with Jean. Yet it was frustrating that he refused to commit. Dom could only hope once Jean had considered the matter carefully and been presented the legal documents and evidence his stance would reverse. Dominic opened his briefcase and passed him the required papers.

Jean studied them and then handed them back. "I presume copies are out of the question."

Dom gave a short laugh as he gathered the pages and placed

them in his attaché case. "Don't pretend you haven't the authority to handle this. You're familiar with the drill."

"All right. Perhaps it's better if you wait here while I make the arrangements."

"Remember, go carefully. Absolutely no one must suspect or the result could be catastrophic."

Jean agreed and left.

Dom wondered what they'd find. He was hoping for hard evidence such as stolen jewels, marked bills, maps, contact lists or plans. Any one of those would be enough to stop her.

Jean returned and led him into an area lined with safe deposit boxes. He closed the door for privacy and handed over the key to Dr. Madelaine Dubois's box.

Dom reached up to unlock it, gave him the keys and stepped aside.

Jean picked up the drawer. "Follow me." He went into a smaller room, motioned Dom to be seated and set the box on the table before him.

Dom realized that at any moment Jean might recant or unseen forces could intrude and mess this up. Dom reached inside the drawer, settling on a velvet pouch. He drew it out and opened it with a silent whistle at the unbelievable array of luminous sparkling diamonds it held.

He would have to proceed cautiously. His first choice would have been to summon the jeweler from Amsterdam to ascertain if these were indeed the jewels stolen. Yet he might alert the thieves. Pia, alias Leah, had to be secured before any overt moves were made that might send the terrorists scrambling to cover their tracks. Dom knew from experience Banque Genevoise de Gestion retained an appraiser on staff. He asked Jean for the name and contacted Interpol's Paris headquarters for clearance verification.

Meanwhile, there were the other items to examine. He unearthed a bag of miscellaneous Middle Eastern currencies. No surprise there. Dom's mobile rang. "Bonjour Francois, what do you have for me?"

"Fortunately, the agency has an appraiser in Geneva. Be on the lookout for Will Mercer." Francois went on to give a brief description of the man. "Keep me posted on what's happening there. Nice work."

Dom hung up and explained the agreement to Jean, who then made arrangements for Mercer's arrival.

Dom continued going through the box but was disappointed in the rest of its contents. Finally, he reached for the envelope at the bottom and found a cashier's check in Saudi riyals for the equivalent of fifty million US dollars. The ease with which Sara had collected the money and jewels to target the West was deeply disturbing.

A brief time later Mercer arrived and duly identified the diamonds as those stolen during the latest heist in Amsterdam. He photographed the stones and replaced them with paste copies the department had made in advance in anticipation of such an opportunity. The check was also retrieved and a marked counterfeit copy was left in its place, in order to alert the authorities if and when it was cashed. Jean locked the box and returned it to its usual spot. Around-the-clock surveillance was officially in progress. It had been a good day's work. The terrorists' organization had taken a hit in the neighborhood of 100 million Euros considering the jewels and check.

Though Dom was tempted to refer to the possible attacks and the devastation to the financial markets, he refrained. Jean would have already considered the ramifications. His shrewdness was legendary in finance circles.

Dominic caught a cab to the airport, boarded his flight and landed in Paris about midnight. Francois met him at the baggage exit. The drive home gave them a chance to discuss the events of the day and Dom's scheduled meeting with Ari later in the morning. He leaned back against the headrest with a grunt of contentment and closed his eyes. "The agency needed the break we caught today."

"Please, don't go to sleep on me now. Fill me in on the rest of the details," Francois begged.

Dom straightened and began to rehash the day and they adjusted their strategy. By the time they reached the Trudeau estate they had covered a lot of ground. The two said good night, jubilant over their momentary success, well aware there were potholes strewn along the bumpy road to victory.

Dom let himself into the house and poured himself a drink before trudging upstairs to his bedroom. He surveyed the room he'd slept in since early childhood with satisfaction. This one place in his life never changed, he thought with a touch of nostalgia. He intended to do everything in his power to keep it so, even if it meant leaving.

He undressed, showered and put on pajamas, then slid into the massive walnut four-poster bed. The one that his father and his father's father and so on had slept in before moving into the master's suite, until death had ended their stay there, and the next generation took possession.

Above all, a man must remain true to his principles and beliefs. To forfeit his plans and desires for the betterment of mankind was creditable. Not in any lofty sense, but for the well of contentment it brought deep inside where it mattered. Dominic fell asleep on the thought.

30

Sun streamed into the east bedroom window, waking Dominic after only three hours of sleep. He dressed and drove the Bentley to the office. He preferred the Rolls, but too many of his friends might recognize it and he was keeping a low profile.

He entered Interpol, looking as confident as he always did, rested and immaculate. It was nice to be in the care of his valet again. His day passed in meetings and briefings on how to counter the alleged attacks the agency's intel had exposed.

Dom was powerless to prevent his next move, repugnant though it might be. It was time to start the third act, which in all good plays led to the denouement. Dominic dialed Abby. He avoided using names in case the lines were bugged. "Chéri, I've missed you."

"Maybe you should call more often," she said in a sexy contralto.

"I've been out of the country. I got in last night."

"Should I expect you to drop by later, say about eleven?" she asked.

"Don't I usually when I'm in town?"

"Hurry, darling, I have a special present for you."

Despite his misgivings and aversion to her games, his pulse leapt in response. "Au revoir."

Dom had been cultivating Abby for months while she toiled under the mistaken presumption, she was flipping him. He hoped to sell her on the idea of redeeming herself through the agency. Interpol had given him the green light to make her an offer. He knew Abby aimed to turn him into a double agent for hire with her as his handler. When she moved to the Middle East, she'd require new contacts to remain viable. He was a significant part of the bundle she wanted to exchange for money and services rendered to the terrorists she'd sold out to.

Dom had a different plan. He would allow Abby to handle him as long as she continued to work undercover exclusively for Interpol. Behind the scenes, Abby's status was negotiable in spite of the CIA intel she'd sold to terrorists. Her agreement to his plan might provide her with some sort of reprieve with the agency should she wish to live in the West or communicate with family and friends at a future date.

Late that evening, Dominic dropped by Abby's place. She wore an enticing short, cotton knit, black dress meant to ignite his imagination. She handed him a glass of red wine.

He nuzzled her neck. "Hmm, you smell good."

"So do you." She wound her arms around his shoulders and kissed him, then drew him across to the sofa. "Have you eaten?"

"Yes, earlier, and you?"

She nodded.

He took an appreciative sip of the Cabernet Sauvignon. "Very nice." She knew her wines. "Abby, I hear you're about to cross over."

"Like to join me?"

"Perhaps, it depends on you."

"Truly?" Her eyes lit and she grasped his arm.

Dom picked up her hand, intertwining it with his own. "Tell me about Sara."

She laughed. "I might as soon give you my head."

He met her gaze. "Trust me. I have a plan. Sara won't be able to hurt you."

Abby drew back, clearly uneasy. "You're aware I can't talk about this. We agreed."

"My dear, you've been using every wile you have to favorable effect, attempting to play me. Well then, go ahead and play me." Dom leaned over and kissed her. They would finish the discussion later. The agency was banking on her accepting their offer. Dominic was glad he had changed into shorts before he left home. He lifted Abby in his arms and carried her outside before tossing her into the pool and following her in.

She came up sputtering. "What is wrong with you?"

He swam to her side. "We both needed to unwind and cool down a bit before we started negotiations. Come on, let's swim." He led and she followed. They were both avid sports buffs and seasoned swimmers.

Fifteen minutes later, they were loosened up and ready to quit. Abby shook out her wet hair, wrapped it in a towel and pulled on a robe, before marching to the bath. Dom strode into the guest room where he showered and changed into the clothes he'd stashed in his briefcase.

Refreshed, they sprawled out in the living room and began the bargaining process. Dominic knew what he wanted and didn't deviate. He also possessed a fair idea of what Abby was after and had come prepared to offer her a deal that would be difficult to refuse. It took some time hammering out the details, but he understood how to manage her. She might be a spy, but he was the master at this game.

"You, sir, are treacherous," Abby said several hours later, after having agreed to Dominic's terms.

He shrugged. "Admit it. With the trouble you're in with the CIA, the offer is immensely to your advantage."

She tipped her head back against the couch. "You promised to put in a good word with Langley as well."

"Consider it done."

She sighed. "I would have accepted almost any terms that resulted in our being together. I care for you. Maybe too much."

"Chéri, there's no need to be melancholy or melodramatic. Come here."

She settled beside him on the sofa with a frown.

"I promised you we'd do this together. Stop worrying." He squeezed her shoulder and then stood.

"You're not going?"

"It's past two in the morning. I have an eight o'clock appointment. Walk me to the door and then get some sleep. You should be on your toes tomorrow."

After they parted, Dominic drove home. He steered the car up the drive, almost envious of the servants who lived there year-round. He was seldom in residence and, regrettably, would soon be departing for Syria on a task he must undertake for his country. Dom let himself in the house, locked up, then walked across the granite foyer and up the curving staircase to his room. He phoned Francois.

"It's all settled. She's agreed to our terms. I'll be leaving with her."

"Good," Francois said. "Any intelligence on the attacks the wires are full of?"

"No, I couldn't risk scaring her off, but I'll get it out of her later."

"I know you will. France is counting on you."

"Me and hundreds and thousands of others. Not that I don't appreciate the sentiment," he said caustically.

"Dominic, what's got into you? You of all people understand what's at stake."

He understood too well. He'd practiced discipline his entire life. He finished the conversation and threw the phone on the floor. He couldn't remember ever being this angry. Why must he sacrifice his family, his home and Gayle, to keep them and everything he loved safe? But he knew the answer. France was his country and the world his neighbor. Duty and honor called and he could not refuse.

31

G ayle lowered the van's visor to block the glaring afternoon sun from her and Mitch.

Unseemly was the only word she could think of to describe her behavior. She was sneaking about like a hornworm after a tomato. How could she suspect Abby? Gayle knew what it felt like to be dissed by the CIA. When they'd discarded her, Abby had stood by her and tried to help. She couldn't believe Abby and Dominic had carried on an affair when he was engaged to her. An affair that according to Kara and others was ongoing.

Gayle drove the van to Abby's place and waited with Mitch. She climbed into the back, while he stayed seated in the front. The darkened windows allowed her to see out, while providing privacy to those inside. They had picked up lunch at a drive-through on the way and ate while they watched the entrance to Abby's place.

"This must be hard for you," Mitch said.

She shrugged. "I have to give her the same benefit of the doubt I would've appreciated."

Mitch frowned. "If she's a traitor, she's being watched. If we're spotted with her, we fall under suspicion through association."

"I've covered our tracks well. The van is registered under an alias. We're both wearing disguises."

"Sorry. I keep forgetting you're a trained agent. I'm obviously a novice at this."

"We're a team and that has broadened our capabilities enormously. Mitch, you are a vital part of this."

"Thanks. Hey, isn't that her?" He moved to ease himself into the driver's seat.

"Better let me drive. There's a technique to following a car and remaining unobserved."

"What kind of technique?"

"You'll see soon enough. Keep your eye on her."

They trailed about a block behind. Gayle's stomach churned. She dreaded the discovery of her friend's betrayal.

"You're going to lose her," Mitch said.

"It's okay." She swung the van left then right. The GPS monitor she'd attached to Abby's car was allowing Gayle to remain a safe distance behind. She checked her rearview and side mirrors, aware of the others following her.

Mitch threw her a harried look. "There's a dark blue sedan creeping up on your left. It's been behind us almost from the start."

"Relax. We're fine." She pulled to the curb, stopping in front of a grocery store. The blue sedan continued following Abby. "I'll be back in a minute," Gayle said.

"Seriously?"

"Yep." She got out and ran inside, a diversion to anyone who might be tailing Abby. Gayle remained in the store for a few moments, then returned to the vehicle. The van's metal bracketed license holders held two plates each, making it easy for her to change out the back and front.

She climbed into the van. "The GPS device I attached to Abby's car places her at Dominic's house in the city. He stays there often when his parents are in town." Gayle put the van in gear, heading to Dom's. She parked beneath a weeping willow several streets away. The leaves provided some camouflage. She glanced across at Mitch. "Would you rather wait here?"

"What exactly are you planning to do?"

"As you said, we're not the only ones tailing her. Let's sneak around to the back of the house and listen."

"From outside."

"I have a key. Remember, Dominic and I were once engaged." Gayle would have preferred doing this alone. Her brothers insisted she needed a partner. Mitch was a tremendous help, but subterfuge wasn't his forte.

She slipped out of the van and Mitch followed. They entered Dom's home without incident. Gayle heard voices coming from the den, and when she peeked in her breath caught.

"Please, darling, it's a chance for us to be together openly, at last." Abby wrapped her arms around Dominic and he kissed her.

A wrenching pain tore through Gayle, startling her. She blinked back tears, reminding herself she was over Dom. Impulsively, she stepped into the room, her gun pointed at them. "Isn't this cozy, my friend the spy and my jilting fiancé?"

"Gayle?" Dominic said in a strangled voice. His gaze roamed over her, taking in her disguise.

"Sit down," she said in a voice devoid of emotion. "Mitch, pat them down for weapons, but stay on guard."

He winked as if to reassure her and moved to obey.

"Don't be absurd," Abby said. "You wouldn't shoot either of us."

"Are you willing to take the chance?"

"What are you doing here?" Dom asked, a forbidding twist to his mouth.

Her muscles tightened, bracing for a blow. "I came for the truth."

Dom squeezed his eyes shut briefly. "I've certainly made my lack of interest apparent. You've got to accept the fact that we're finished." His icy gaze met hers and Gayle saw he had himself under rigid control.

"I'm not interested in our past," she lied, needing to understand how she could have been deceived by him. "Tell me why someone is impersonating me, and who's trying to kill me? And what has happened to CI's missing crew?"

Abby broke in. "Wow! Don't forget to collect two-hundred dollars and a Get-Out-of-Jail-Free card as you pass Go. This isn't some little board game we're playing."

"Cut the sarcasm. Being a traitor doesn't make you any smarter."

She sneered. "You don't know much—"

Dominic interrupted. "Abby! Stop and think before giving in to the heat of the moment." He studied Gayle. "I'm sorry our breakup caused you pain. I can't help how I feel."

"Honesty might have helped."

"I'll give you that. Still, it's probably best you leave."

"Nice try to snowball me. I'm waiting for answers."

"I have no idea what you mean."

His look of pity mixed with disdain irked her. She wouldn't let him psyche her out. "Agent Trudeau, isn't it? Or should I say double agent? Yes, I've learned a lot about you, stop being disingenuous. Interpol read your team in on the CI plane crash, and you watched it burn."

"Don't be delusional." Despite his swift comeback, a flicker of surprise crossed his face and confirmed her suspicions.

Mitch scowled, moving threateningly toward Dominic. "What do you know about CI?"

"Nothing. It's obvious she's jealous and making things up."

Mitch's fisted hands dropped to his sides. "Gayle?"

She ignored him and pressed Abby. "Who's impersonating me? Don't bother denying that you know who it is. The expression on your face says otherwise."

"You're crazy. Even if I knew, I wouldn't tell."

Dominic said, "I feel the same. We've nothing to say."

"Not even about the agent you visited in Houston after leaving the scene of the plane crash? Did Abby neglect to mention she was kind enough to give me certain phone records? For some reason, Guy didn't appreciate my call."

Mitch looked stern and unyielding. Gayle's gaze pleaded with him to trust her and save his questions for later when they were alone.

"I've had enough of this fishing expedition," Dom said warily.

Gayle couldn't force them to talk. In a skirmish, it would be two skilled agents against one. If she fired, the gendarmerie would converge on the place.

"Mitch, let's get out of here. They won't reveal any more."

Abby hugged Dom as Gayle left with Mitch.

For Gayle, the sight of the two of them, wanting her gone, hurt. Somehow, she made it to the van without breaking down.

Mitch slid behind the wheel. "Let me drive. Sorry you had to go through that."

"If you don't mind, I prefer not to talk about it."

"We have to discuss what happened back there. What's this about the CI crash?"

"A few lucky guesses on my part." Gayle explained how worried she'd been when Dominic first disappeared. She feared he'd been kidnapped and had asked Abby to retrieve his phone records. "A certain man named Guy Henderson from Houston rang Dom shortly before he vanished. I phoned him and found him courteous until I asked for Dom. He hung up on me immediately. I sensed then something was off."

"And you never told me?"

"It's only recently I realized CI's plane crash occurred the day after Dom vanished. I checked the flight logs for his private plane. He not only flew to Houston but rented a Camry while there. I accused him of being at the crash site to see his reaction."

Mitch pulled into Gayle's driveway and said, "And from the look on his face, he obviously witnessed the crash. Even I could see that much. Does this mean it's part of an Interpol investigation?"

She nodded. "The question is, why are they involved?" Gayle and Mitch climbed out of the van.

Gayle headed inside to her room, needing down time to assimilate all that had occurred. A glance in the mirror revealed her feverish and over-bright eyes. She collapsed on the bed, retreating in an effort to cope, her faith wobbling in the wake of Dominic and Abby's double betrayal. The tightness in her chest grew until she broke down and sobbed. "Lord, help me."

Eventually, her composure returned. In the aftermath of her stormy emotions came questions. How faithful had she been? Certainly more than Dom, who'd left before their wedding and had played her their entire relationship. Yet she had also deceived him, failing to trust him, though as it turned out with good reason. Comparisons were depressing.

In her heart, she knew her failures were more often ones of omission: failure to pray and study the pages of life; to consider others more. When she chose to become an agent, she never weighed the cost to her family. Had her dad's heart attack been brought on in part by worrying about her?

Not much had changed since she'd gone into hiding. Those who were out to murder her remained as intangible as their motives. What could she possibly know to their detriment?

Father God, high in the heavens, reach down from your height. Penetrate this opacity with your brightness. Help me understand Dominic and Abby's betrayal with your love and compassion. Forgive me.

32

Abby had arranged to meet Dominic at Louis's Bistro that afternoon. Gayle's intrusion had unnerved Abby. A reminder to Dom about her own assets would not go amiss.

She reached for a pink Chanel suit that emphasized her femininity. At about the age of thirteen, she'd realized that her resemblance to Audrey Hepburn was a gift when dealing with men. Abby dressed and combed her hair, pausing for a final glance in the mirror. Pleased with her image, she picked up her purse and left.

A taxi took her to Louis's Bistro. Gayle had foolishly believed the place was special to her and Dom, but it was Abby he met there now. When she arrived, Dom rose to pull out her chair, taking in her ap-pearance with a warm glint of approval. He had already ordered for them. After they were seated, he took a long sip of coffee. "Abby, tell me, what exactly is going on?"

Unreasonably, she resented his request, but she checked her emotions and tossed him a seductive glance, stretching to clasp his hand. "Sara was not happy to hear you will be joining us in Syria."

"How disagreeable. Why not?" He studied her for a moment and then sighed as if disappointed. He intertwined their fingers and kissed her palm, lingering over the act.

Abby wanted to curl into his arms and savor his nearness but shook off the feeling, striving to focus. "Sara's suspicious of your motives and she doesn't trust you. Let's go to my place to talk."

Dom's other hand shot out, and she flinched at the firmness of his hold. "Don't play with me. We both understand what's at stake. I offered you the best deal I could. If you want out, tell me now."

She needed to retrench. "There are myriad shades of truth, and grays in between."

"Not for me. This is my neck at risk."

"I'll try to persuade Sara. Let's forget it."

"No," he said coldly. "I want some assurances before we go any further."

"I gave you some." She regretted meeting with him because it had served to exacerbate their problems.

He stood, distancing himself. "Trying is not good enough. Either you deliver or we're finished."

"Like that?"

"Yes." He laid some money on the table and left without another word.

Abby had to think of a means out of this impasse. She hadn't wanted to kill again, yet her choices were narrowing. And she chose to survive, even if it meant murdering those who meant the most to her.

Back at Interpol's Paris headquarters, Dominic needed answers. Soon Ari would arrive and Dom wasn't sure how to tell him that Sara was alive and was suspected of working with terrorists. Worse—she was the alleged leader of an active cell. Why else would she have avoided Ari these last five years?

Dom gave Sara credit for being cunning. The wiretap on her phone had revealed several coded messages intelligence was still unable to crack. She consistently lost the agents tailing her.

Dom stared at the streets below, breathing in the glamour and sophistication of Paris in the summer. His stomach clenched at the sight of Ari climbing out of a cab and entering the building. Several minutes later Dominic braced himself as his friend strolled into the office. He rose and hugged him. "Ari, it's great to see you."

Ari stepped back. "Dom, let's not draw this out. I couldn't take it. I've waited five years for this moment."

"*Ça va.*" He gestured to two cushioned chairs and they settled across from each other.

The upholstery always made Dominic think of his mother and he found courage when he glimpsed it. She had chosen the fabric, an intricate Moorish pattern woven into satiny tapestry because it represented the strength she saw in him.

Dom forced himself to focus. He would let Ari deal with Sara. "Your wife is alive and living in Paris under the alias of Doctor Dubois. She's director of the Cremont Sanatorium and acting chair of the board."

Ari's eyes widened. "Sara, a doctor! Impossible. It is too incredible to believe. How could she possibly have qualified for such a position in five short years? No, no, no."

"The agency concurs." Dominic went on to fill him in. "We were hoping perhaps you could help. She has no idea you're a double agent."

Ari looked as if he'd been sandblasted. Dom knew his friend had his own method of dealing with pain and bewilderment, and that was to erase every trace of it from his face. But today his pain was too great to hide entirely. "I'm sorry. I wish I could have given you better news, but—" Dom shrugged.

Ari seemed to gather his wits. "It's a shock, though not as much as you might think. When the years rolled by without a word from her, I surmised her disappearance had to be one of three scenarios and none of them pleasant to contemplate."

Dom rose, crossed the room to the coffee pot and poured out two cups. He handed one to Ari and sipped the other one himself. His friend held on to the mug like it was a life preserver and he was lost in the middle of the ocean. "If you need anything—"

Ari shook his head, appearing half-drowned and dazed. He continued where he'd left off. "At first, granted, I was at a loss and scared senseless, sick with fear. Eventually reason clicked in. It took me two years to admit she might have instigated the vanishing act."

"You're too hard on yourself. You always have been. It's her loss."

"Sure, I compute that here." He pointed to his head. "But in my heart, it's a whole different terrain. Black isn't white and I'm not who I want to be. It hurts."

Dominic was treading in deep water, uncertain what to say or how to react. What he had gone through with Gayle couldn't compare to the tempest Ari had endured.

"I knew that Sara was dead, kidnapped or she'd chosen to disappear. If she had stopped loving me, divorce would have been simple enough. I was educated in Britain and didn't adhere to strict observances of the Muslim faith. I always found it suspicious that her friend Pia Helmut went missing around the same time. Has she turned up as well?"

Dom nodded. "She's a patient in the sanatorium where Sara works. Her story is unclear. Though it appears she's been held captive and possibly driven mad."

"It's as if the Sara I knew is dead. This other woman can't be the girl I married. Not the wife I strolled on the beach with, holding hands at sunset." His fist pounded the table. "I know it's her, yet I'd give anything if it wasn't."

"You need closure."

"I've needed it for five years." His gaze, glazed with pain, met Dom's.

"Pull yourself together. Go visit her. You need to see her to move past this."

"Then what?"

"Someday you'll meet the right woman for you. Not a terrorist who probably deceived you from the beginning."

Ari held up a hand. "Stop. Please, don't say any more." He broke down and heart-wrenching sobs filled the room.

Dominic understood Ari was grieving his lost wife now as he never could before. Dom waited quietly, regretting his inability to help and wishing there were words to ease his friend's pain.

Finally, Ari came to the end of his tears. His lips curved faintly, more a tired effort than a smile. "Whatever you're planning, count me in."

"*Merci, ami.* We're trying to save three cities and millions of innocent people from disaster. It won't be easy."

Ari rose. "Where am I staying?"

"Somewhere Sara won't suspect. Let's get you briefed, then we'll plan strategy."

33

Determined to confront her nemesis, Gayle had to choose a time and site to her own advantage or risk losing more ground. Her Transway office was the logical place. She could enter the building in disguise and discard her camouflage, metamorphosing into Ms. Regan, general manager of marketing at the appropriate moment.

The trick was to pose as someone who could safely approach the impostor and get rid of her through intimidation. After some reflection, Gayle realized Dom's mother was the sole person in Paris who had succeeded in intimidating her. The more she considered posing as Mrs. Trudeau, the more likely choice the woman seemed. Most likely, the pretender had never met Madame Trudeau, and the disguise shouldn't be difficult to pull off. Gayle's decision made, she prepared for the upcoming confrontation.

A search through the closet unearthed an attractive wig with a sophisticated frosted hairstyle suitable for a female aristocrat in her fifties. Next, she applied cosmetics and was pleased with the results. The mirror told her she looked enough like Dom's mother to fool any casual acquaintances encountered.

A rummage through her wardrobe uncovered a demure blue silk jacket and skirt. Fortunately, Madame Trudeau was about Gayle's height and possessed a trim but generous figure similar to her own. She slipped on the outfit and stepped into a pair of heels, amazed by the transformation.

Gayle put on zirconium wedding and engagement rings, adding diamond earrings and a brooch for the finishing touch. She picked up her purse and dropped in an old-fashioned quizzing glass for dramatic flair.

She walked into the breakfast room in anticipation of her brothers' and Mitch's reactions.

J.O. glanced up first. "Excuse me, ma'am, may I help you?"

Gayle shrugged in a helpless manner and broke into a torrent of French that left the men gaping and murmuring between themselves in an effort to figure out why this strange woman was in the kitchen.

"Sis, can you come in here a moment?" Jason called.

Mitch frowned, studying her closely and then his face lit in comprehension. "Gayle, it is you, right?"

In surprise J.O. examined her more carefully, then shook his head in consternation. "Who are you supposed to be impersonating?"

She laughed in sheer delight at fooling them. "I'm disguised as Dominic's mother."

"You look ridiculous," Seth muttered. "Tell her, Mitch."

He grinned. "I think what your brother means is the sight of you a bit heavier and older than usual is unexpected."

"It's not what I meant," Seth said. "What possible reason could you have to pretend you're related to anyone in that family? I would think you'd be finished with the Trudeaus after the grief they've caused."

"At least hear me out." Gayle filled them in on her plan, answering their questions and patiently bearing with the ensuing heated discussion. J.O. applauded her genius, while Jason and Seth argued it was too dangerous.

Finally, Mitch intervened. "If Gayle has no objections, why don't I go with her? I have legitimate business at Transway, lobbying on behalf of CI." He glanced at her quizzically.

"Fine. But we can't be seen together."

"It would appear suspicious," he agreed. "However, we could

enter the building separately and have our phones **ready** to text the other should any difficulties arise."

His sincerity strengthened her, the warm tug within her reminiscent of a younger Gayle, her small hand tucked into her dad's as they walked in the garden.

She and Mitch shared a brief smile, its lingering rays buoying her spirits as they discussed means and methods. Their plans made, they left, heading to the nearest métro station.

"My brothers are overprotective. It's absolutely embarrassing. I wish they'd remember I'm an adult and a trained agent."

"They are proud of you and with good reason."

"Thanks."

They entered the station and rode the métro downtown, standing in the crowded, noisy aisle until their stop, then walked to her office. Mitch's light chatter seemed designed to soothe her. But she was too keyed up to respond.

When Transway's offices appeared a block ahead, she and Mitch separated. Gayle entered the building, concentrating on the persona she was attempting to portray. With a surge of half confidence and half bravado, she barged into her former office to confront the phony Gayle. "How dare you persist in harassing my son!"

The impostor half rose from behind the desk. "I have no idea what you're talking about."

Gayle perched on the edge of the chair across from her, playing Madame Trudeau the aristocrat to the hilt. "Hmm. As if I didn't answer the telephone myself. These calls and visits must stop or I'm pressing charges."

The pretender's scowl eased. "There's no law against phoning and visiting anyone, is there?"

Gayle raised the quizzing glass to her eye for full effect. "Mademoiselle, you are impertinent. Summon your supervisor. We're going to settle this today."

The fake Ms. Regan looked unsure of how to proceed. Then she assumed an abrasive bluster. "Are you going to leave or force me to summon security?"

"By all means, summon them."

"Get out, now!" Rage dilated her pupils, twisting her face into the unfamiliar image of a dangerous stranger.

Gayle met her gaze, commanding the full force of the Trudeau persona she had assumed. "Mm. Now that I've observed you, I feel something is not quite as it should be."

A tremor of fear radiated from her nemesis. "I don't know what you mean. I'm giving you one last chance to leave." She grabbed her purse and cell phone. "I expect you to be gone when I get back from lunch, or else." She rushed out, leaving the door open.

Gayle closed it, surmising her double was flying on trembling feet to Clyde. Good, she was rattled. Gayle wanted to unnerve both the woman and Clyde until they eventually slipped and exposed themselves.

The visit had been planned for a time when she knew Helen would be at lunch, allowing Gayle to change her disguise without too much fear of discovery. She removed the wig and stashed it in her purse and then wiped off the excessive make up that she had used to age her face. The blue silk suit was fine. The matronly shoes were dropped in her bag, and a pair of high heels retrieved and slipped on her feet. Gayle sat behind the desk as if she belonged there, which she did. Swiftly she scanned the latest reports and briefings and settled in to await her PA's return and Clyde's entrance.

When Gayle heard Helen stirring in the outer office, she buzzed her assistant. "Do you have those papers on the Bridgemont contract for me to sign?"

"They're not back from legal but I have the others ready."

"Bring them in."

Helen entered and set the documents on the desk. "I've double checked. Everything's in order."

"What would I do without you?"

Helen's mouth curved into a surprised smile. "How nice to hear you sounding like your old self again . . . before this trouble started."

Gayle warmed to learn the fraud might be aping her, but the copycat's behavior and personality must leave much to be desired.

Helen left, and moments later, Clyde burst into Gayle's office. He paused, a flash of recognition in his eyes. He looked startled to see her calmly at work. "Clyde, have a seat." She lifted the prepared contracts from the corner of her desk and passed them to him. "These documents are signed and ready to go, but I'd like you to give them a final proof."

He studied them while she caught up on several briefs. "They appear to be in order," he said. "Would you like me to get them out today?"

"No, Helen can take care of it." She gazed at him inquiringly. "Was there anything else?"

He cleared his throat. "I guess not."

She busied herself reviewing the correspondence as he rose reluctantly, clearly unsure about how to resolve the dilemma of Gayle being there, in her own office. Gayle could tell he was worried. To confront her might result in a comparison and an investigation of the two women, and thus end his plans. She watched as he walked out slowly, glancing over his shoulder with a puzzled air.

She didn't dare risk making her stand then. Better to scout the terrain first. Once again, she closed the door, then rifled through the files for the address and keys to the impostor's dwelling.

Gayle found the woman's address on the company roster and guessed her keys were probably in the locked, bottom left drawer of the desk. She reached into the space above the center drawer and detached the desk key she kept hidden there. She unlocked the bottom left drawer and retrieved her double's spare keys.

Gayle dropped them into her purse and left, stopping only to leave instructions for Helen. She caught a cab to the woman's address, suspecting it might be bogus. The driver pulled up to a dark empty warehouse that screamed danger. Gayle stared at it, unsure what her next move should be.

"This is it, mademoiselle," the driver said.

"Give me a few moments."

"With pleasure. The meter's ticking."

If this had been an apartment in an upscale neighborhood, she wouldn't have hesitated. But? No. She decided the smart move was to get reinforcements.

Abruptly a prickle ran up her spine. With a shudder at the sensation of being observed, she wondered if the CIA was onto her. What if they believed she was the pretender?

"Take me to the nearest métro, and hurry," she said, wanting to ensure no one followed her home.

Several minutes later, the driver stopped at the station. Gayle paid him and got out, reining in the urge to run as she lost herself among the crowd.

Then she remembered Mitch. She'd left without telling him where she was going. What if he encountered the impostor and thought it was her? He might give away their plans, or worse, put himself in danger. Gayle would never forgive herself if Mitch were harmed while helping her.

She sent him a text to meet her at home, then rushed to board the métro. What had she accomplished? Besides fomenting the waters, had she placed her enemies on the *qui vive*? She was certain now that Clyde was in on the scheme to ruin her. Hadn't he come running as soon as her nemesis left?

Gayle exited at her stop and trekked the few blocks to the house. She entered to find everyone in an uproar over her absence.

"What were you thinking, taking off like that? Do you realize you could have been killed?" Mitch challenged.

Her temper flared and she mentally ordered herself to calm down. "I wasn't hurt. Besides, I was doing my job."

Mitch grasped her shoulders and shook her gently as if to get her attention. "What you did was thoughtless. We're supposed to be a team. When you disappeared, it stressed everyone. Don't you get that we were worried sick about you?"

He had a way of making her seriously consider her actions in order to understand how thoughtless she'd been. Gayle swallowed, tears gathering in the corners of her eyes. "I'm sorry. I didn't think. I'm used to going it alone. I'll try to be more thoughtful."

Her brothers' relieved sighs whispered across the room. She studied Mitch, wondering if he cared as much as he sounded like he did. Gayle resigned herself to the inevitable and filled them all in on her afternoon.

J.O. said, "One of us should have been with you. We're your backup, use us."

"I appreciate how you have all been there for me. Give me credit for deciding to get reinforcements when I arrived at the warehouse instead of entering by myself." An interesting discussion followed about the warehouse location and how to investigate it.

"Why not have my friend in intelligence check into it for us?" J.O. offered. "He has access to resources we lack."

Everyone agreed, and Gayle asked Mitch how he'd fared at Transway.

He grinned. "Your nemesis agreed to see me and after some conversation she drew up a renewal contract. It's signed and sealed."

"Marvelous. Though it might not be legal."

"Precisely, Sis," J.O. cut in, "which is why I think you need to assert your claim. Otherwise, you could be liable for damages when the situation resolves itself."

"If only it would resolve itself." Her shoulders slumped. "How do I go about contacting my superiors without landing in jail?"

"Let me consult one of my sources who specializes in such cases. I'll get back to you."

"Naturally," Seth said. "You and your unlimited sources."

"He's right. You always seem to know the right person for the job," Gayle said.

As the group began to break up, she informed them she was going shopping and would return later.

Mitch's gaze seemed to linger on her, and Gayle enjoyed the feeling as she strode outside and down the sidewalk.

She caught a cab to rue des Franc-Bourgeois and went into the corner boutique. It carried the exclusive designer jacket and purse she'd recognized in the impostor's office. Gayle had often shopped there. The store carried a line that was particularly attractive on someone of her size and coloring. She described what she wanted to the clerk.

"We sold out some weeks ago, Mademoiselle Regan. In fact, I seem to remember you bought the same items about a month ago. Let me check." She rifled through her PC files. "Yes, here it is. We delivered it to you on the tenth of June."

"What address did you send it to?"

"Apartment Two B, Seventy-five Park Place. The manager signed for it. I wonder what could have happened. I'll ask Thomas when he gets in. He handles the deliveries."

"I'll check with the manager when I get home. He may have set the package aside and entirely forgotten it." Gayle smiled. "You've been an immense help."

With a casual wave she departed and caught a cab. As it neared 75 Park Place, the neighborhood became more upscale. It dawned on her that Clyde also lived in the area. She pulled up his address on her mobile and discovered it matched his accomplice's. Were they romantically involved?

The taxi came to a halt. She paid the driver and got out. A glance at her watch reassured her. Gayle had a couple of hours before the two left Transway if her timing was right. She knocked on the manager's door and apologized for forgetting her key. This way she could still get in even if the keys from the impostor didn't fit the lock.

"No problem, Ms. Regan," he said. "Drop it at the office on your way out."

"Will do. Thanks again."

She rode the lift up to the second floor, located 2 B, and let herself in. She paused in the entry, surveying the area. "Clyde, honey, are you in?" she called out just in case someone was there, but there was no answer.

She glanced around and then walked through the entire home, getting her bearings. There were two bedrooms, one converted into a study. Where was the most likely place to hide important information? She started in the bedroom, assuming the study belonged to Clyde. If his relationship with the woman was long standing, the room might be shared.

The wardrobe in one of the closets could have been her own. Strange to think someone unrelated looked so much like her. It gave her an eerie feeling, knowing this woman knew her so well. How was it possible? A quick search through her belongings revealed nothing.

Next, she tried the study desk and the PC on it. The files and directories were password protected. On a hunch she typed in *nemesis* and was in, staring at a detailed profile on herself. It listed her likes, dislikes, favorite people, places and phrases, even her family and friends. But it gave little insight into the impostor's motivation.

She pulled the woman's key chain out of her purse and tried one of the keys in the apartment lock. It fit. The second one on the ring looked like a safe deposit box key and the other might be to the warehouse.

Gayle left with a niggling sense of having overlooked something. What could she have missed? Then it hit her. Someone close to her had provided the pretender detailed information about her. Was Abby somehow involved? Could she be the leak?

34

Abby chose to betray Sara on her own terms, not Interpol's or Dominic's. Any plot to undermine Sara required subtlety. The plan must make her appear guilty and yet be clever enough to keep her from knowing who sold her out.

Ideally, Abby planned to work it so the agency believed she was not only a heroine but had never been a traitor. She needed to convince them that her strategy all along had been to save Leah a.k.a. Pia. Abby's inability to rescue Pia would ensure she conveniently died and Abby's reputation was restored. Sara would make a convenient scapegoat for any fallout.

Abby knew Doctor Langston would be impressed by her efforts. Aside from the fiction she'd fed him, he knew nothing about her. She had already let several hints fall that all was not as it should be at Cremont.

Abby packed a light bag and prepared to meet Dominic. He was her payback for everything she'd lost. He might be a counterspy with an agenda, but for now he suited her purposes and longings. How often did the two coincide?

Sara was a problem, but Abby knew how to handle her. She stuffed the Beretta in her shoulder holster, slipped on a jacket, then locked the apartment for possibly the last time.

There was no returning. The past was finished. She crossed to the elevator and rode it to the parking garage. She placed her bag in the back of her minivan and drove to the sanatorium.

Most of the administrative staff hadn't yet arrived. She parked at a shady spot in back and went inside. On the lift going up, she considered her options carefully.

As Abby entered her partner's office, Sara glanced up. "Isn't this risky, meeting like this?"

"We have to talk."

"There are telephones." Sara arched an elegant questioning brow. "What's this about?"

"It's about control. I'm taking all the risks, while you're sitting in your nice office in the clear."

"That's not true. Interpol is watching my every move, waiting for me to slip."

"My point exactly. You're not engaged in nefarious activities. I am, and I'm the one who has been found out."

Sara rose. "Don't blame me for your own stupidity. Get out, and don't come here again whining as if you weren't paid plenty for each job. You acted like a starved coyote, greedy for every installment." She threw her a look of contempt.

A slow steady rage burned inside Abby. "You're right. This kind of talk is useless." She drew out the Beretta, the silencer in place, and pulled the trigger.

The bullet slammed into Sara's chest and she fell.

Abby whipped the pistol back into her shoulder holster and fled.

Outside in her car, an insanity of sorts took hold of her and she began to sing shrilly. "Someday you'll find him. He'll be waiting beyond the horizon singing the blues. Turn his life around and be like you." She laughed hysterically. "A pocketful of money and no honey. Round and round, up and down, how many times 'til in you go, out the chute, into the circle and . . ."

She cried. Sara! She'd killed Sara. Her only friend in this world of deception. Abby saw her lying there in a pool of blood. The face once set with determination, shriveling in desperation and drawing her last breath.

Wait. Sara wasn't her friend and never had been. Abby was a tool she'd used. Sara had twisted and deluded her until Abby fit her designs and purposes.

By the time the authorities discovered Sara, Abby should be safe in Vienna. Later, there would be consequences. Still, she'd made the only possible decision given the alternatives. She'd disposed of Sara and arranged for the two star-crossed lovers' reunion in one skillful stroke. Neither Gayle nor Dom possessed a glimmer of insight vis-à-vis what was about to occur.

Perry Langston stared out his office window. For some time, he'd worried Leah might be in danger. Interpol Agent Francois Rodea's recent confirmation of the peril she was in had left Perry in a near state of panic. He'd come to care for the complex woman he matched wits with during her therapy sessions. He supposed she was one of his favorite patients, although it was unethical to admit it.

Interpol's covert presence at Cremont meant the situation was threatening, and the agency's precautions further pointed to concern for Leah's welfare.

Perry thought of his home in Houston. He had spoken with his parents during the weekend. Recollections of his family around the dinner table on Sunday after church, eating roast beef and gravy, Mom's homemade rolls and apple pie, left him nostalgic.

Leah would be safe in America. Yet the idea was absurd. The authorities wouldn't allow her to leave until the case was resolved. Was he falling in love with her? He'd never wanted to bring a patient home before. Then again it was his first case involving a criminal investigation. Gayle would laugh to see him now. Practical and easygoing Perry was half out of his mind with worry and anxiety.

To his relief, Francois contacted him late that morning to let him know the agency was removing Leah to a safe house. One of the agents, acting as a medic at Cremont, would take her there in the afternoon. Perry was to meet them at a métro station near the safe house. With her history, Francois considered a doctor's presence necessary to reassure her. Perry concurred.

In the afternoon, he stepped off the train. Leah strolled toward him, revealing a side of her he'd never seen. She appeared to be floating with the breeze.

"You came. I never believed it was possible to be free and to have such a friend as you." She looked dazed, dreamy and apprehensive all at once.

"Naturally, I came." Perry acknowledged the agent, then took her arm and guided her down the street to the designated safe house. The place was a modest two-bedroom apartment with a small kitchenette and sitting room. He patted Leah's arm. "This is where we'll be staying until you're entirely safe again."

Her eyes glowed. "Safe . . . " In her voice, the word connoted all the yesterdays, today and tomorrows wrapped into a cloud of yearning.

He clasped her hand and she let him. He'd never met anyone braver. Perry realized he loved her. And when she looked at him with those worshipful eyes, he knew she felt the same.

He longed to dress her in lovely clothes and give her the things she'd done without. How had she survived five horrible years at Cremont? He had to prepare her for the interrogations to come regarding the death of her husband. To get through this, they must confront the truth together.

"Leah, I'm asking you to trust me and try not to be frightened no matter what I say."

She nodded, solemnly.

He led her to the sofa in the small living room and sat across from her. "I realize it's painful for you to remember. However, unless you face this situation, you'll never be able to move forward, emotionally or legally."

"I understand."

"The authorities have questions that must be answered. I don't want to hurt you, but we've got to know what happened the night your husband died. Remember, I'm on your side."

She bowed her head. "Those horrible men, they came and told me Walter was hurt and he needed me. I believed them. I was frantic. I left with them immediately." She sobbed.

"You can get through this," he soothed.

Her hazel eyes awash in tears, she continued. "They took me to the sanatorium where I spoke briefly with Sara, my old college roommate. She told me Walter had been murdered and the authorities believed I had done it. She said it was better if I hid there for a while until the police realized I was innocent. She warned me if I said anything, the men who killed Walter would get rid of me too. Sara said, the only reason they kept me alive was because she'd intervened."

Leah drew in a deep breath and continued. "Before I was even aware of it, I had been admitted as a patient to the asylum. At first, I protested and tried to tell people the truth. As a punishment, I was given shock treatments and forced to endure other horrors. Eventually, I pretended I was insane and believed whatever they said. It was the only means I had to survive. Some days I wanted to die."

Perry ached for the agonies she'd endured and promised himself he would change all that. From now on, her life would be different. He wanted to hold and protect her always, but he knew she was strong and independent or she would have never survived. He had to move slowly. Let Pia find her way and get through this, then they could revisit their feelings. "Thank you for sharing the truth. Now, go to bed. Choose whichever bedroom you want. I'll take the other. The agent will sleep in here." He watched as she pondered her choices.

"I'll take this one."

"Fine. I'll carry your bag in." He picked it up, followed her into the room and set the case on a table in the corner. Perry touched her shoulder briefly. "Sleep well."

"You won't leave?" she asked with a diffident air.

"I'll be here. Try not to worry. Everything is going to be okay from now on. I'll trade with the agent and take the sofa tonight in case you need me."

The fear in her face receded a bit. "Thank you."

He left her, closing the door behind him.

Francois arrived shortly afterward, and Perry filled him in on what Leah had said. To his surprise, the other agent handed Francois a tape of Perry and Pia's earlier conversation. Perry had no idea anyone had taped them, and he was especially glad Leah, or rather Pia, hadn't as well.

Francois said, "Your cover is arranged. We will tell the administrators of the sanatorium that you have been called home because of a family emergency. One of our agents will be your replacement. We need you to be free to give Pia your undivided attention."

"What's going to happen to her?"

"She hasn't broken the law. Her captors forced her to pretend she was insane. Once she testifies and we have them in prison, she'll be free to return to her former life. She'll need to lean on you heavily to get through this. Are you up to it? It may take some time."

"Naturally. She's my patient and I feel deeply for what she's been made to suffer." His personal feelings were better kept to himself for now.

After Francois left, Perry bedded down on the sofa. It had been a busy day. He fell asleep, the strange play of events running though his mind.

35

Dom set the phone down with forced calm. What was Abby up to, orchestrating a meeting between Gayle and him? What could Abby possibly have to gain? How could he face Gayle's scorn after everything that had transpired? True, she had deceived him too, but she'd never intentionally hurt him. Their last meeting had been a disaster. Yet Gayle's call had taken him by surprise, and he found himself agreeing to see her, though her presence might endanger them both.

Gayle brought a shaky hand to her forehead. She'd worked months for a break like this in the case, but she suspected it was a trap. When Abby phoned earlier, Gayle had been stunned to learn Dom finally wanted to level with her. It was a boon she couldn't possibly ignore, despite the source. If she were ever going to have closure, she desperately needed answers whether she liked them or not. Images of her last confrontation with Dom turned her stomach to *blancmange*. She'd eaten the creamy gelatinous dessert on her last date with Dom before he'd vanished. After some reflection, she conceded the necessity of meeting him alone where he could speak freely without fear of endangering his mission. She had questions only he could answer.

Gayle checked her luggage and boarded the flight to Vienna, her nerves as tangled as the wisteria vines along her mother's back fence in Houston. She'd left her brothers a note, saying she was fine and would be out of town for a while. She didn't want to worry them, but she had a job to do.

The flight to Vienna was almost too brief. Gayle hadn't bothered booking a hotel as she didn't plan to stay. She hailed a taxi and headed downtown. The cab turned onto Kärntner Straße, near the pedestrian shopping area, passing the ultimate in baroque and Gothic architecture. The magnificence of the Burg and the Imperial Court Theaters and Vienna City Hall failed to dispel her agitation about the looming confrontation. Scenes from her and Dom's past flashed through her mind, Gayle's anger deeper than any hurt.

Their love had died stillborn, unable to withstand the pressures, doubts and lies. Yet, she understood his dilemma too well, being an agent herself. Dom, however, had left her exposed and vulnerable before his family, the press and the entire country. Worse, he'd placed her in jeopardy, refashioning her into an assassination target for his enemies. No, she couldn't forgive him. Love might be blind in the movies, but this was real life and hers was on the line.

Gayle got out of the cab and crossed the street, stepping into the vigorous stream of hurrying pedestrians. She envied them their complacency and the ease of movement she'd once taken for granted.

She glanced at her watch and steeled herself from straightening her hair or checking her makeup. He didn't deserve her consideration. The café appeared silent and closed. A warning chill crept up her spine. She reached for the door and it swung open. The darkness clung to her like an unwanted lover, and a clawing need to flee ignited. She stumbled toward the bar, forcing herself to embrace the shadows. She pulled out a high-backed stool, wincing as its metal legs scraped against the tile floor. Her heart seemed to squeeze up into her throat.

Gradually, her gaze adjusted to the hovering gloom and she moved to one of the tables, taking a seat against the wall to eliminate any surprises from behind. Her hands slipped into her pocket. The grip of the Derringer's smooth metal against her palm reassured her.

Abruptly the lights came on and at the sight of Dom, her temper flared. They stared at one another. The taut silence crisscrossed the threads of deceit he'd stitched and woven into yards of seamed differences throughout their relationship.

"Gayle, I never thought you'd really come."

"I'm sure you didn't," she said dryly.

He moved toward her, and she shook her head, raising one hand in a gesture of self-preservation. "Stop. If you imagine I flew here for some romantic tryst, forget it. All I want from you are answers."

"Would it be too much for us to be civil?"

How clever of him to insinuate she was at fault. "You owe me the necessary intel, past and present, to protect myself."

"My advice is to walk out of here and get as far from me as you can." Eyes as warm and blue as the sea studied her, their message contradicting his words.

"I intend to do exactly that, but not without some answers first." He was still devastatingly handsome, but she was remembering the pain of failed expectations and soured hopes.

"Gayle, slip off those rose-colored glasses. Do you want me to fill in the blanks left by your own people?"

She stared at him coolly. "Frankly, I'm disappointed. I anticipated some originality. How boring of you to spin this and blame the CIA."

Dom hesitated and then handed her a card bearing the name, Hotel Sacher. "I'll expect you for dinner. Shall we say seven?" He pivoted and walked out.

She needed to know what he was planning. Gayle rushed to follow but he was already in a taxi, driving away before she could reach him. She climbed into the nearest cab and ordered, "Follow that car," wincing at the triteness of the phrase. The driver promptly lost him. She gave up the search and checked into the Hotel Sacher.

She asked the clerk, "Is Dominic Trudeau in?"

He checked the register. "I'm sorry. He isn't here. You might check with Hotel Graben. We generally refer any overflow to them."

"Thanks." Gayle rode the elevator up to the third floor and tipped the young man who carried her bag into the room. She crossed to the window and gazed out at the Wiener Staatsoper. Dom's family likely had season tickets to the Opera House. The Sacher was only a short walk from Saint Stephens Cathedral, the Hofburg Imperial Palace and Vienna's elegant Ring Straße. Then money had never been a problem for Dom.

Still holding the card he'd handed her, she dialed the desk and asked for the room number he'd scribbled on the back of the card.

"*Es tut mir leid, Herr Ropell ist nicht in.*"

"Did he say when he'd return?"

"*Nein, aber sie können ihn später zurückrufen.*"

Gayle sighed. "All right. I'll call back later." Was Herr Ropell a pseudonym for Dominic or had she lost him again? Was she destined to be diverted at his whim? She'd have to meet him for dinner to learn more.

Tired, she lay down for a short nap and fell into a restless sleep. She awakened and sat up with a start, struggling to shake off the dreams evoking the past and the man she'd once dreamed of marrying.

She called Paris and spoke briefly to Seth, and was surprised to learn he and Jason were planning to fly to Houston.

"It's where the investigation into CI's missing preflight external check crew is leading us. Also, the trip will give us the opportunity to check on Mom and Dad."

"Give them my love. Text or phone me how they're doing."

"Sure. By the way, you haven't said where you are."

"Vienna. I'm meeting with Dominic, finally, to try and get some answers."

"Sounds dangerous. I'm not sure Mitch is going to forgive you for rushing into danger this time."

"His friendship doesn't give him the right to run my life."

"So, he's simply a friend?"

"What else?"

"All right. Where did you say you were staying?"

"I didn't."

"Come on, J.O. will tear a piece out of me if I don't find out."

She knew her eldest brother well enough to realize he would be annoyed at not knowing her whereabouts. "I'm at the Hotel Sacher, but I need space here. Tell the fellows to back off."

"Like that's ever going to happen. But I'll do my best to distract them for you. Stay safe, Sis."

"Take care of yourself too."

Gayle hung up, and her thoughts went to the evening's meeting with Dominic. She needed to stay focused on her survival. If only seeing him hadn't resurrected a myriad of feelings she believed she'd put to rest.

36

Seth hoisted his bag into the overhead compartment of the Houston-bound jet and slid into the seat next to his brother. "How do you think Dad really is? Mom always puts a positive spin on any news for our sakes."

Jason stared down at his hands with a sigh. "Another ten hours and we'll know."

Seth's jaw tightened at the thought of what they might discover. The plane cleared for takeoff, sped down the runway and angled toward the sky until it settled into a comfortable cruising altitude above the sea of clouds. The attendant came around with the beverage and snack cart. Seth accepted a glass of juice.

Jason refused any refreshment and slipped on a pair of headphones. "Wake me when we arrive."

Seth considered CI's missing external check crew, which included Mitch's friend, Ryan. Mitch kept in close touch with Ryan's wife, Laura, supporting her and the twins in the desperate search for their father. Seth planned to interview her first.

He glanced across and saw his brother was already dozing. Seth leaned back and closed his eyes. He might as well get some rest.

Several hours later, Jason shook him awake. "Bro, we're almost home."

Groggy, he ran his hand through his hair and gazed out the window, warmed at the sight of the green foliage shading the landscape. "It's good to be back."

"No place like it."

The 747 landed. They gathered their bags and exited through customs, happy to stretch their legs. A shuttle took them to the outlying parking lot. Jason threw their gear inside the Highlander and Seth drove downtown, taking the 288 exit off of US-59 to the Methodist Hospital.

The two entered the vast medical complex through the parking garage elevator and minutes later walked into their dad's room.

He lay sleeping, tubes and monitors hooked up and swirling about him like a freeway spaghetti bowl, his colorless face a window into his fragility.

Concerned by the change in his father, Seth traded a worried look with his brother, then sat in one of the chairs placed on either side of the bed. Seth clasped his dad's hand, bruised from repeated IV punctures, and held on to it while praying for his recovery. Seth stayed for several minutes not wanting to wake him, then went to see if he could speak to one of the doctors and get an update on his father's condition.

Fortunately, the cardiologist was doing his rounds. "Your father is improving daily. His complete recovery will take some time." The doctor's pager beeped, and he paused to peer at it. "I have to go." He lifted his hand in a half wave and strode down the hall.

Seth retraced his steps to his dad's room, striving to focus on the positive words, "improving daily." He repeated the prognosis to Jason who meanwhile had learned from the nurse, their mother had stepped out to the cafeteria.

The two trooped downstairs to find their mother sitting at a corner table. She glanced up and her eyes widened as she rose and hugged them tightly, tears streaming down her cheeks. "It's wonderful to see you." She dabbed at her eyes with a tissue. "Let's get you boys some coffee. When did you get in?"

"We came straight here from the airport," Jason said.

They poured some coffee and joined her at the table, speaking lightly of their trip.

"I want you both to know your dad and I are fine, though it has been a bit of a strain."

Jason grasped her hand. "Mom, you should have told us. We would have come immediately."

"Honey, it's why we didn't. Your father and I wanted you to take care of Gayle because we sensed she was in trouble."

"Mom, she's okay. Set your mind at ease." He brushed a strand of hair off her forehead, needing to touch and reassure her.

The three of them talked for a while, then returned upstairs to his father's room. His petite mother had lost weight, and Seth worried she couldn't afford the loss.

She smiled. "I told you boys not to come, but it's nice to see you and I won't scold. How is Gayle?"

"Great," Jason said. "Like a cat with nine lives, always landing on her feet."

"I'm glad. If ever there was a child who could tumble into the brambles, it's our baby girl."

Seth choked back a laugh, imagining his sister's reaction. If their mother only knew, her daughter was one tough agent. "Have you forgotten she's GM of marketing for a major airline with impressive responsibilities? Gayle's grown up."

"Of course, she has, and it doesn't change a thing. You boys will always be my babies too."

Her sons swiftly reverted to the subject of their father's condition.

She filled them in on what had been happening. "Your dad's doing well, considering . . . He's at his best in the mornings and is able to talk a bit with me then."

They visited a while longer and then left, going in different directions to make better use of the time. Jason accompanied their mother home and planned to concentrate on following up leads and phone work in hopes of locating some of the missing CI crew members.

Seth punched Ryan's wife's address into the Highlander's GPS and drove off, his thoughts on the airline mechanic's disappearance.

He parked in a middle-class neighborhood typical of Houston in the '70s. The modest brick homes had sweeping lawns of thick green Saint Augustine with sidewalks leading up to the front doors. Giant globes of pink and blue hydrangeas leafed out against the houses. Purple, raspberry and white blooming crape myrtles lined the streets and drives.

He ambled up the sidewalk and knocked.

"Who is it?"

"Seth Regan. We spoke on the phone earlier."

A striking blonde invited him in. "Hi, I'm Laura. Come on into the den, where the boys are. Would you like some iced tea?"

"Thanks. It's hot out today."

"Isn't it always. Please, have a seat. Excuse me. I'll be a minute."

Seth sat and studied the twins playing quietly in the corner. He didn't know a lot about children, but he had heard friends speak of the terrible twos. These kids appeared almost angelic with their happy giggles.

"Here you go." Laura handed him a glass and then crossed the room to give the boys small boxes of juice with straws.

"Yum," they chorused in obvious delight.

She sat across from him. "I'm not sure I can add to what's already been said."

Seth cleared his throat. She possessed a sweetness that seemed to draw him in, but he resisted. Sugar could be deceptive, and he needed to remain unbiased in his observations. "I'd like to say how sorry I am about Ryan's disappearance. It must be extremely difficult for you and the children."

She nodded, locking her hands together as if to force them to rest in her lap.

"I would appreciate any help you can give us in resolving this for your sake and Mitch's."

"If only we could," she said, wistfully. "Mitch has been great. It's awful that he's been blamed for any of this. If people knew him like we do, they wouldn't doubt his integrity."

"I'm glad Mitch has been there for you. We were college roommates and have stayed close through the years. Like you, I want to prove his innocence. I'll do everything in my power to find your husband." Despite his weighted words, Seth couldn't even spare her the pain of rehashing what must have been the most horrendous day of her life. "What can you tell me about the day Ryan disappeared?"

She swiped at her tears. "I can't get used to the idea of Ryan vanishing like he did, even though it's been weeks."

"Take your time." He took a long drink of tea, wishing there was a tangible way he could help. Instead, he waited awkwardly as she dried her tears.

She swallowed and seemed to gather her composure. "I'm not sure where to start, but I didn't notice anything out of the ordinary. I usually stay busy with the boys. Ryan did as well."

"Why don't we start with that morning. Walk me through the day step by step."

"Ryan got up first. He made the coffee and brought me a cup in bed. I had been up much of the night with the twins. They were both sick with a virus they'd caught from a friend."

"Ryan sounds like a considerate husband. Was he usually attentive?"

"Yes. He could never do enough for me and the boys."

"What happened next?"

She exhaled heavily, her eyes taking on a faraway look. "I remember we ate poached eggs, buttered toast and had a glass of carrot juice with our vitamins. The boys were still sleeping and we enjoyed the alone time. It gave us a chance to visit."

"Was Ryan worried about work?"

"No. He was in a great mood. He was scheduled to go in early, but one of the other men needed the afternoon off and switched with Ryan."

"Do you know who?"

"No. It would be there in the work schedule."

"Has your husband contacted you since he left home that day?"

"He called to say that the preflight external check crew members at CI's facility in Tulsa were ill. Ryan and his crew would be there for a few days filling in. He said he'd call me that night. I never saw or heard from him again." The words seemed torn from her.

"I have to ask if there's any incident or person, in retrospect who stands out as unusual or suspicious?"

"No. Nothing."

Seth rose. "If you think of anything, don't hesitate to call. Here's my card." He held out his hand. "I've enjoyed meeting you and the boys. If you need help, please phone me."

"I appreciate your efforts to find Ryan. Could you possibly give me weekly updates? Mitch has been great, but not about keeping me informed."

"Sure. I'll be glad to, but I may not have any news for a while."

"Still, it's better than wondering and imagining the worst."

Seth realized he was still holding her hand and dropped it. Her courage had won him over. He only hoped he could find her missing husband.

37

Following a sumptuous dinner served on the patio of Dom's hotel suite, Gayle tarried. They stood side by side, lost in the Vienna sky. The evening possessed a dreamy surrealness.

Throughout the meal that she'd been too anxious to appreciate, their talk had remained impersonal and light. Afterward he began a determined assault on her defenses. She took in the breadth of him, wishing for the impossible. How could she ever trust him again? She cautioned her wildly beating heart. He hadn't explained his actions yet.

"Gayle." He reached for her.

She stepped back. "Stop, too much has happened. I'm not ready to forget or forgive. What's this really about?"

He gave her a long steady look. "I've always loved you, however it may have appeared."

"You deserted me and left me to face your family and the press alone. Those are not the actions of someone in love."

He seemed to shrink. Then as if gathering some hidden strength, he straightened and motioned for her to take a seat.

She sank onto the cushy patio chair. Dom sat across from her, near enough to touch.

"Missing our wedding hurt me as much as you."

Gayle searched the depths of his blue eyes, wanting to read him. Was he making a play to get her back? He must be delusional to think she'd consider it. He appeared to be all tenderness and concern, acting as if his desertion had never occurred. She had already learned that his feelings were fleeting, and his love was not the kind she dreamed of.

She shook aside her memories of them together. There was no them. She had to stay focused on the intel she needed from him. "Why did you bring me here, if not to explain?"

"For your own safety and to plead with you to stay out of this. I don't want you to be hurt more than you have been."

"It's a bit late for your concern."

He grasped her hand. "I'm not talking about your feelings, but your life. This is a treacherous game we're caught up in. I couldn't bear it if you were hurt."

She removed her hand from his. "If you're that concerned, tell me what's going on. I would be safer forewarned."

"Chéri, to do that would increase the danger you're in."

"Dom, I'm asking for the truth. Are you connected to what's been happening to me?"

"I can't confide in you."

"I see," she murmured, his words setting the final seal to the end of their relationship. If he cared even as a friend, he'd tell her enough to protect herself. Without trust, they could go nowhere.

"Gayle, you believe you understand, but you're wrong, my darling."

She studied him sadly. "I'm confused. Why am I here?"

"I had hoped to dissuade you from further interference. Interpol has the matter well in hand."

"When are you going to level with me? After everything I've been through, I deserve some answers. I've lost my home, all my savings, belongings and my job. I've been knocked out, nearly blown up and shot at."

He countered. "Were you ever going to tell me you work for the CIA?"

Instead of answering she attacked. "Don't think I'm not aware of the other women in your life. While we were engaged you were having an affair with Abby and maybe others."

"It's not what you're imagining. What I did was for my country."

She rolled her eyes in disbelief. "What kind of a man proposes to a woman, then leaves her to face his enemies?"

"One who has no choice. There's too much at stake. And yes, our relationship was expendable. I never meant to wound you, but I had a duty to my family and country."

"I don't recognize you anymore, you're a stranger."

"I don't feel like a stranger." Dom took hold of her hand and helped her rise. He cupped her face and with a lingering look drew her next to his heart and kissed her with a gentleness that nearly crumbled her resistance.

This man, once the love of her life, was possibly her nemesis. She inched back warily. "I want answers, not soft words whispered in my ear."

Abby stepped from the shadows with her pistol aimed at Gayle. "You're going to get some answers but not to your liking." She smiled at Dom. "Good work. I knew you could get her here if you set your mind to it."

For a nanosecond, Gayle stared at Dom in shock. Then she ran from the patio, terrified he'd catch her. She heard him shouting in the distance.

"Gayle, wait, please. Come back. You don't understand . . ."

And it was true. She understood little. Tears blurred her vision as she ran.

What was happening to her was an enigma, a conundrum beyond her perception. She needed help.

38

The thunderstorm that struck Vienna the night before reminded Gayle of Houston weather. Her dinner with Dom and Abby's threatening appearance now seemed unreal. Gayle had returned to her room and slept. Her dreams had been of safer and happier days. The kaleidoscope of perfumed roses in brilliant colors were evocative of the feisty grandmother who'd taught her to confront life's challenges with spirit.

The scene shifted to a sandy beach with the sunrise etched in flamingo and coral pinks. Waves tickled her feet. Gayle's dad scrambled eggs over a driftwood campfire. They shared a smile, enjoying the moment. She'd learned integrity and diligence from him.

Then abruptly she found herself in darkness, teetering on the edge of a precipitous cliff. She awoke with a sense of impending doom as if last night had been a portent, signaling some imminent disaster.

She remembered running from Dom's suite in a panic, stunned, hurt and frightened in turn. The rumors about Abby were true. Gayle should never have come to Vienna—should have forgotten Dominic and moved on with her life.

There was a knock at her hotel door and she braced herself to ignore whoever was there.

"I know you're inside, Red. Let me in."

The last time Elliot phoned, her car had exploded and she barely escaped with her life. Though he had warned her. He'd also alluded to a contract put out on her. Gayle didn't move until his retreating footsteps down the stone corridor grew faint.

God, where are you in the midst of this? Please, give me clarity in this situation.

She dressed and made coffee, feeling better after the first cup. After the second one, her mind blinked on.

Her mobile announced an incoming text from Elliot. "We need to talk. Meet me on the patio of the Kleine Konditorei. I'll be waiting."

Should she chance it? Would he provide intel that could protect her? In retrospect, what choice did she have?

Gayle left without breakfast and headed downtown to the Ring, unable to forget how near she'd come to being blown to bits before. With a sense of trepidation, she rounded the corner, caught a bus to the edge of town and walked to the rendezvous point. Why, after all this time, had Elliot decided to approach her?

He sat at a patio table outside the Kleine Konditorei. "Hello Red." He didn't bother rising but pointed to the food. "There's coffee and strudel."

She slid into the chair opposite him. "You're the last person I expected to hear from."

"I have my orders. If you recall, I broke silence to save your skin a while back."

"You have my eternal gratitude. Yet, how do I know you didn't plant the bomb to begin with?"

"Some things you have to take on faith." He grinned engagingly.

"You'll be quoting scripture next."

"I'm curious. What happened between you and Dom last night, and how did Abby enter into it?"

"So, you're having me followed. Strange how your priorities work. Ignore me until you require some intel. Is this the new game plan?"

"You've been on the CIA's radar the entire time—when you needed us, we've been there."

"Like when my safe house exploded?"

"Exactly. I warned you. Consequently, you were on guard and your training kicked in and saved your life."

"By a nanosecond."

"More than anyone, I have a grasp of what you're capable of."

"You also warned me the agency put out a contract on me."

"Not the agency, but rogue agents who are no longer with the CIA."

"Like Abby, who also arranged for me to meet Dominic here in Vienna?"

"Maybe."

Gayle wanted to believe him and needed an informed sounding board. She met his concerned gaze. "I never thought it would end like this. Why didn't you tell me Dom was with Interpol and was seeing Abby?"

"And have you walk out on us? Not a chance. You were our best link to both Dominic and Abby. The catalyst to help set this sting in motion."

"I don't understand. Set what into motion?"

"Abby's unveiling. We've suspected her of treason for three years but without proof of her betrayal . . . The agency tried feeding her false info, but Abby was too clever to step into any of those traps. Interpol suspected her as well, and chose Dominic to reel her in. Sorry, Red. We used you to squeeze them both."

The CIA couldn't possibly have planned this from the beginning. How could they have known Dom would fall in love with her? The reality of the situation and its inherent danger ricocheted through her.

Appearances were deceptive and truth more subtle than she'd ever realized. Gayle was wary of the agency's secrets and wouldn't forget how they'd abandoned her. She wanted out.

As if he could read her thoughts, Elliot shook his head. "You can't leave with Dominic's life on the line. It wouldn't resolve this. He's agreed to make the ultimate sacrifice by entering into deep cover. Think of the spot you're putting him in."

"I'd much rather think of the quandary he's left me in and how to emerge unscathed. Abby tried to kill me."

"Get a grip. You haven't been read in on the entire operation, just a few moves."

"Whose fault is that? You weren't the one peering down the barrel of a gun last night."

"No, but I've been there often enough in the past."

"Touché." Gayle caved and told him what had happened, omitting those details too personal to share.

In turn, Elliot confided how Dom had persuaded Abby to accept a deal with Interpol. The two would be working as double agents in the Middle East. The CIA, unhappy Abby was slipping from their grip, agreed to stand down and allow the plan to go forward as long as Interpol pledged to share operational intel.

Gayle shied from the obvious implications regarding Dom's relationship with Abby. He'd caused her enough grief and placed her in a situation that could have ended in her death. She refused to be his or Abby's pawn.

"Earth to Gayle, do you read me?" Elliot asked in an exasperated voice. "It's a lot to absorb, and there's no advantage in taking this personally."

She shook off her dour thoughts. "My sentiments exactly. Though it feels a tad personal when someone lures me to a rendezvous and threatens to shoot me."

Elliot smirked. "Yes, I can see how it might. However, in all likelihood, Abby was merely bent on protecting her turf and removing you from Dominic's vicinity."

"Then, why did she arrange for us to meet? At least now, I needn't deal with either of them ever again."

"You're not out of this yet. Dominic has a reservoir of feelings for you. It's to our advantage to pursue those. Let's call it an insurance policy on the intel Interpol has promised the CIA."

Gayle stared at him in disbelief. "I won't do it and you've no right to ask. Besides, Dom doesn't have any feelings for me."

Instead of replying, he pulled out his cell and punched speed dial. "Yes, Sir. Agent Regan's right here." He handed her the phone.

She took it shakily. "Hello. Gayle Regan speaking." She listened and then set Elliot's mobile on the table without a word.

He started to speak, but she stopped him. "Please. Not now. Give me time to consider." She rose, left the table and stumbled to the street.

Gayle didn't know what to think after speaking with the head of Central Intelligence. The trip to Vienna had been a mistake. How could she escape the bombardment of difficulties continually bearing down on her? If only she could relocate downwind of her imploding universe. Her only way forward was to confront the challenges and do what the agency asked.

She knew the relationship between her and Dominic was finished even if the agency didn't. To continue in the pretext was an exercise in futility. Blue skies overhead might be a barometer of fair weather, but not for her carefree sunny days. Storm clouds slid across her horizon and tornadoes touched down where she lived. Those who chose to play dangerously, must be prepared to pay.

Oblivious to Vienna's charm, she trudged down its sidewalks close to tears. Finally, she caught the tram and took a seat to get off her feet. Maybe she could catch an evening flight and be back in Paris with J.O. and Mitch tonight. For a while, Mitch had loomed large in her mind. As they worked together to untangle the web they were both caught in, she found her admiration for him growing. Yet her fleeting and almost fatal attraction for Dominic had left her wary of relationships.

Back in her hotel room, Gayle continued to struggle with her response to her CIA boss's directives. She got down on her knees. *Dear Lord, I'm out of words, but You, the Creator of life, know my heart and needs. Help me yield to You.*

That evening Gayle wandered out on the balcony and stared at the crescent moon in the velvety sky and the shadows on its craggy face. Her future seemed to mock her. Perceptions changed. The heart asked too many questions. No wonder she had difficulty distinguishing reality from the nightmares and fantasies.

She had perceived Abby as her friend, and Dominic, her fiancé. Wrong on both counts. One thing Gayle knew for certain, with somebody out to dispatch her, anyone connected with her remained at risk.

She and Mitch had successfully linked Harri Malone to the diamond heist and by a stretch to the CI crash. Seth and Jason were in Houston investigating the missing crew. It was amazing how quickly her siblings were finding answers. If Gayle hadn't known their brother J.O. her entire life, she might suspect he worked for a government agency or think-tank.

She went inside, slipped off her clothes and showered, then dressed for her evening flight. "God, I have much to be thankful for, despite my present problems. Dad's holding his own in the hospital and mother is strong. Lord, You triumphed over sin and treachery, rescuing mankind. Please rescue me." Tomorrow was another day, another chance to make of it what she could with the help she'd been given.

In the dimly lit hotel restaurant, Gayle sipped a cup of Vienna roast to while away the hours until her departure. She yearned to be carefree, to return to the days when change wasn't her enemy. Outside the city beckoned.

Gayle left the restaurant and walked through the downtown area, engrossed in her thoughts. Thirty minutes later, she whirled halfway down the block, surprised to discover she was lost. She became aware of a hulking man, who stopped and turned when she did. Was he tailing her? She took the next corner rapidly, and he followed. Too late Gayle realized the street was deserted. Frightened, she jogged to the left and then the right, slipping inadvertently into an alley. The stranger grabbed her. His hands closed around her throat and squeezed.

She fought him, her flailing arms and kicks useless against his strength and the burning pain in her throat. Gayle heard a shout, and suddenly free, fell to the ground.

The man ran, glancing uneasily over his shoulder. Elliot stood there, his pistol drawn and extended until the man vanished. Then, he knelt on the cobbled pavement beside her, examined her injuries and helped her rise. "Let's get you to the hotel."

She struggled to speak over the pain in her throat. "Thanks. You arrived just in time."

"Now are you convinced there is a contract out on you?"

"Yes."

Despite his scowl she read the concern in his face. "Red, don't miss that midnight flight. I'm not some brave young knight like Lochinvar."

"No, I never imagined you were." She had never felt more abandoned and alone, then he'd appeared. She might have died. "Elliot, have you ever been in love?"

"Only with every agent I've ever handled."

"I certainly never noticed."

He paused and drew her close, whispering softly, "Especially and irrevocably with you."

He was going to kiss her. Curious, she waited expectantly.

His lips found hers in a tender kiss of warmth and friendship.

Before she could object, he wrapped his hand around hers and tugged her down the street alongside him.

She gave him a cross look. "If I develop a crush on you, it serves you right."

"I personally have no objection, however, were I to receive orders to eliminate you it might prove awkward."

"Are you never serious?"

His gaze met hers, enveloping her like a warm breeze. "I'm crazy about you. Now, let's get you to Paris where the assassins aren't as deadly."

"Whatever you say," she agreed, slightly bemused. His flirting was meant as a diversion—a gift to a friend in desperate need of reassurance. It was an act of kindness neither of them would view seriously. Neither of them was in the habit of encouraging such intimacy with colleagues.

39

Dominic awoke, the panic of the scene with Gayle the night before still vivid in his mind. Worse, there was nothing he could do to stop the sequel Abby had set in motion from playing out. He'd fooled himself into believing he was getting over Gayle, only to find that his love was as fervent and hopeless as ever.

Abby had manipulated them both into the Vienna meeting. But who could have predicted her attempt to murder Gayle?

When Gayle walked through his hotel door, he had been in Eden, the dreams he'd disavowed possible. Then Abby arrived and put an end to the fantasy. Gayle was far better off marrying some American. Dominic's duty would always come first, alienating them. Besides, Gayle believed he wanted to get rid of her. And who could blame her?

Dominic rose and dressed. After breakfast he dealt with several loose ends, reining in his thoughts of her. By the end of the day, he was feeling more resolute and somewhat restored.

He hadn't seen Abby, who seemed to have vanished after the drama with Gayle. It was time he checked in with his Paris team.

The next morning Dom boarded a plane out of Vienna and landed at Orly-Ouest, about nineteen kilometers south of downtown Paris. He picked up his car and drove to headquarters, not minding the drive or the July heat Parisians complained about. The journey gave him a chance to say goodbye to Paris. Her beauty, culture and history had been both tutor and lover, her enchanting face doused in the sweet perfume of yesteryears and modern intrigues. The kilometers kept pace with his melancholy reflections.

Forty-five minutes later, he parked and entered Interpol's modest three-story building. As he strolled into his department, Ned, his IT expert, and several special investigators were eating lunch. They sat up straighter as he approached.

Ned practically inhaled a bite of his sandwich, then swallowed, struggling to speak. "Welcome back."

Dominic raised his eyebrows quizzically, then greeted his operational director. "Any news?"

Bob grinned. "We've cracked the code. Wait until you see the scripts."

"Great work! Francois has seen the reports?"

Debra nodded. "I set them on his desk about an hour ago."

Dominic headed for Francois's office. He found him barricaded behind his desk. "I hear we've caught a break."

Francois motioned him to a nearby chair and passed him the scripts. "If these are spot on, we have six weeks to stop the attacks."

Dominic rapidly read through the pages. "This is terrible."

"There's more. Sara's been murdered."

"Now that does surprise me. How did it happen and when?"

"Shortly before Abby left for Vienna, according to the coroner. Interesting timing, her leaving then, wouldn't you say? The shooter used a silencer."

"Was Abby seen near there that day?"

"Not according to any of the witnesses. Sara was already dead before most of the staff arrived."

"The murder took place in her office at Cremont? Any hard evidence Abby was the shooter?"

Francois frowned. "Not yet, though the woman has been nothing but trouble."

"That must be why you're anxious for me to join her."

Francois gave him a hooded glance. "If you could get Abby to reveal what she knows about these terrorist plots, it might not be necessary. The agency is counting on you to pull her in."

"I'm aware," Dominic said dryly. "Any leads from our discovery of Sara's safe deposit box in Geneva?"

"It's still under surveillance, but thus far no action. I appreciate the bank's cooperation, and I believe we have you to thank."

Dom smiled faintly. "Yes, Jean and I go way back, but he wouldn't have moved like he did without the proper documented evidence. He is strictly by the books despite his sympathies lying with us. Has there been any more chatter linked to the attacks?"

"No more than usual. I wonder if any of Sara's comrades knew about her Swiss stash?"

"Hard to believe the brotherhood would allow Sara or any woman sole access to major funding. You're thinking Abby knew? It would give her a million more reasons to shoot Sara."

"True. Between the cashier's check and the jewels, we're talking huge motive. Naturally, our men are following her."

Dom nodded. "Good. My contacts in Vienna lost her."

"Interpol brought in a separate team and didn't alert the locals. The agency deemed it best to keep it under wraps."

"Smart move. I wish you had told me."

"Until your Paris arrival, you were considered a Vienna local."

Dom knew the agency's quarantine procedure was used in handling certain delicate situations. "Where is she?"

"Holed up in Vienna. I understand there was quite the dramatic scene between Abby and Gayle."

"Too theatrical for my taste. I want this finished." Something else had been bothering Dom. He had a hunch it might tie in with Abby's pursuit of the money and jewels. "Abby's attempt to shoot Gayle, with me as a witness, seemed out of character. Maybe it was a distraction to throw us off and to enable her to get to the bank."

"Possibly. I would sure like to be in the field on this one."

"Don't tell me you're yearning for bygone days. When we met in Switzerland, you were ready to pack it in."

"*C'est la vie.* May I offer you a cup of coffee?"

Dom rose. "I've got to regroup with my team."

"Then go on, get out of my office and get to work."

Dom left with a casual wave.

Clyde walked along the Champs Élysées, feeling smug about how his embezzling of the marketing division's pension funds had gained him prestige in the brotherhood. No one besides himself and his half sister Sara knew their father was Syrian. Clyde's grandparents had made sure their Syrian heritage died with his mother's death. He'd been four years old when his grandparents left him at the orphanage, ex-plaining they wanted no contact with the little foreigner. Clyde's father Harri Malone found him when he was eighteen years old and arranged for him to attend college.

Harri often visited, telling Clyde about his Shiite heritage and of the hatred the West bore them. Thus, Clyde's monthly initiation and training began. His father's truth, previously unknown to Clyde, became the opus of his personal symphony, and finding it changed him forever.

He now had a mission: destroy the West. To accomplish the goal, he needed to keep his job at Transway until he had embezzled enough Euros to finance the operation. He was close.

No one at Transway, except Gayle, had suspected the abnormal volume of pension fund trading in foreign markets or the sudden activity in routinely dormant accounts. Everyone except Gayle had underestimated his abilities and intelligence. But she was slated to die, and her enemies were lining up to take her out. He'd made sure of it.

Sara had been immensely helpful. It was on her orders he'd made his first hit and strangled his partner in crime after their failed attempt to murder Gayle. Sara was Gayle's double, her nemesis, impersonating and routing her at every turn. With his sister's training, it hadn't been difficult to fool everyone into thinking she was Gayle.

Sara was a master at disguises. She'd had several custom wigs made in Gayle's hair color and style, and bought suitable clothes. For months, Sara practiced making up her face to look exactly like Gayle. Facial features and lines, the shape of the eyes and brows, nose and mouth, skin color and other fine details were drawn and shadowed in to make Sara the image of Gayle. Even Clyde had difficulty distinguishing the real Gayle from her impersonator.

When Gayle first started work at Transway, Clyde had secreted a video camera in her office that had recorded the way she moved her hands and walked and how she spoke. Sara had used these and worked hard at her portrayal of Gayle over a lengthy period of time, and it was spot on, he thought proudly. They'd fooled everyone.

One day, Sara and he would take their rightful place in the brotherhood as Harri's children.

Clyde paused outside the small coffee shop where he was to meet Sara and glanced at the headlines in the newspaper on the newsstand in front of the place. For a moment, he couldn't move. Fear and shock paralyzed him.

Blood rushed to his face, his heart pounding. He knew whose fault this was and where to put the blame. He'd find Gayle and when he did, she would die. She'd destroyed his family. Sara was dead because of her.

40

Gayle returned to the Hotel Sacher, mulling the stranger's attempt to strangle her. Though grateful for Elliot's intervention, she was more aware than ever of the dangers stalking her. Two attempts on her life in two days was like being catapulted into an alien cosmos. On faith, she accepted that one day her universe would return to normalcy. Shoulders tight and elbows pressed into her sides, she struggled for composure and thought of David's words as his best friend's father Saul sought to murder him. "I had fainted unless I had believed to see the goodness of the Lord in the land of the living. Wait on the Lord and be of good courage and He shall strengthen thine heart," (Ps.27:13,14).

She must be close to her adversaries' secrets for them to boldly attack her on the streets of Vienna. In the same psalm, David wrote, "The Lord is my light and my salvation; whom shall I fear? The Lord is the strength of my life; of whom shall I be afraid? . . . Hear, O Lord, when I cry . . . Hide not thy face far from me. . . ."

Gayle recalled many instances when God had delivered her from her enemies and praised Him for His faithfulness to her. "Thank you, Lord."

Comforted, she rose and rang J.O. for a progress report. "Hey, big Bro."

"I wondered when you'd break down and give me a call. How are you, Sis?"

"Besides being attacked two days running, I'm okay. How are things on your end?"

"Mm. I don't like the idea of someone using you for target practice. When are you coming back to Paris?"

"I'm booked on the evening flight."

"Good," J.O. said, relief in his voice. "Dad's improving. The doctor says he'll be released tomorrow."

"Wonderful. Mom must be thrilled."

"Yep. We all are."

"Any word from Jason and Seth?"

"Jason discovered that two of the missing CI crew had died in unrelated car accidents. The copilot doesn't seem to have any family. Seth has met with Ryan's and the deceased pilot's wives. Both women seemed cooperative and anxious to help."

"Isn't the chief pilot's wife the one suing CI?"

"Yes, but she speaks highly of Mitch and the company. Problem is, she's dying of cancer and wants to leave some provisions for her children. Can't say I blame her."

Gayle said, "It's heartbreaking, and the judge and jury will feel the same if the case ever makes it to court. Maybe we can prove Mitch is innocent before then."

"Let's hope so. Meanwhile, give Mom a call on her cell. If she's at the hospital, you can talk to Dad too. They'd love to hear from you."

"Sure. Before I go, have you or Mitch learned anything else of interest?"

"That's a loaded question, one I feel much better answering in person."

"Okay. See you tonight." She hung up, phoned her parents and enjoyed a brief chat. Her dad sounded in good spirits and on the mend. Her mom seemed to be holding up under the strain. They said goodbye.

Gayle packed her small bag and checked out of the hotel, relieved by the unexpected release from guilt. The breakup with Dominic was not her fault. His vanishing act had little to do with her and everything to do with his career and duty. She had once thought he was exceptional, and maybe he was. But Dominic wasn't for her. She deserved much more, a husband who loved her. One who didn't carry on with other women regardless of national security and pending attacks. A sense of buoyancy filled her at being freed from the burden of their past.

Gayle caught a taxi to the airport and was in Paris and home by midnight. J.O. and Mitch were still up and, judging from the fierceness of their hugs, glad to see her. She sank onto the couch next to her brother.

Mitch passed her a bottle of water and pressed her shoulder briefly. "We were worried about you."

"Thanks, but I'm a big girl now."

He dropped into a nearby chair. "I never doubted it." He studied her a moment as if trying to analyze what had changed. "You met with Dominic?"

"And Abby. Though the visit was cut short when she tried to shoot me."

Mitch's eyes darkened with anger. "I'd like to get my hands on her."

His concern warmed Gayle, and her gaze was drawn to him. She had forgotten how handsome he was. "Relax. I'm fine."

"I'm glad to hear it."

She realized that he made her feel safe. The feeling must come from having him and her elder brother nearby. J.O. had been rescuing her since she was a tyke in diapers. She filled them in on her trip.

J.O. handed her a report on the warehouse.

Gayle scanned the brief. The warehouse turned out to be a gathering hole for suspected terrorists. The CIA had been watching the place for a year and maintained video surveillance. Her visit was noted in the report. "Wow. You certainly have connections."

"Yes, and they want you to stay away from that location. You could have blown their investigation."

"Don't worry. I don't plan on returning." It stung that while she was persona non grata, J.O.'s friend, in the agency's upper echelons, kept him in the loop. Gayle had decided to begin anew and retrace the fraud at Transway. In her absence, Clyde and her nemesis had gained even more access to the accounts. What if they were embezzling from the marketing department's pension plan and funding terrorists?

"Before you left," J.O. said, "we discussed your coming clean with Transway about what's been happening."

"You were going to check with a lawyer friend to figure out the best way for me to handle it. What did you learn?"

"I set up an appointment for you to meet with him tomorrow afternoon. As your impostor has disappeared, the process should be a mere formality."

"What do you mean she's disappeared? When did she leave, and what makes you think she won't be back?" The news seemed too fantastic to be true. Could Gayle's ordeal be almost finished?

Mitch squeezed her hand in congratulations.

"She disappeared the day you left for Vienna. No one has any idea where she is, but the authorities are working on it," J.O. said.

"Has anyone questioned Clyde? What if, in my absence, they've been embezzling funds and left a trail pointing to me?"

"Transway might find it difficult to believe you haven't been working there all along. But the doctor and the family you stayed with can verify you were indeed attacked and were off the job when the pretender assumed your identity and took over as GM of marketing."

"Thank you for all your help, J.O. And you too Mitch."

"What puzzles me is why the agency placed you in marketing to investigate embezzlement? Wouldn't the accounting department have been a better fit?" her brother asked.

"Transway is a huge multinational company, and as such, its marketing division has its own pension fund. Irregularities had been reported, and the company had reason to suspect Clyde might be implicated in the fraud and embezzlement. Also working in marketing gave me access to company clients and an opportunity to vet them as well."

"You'll straighten it out soon enough." J.O. yawned.

"I'm keeping you awake," Gayle said. "You should have gone to bed hours ago. We can talk in the morning."

"As if I could have slept with you still out there," J.O. groused.

"I'm too keyed up by the news to sleep, and I'm hungry. I think I'll get something to eat."

Mitch rose. "Come on, we can raid the fridge together."

She hugged her brother goodnight and followed Mitch into the kitchen. He pulled her close. "I missed you."

"Me too." She edged back.

"But not quite as much, I see."

She touched his face, and he held her hand against his cheek. "Mitch, I need some space to sort out the confusion that's become my life. I honestly don't know how I feel. A lot has been happening fast. Please, bear with me."

"Fine," he said gruffly. "It's late. Let's turn in. We can speak about this later."

"You must be anxious about what's going on in Houston with the Fed's investigation of CI. You can talk to me."

"It is what it is. I'm grateful Seth and Jason have had a few break-throughs, and hopefully, they will uncover the truth and end the FBI's scrutiny of CI."

"I hope so too." They talked a few minutes more, said goodnight and then she headed off to bed with a wave and a grumbling stomach.

J.O. had left her belongings in her room with a bottle of water on the desk. She grabbed a package of cheese and crackers from her bag, devoured them, swigged down some H2O and opened her laptop.

Time to remote into Clyde's PC to discover what he'd been up to.

Access to his passwords made it possible to keep track of his finances and emails. Strange how nothing appeared to have changed. Gayle exited his computer, then linked into her office to check on her department's employee pension fund. It was important to ensure no one had tampered with it in her absence.

She blinked rapidly at the screen, wanting to dispute the numbers. How was this possible? Millions of dollars had been misappropriated. Stricken and a bit queasy, she slumped in bewilderment, her mind scrambling to understand.

The recent disappearance of Clyde's partner-in-crime, a.k.a. Gayle's nemesis, was both suspicious and inconvenient. The impostor had wired fund assets to discretionary accounts she'd set up in Gayle's name. And those accounts had all been emptied!

Dear God, wasn't it enough her enemies had tried to murder her and steal her job, possessions and assets? Was she slated for prison as well? She scraped a hand across her face in a vain effort to temper her roiling emotions. Too many questions needed answers.

While tracing the money, she found records of where several key employees had inquired about the missing finances. The impostor had used Gayle's name and office email account to assure them the resources were safely invested.

In another memorandum, the employees had checked with the CFO about her unlimited access to the marketing division's pension fund. He had assured them Ms. Regan had clearance from the top. In the beginning, the CIA had arranged for Gayle to meet Transway's CEO and CFO. They knew exactly why she was there. Unfortunately, they had no idea she had been replaced by an embezzling impostor.

Gayle was aghast to find $3,276,000 was used to purchase a resort, on behalf of the limited liability corporation, which she supposedly held under the name of Green Valley Holdings.

Ostensibly, she had reassigned another three million to Green Valley Holdings, describing the transaction as an investment in a fixed income banknote. In reality, the three million was used to secure a majority interest in a golf resort. An additional, $425,000 cash loan had been obtained from a private lender using the same note as collateral.

The forged documents were sloppily drawn up in a bogus attempt to make the transactions appear legal. Clyde and the impostor had set Gayle up to take the fall, while the two absconded with the cash.

Plus, there was a wire transfer of $275,000 stolen from the pension plan and moved into another phony account. Multiple entries showed the money had been spent for personal purposes. Her hands moved jerkily on the keyboard, her gaze bouncing across the screen. Thank God Kara worked at Transway. She had insight into what was going down and could vouch for Gayle if it became necessary.

In all, she found more than seven million dollars had been diverted by Clyde and his cohort. Where was the money now? Could Clyde be working with the terrorists to raise enough cash to destroy Paris?

The weighted hammering in her chest hardened into an acute sense of resolve. She copied the trail of financial records and memos and emailed the evidence to Kara and Elliot, officially informing the agency of the fraud.

With the idea that J.O.'s connections might help, Gayle woke him up and explained the situation. "Notify your friend. I've already alerted my handlers."

He ran a hand through his disheveled hair. "I'll take care of it. You go back to bed. It's almost three in the morning."

"No. There's too much at stake." She dressed, grabbed her gun and badge, then woke Mitch and asked him to ride with her. Gayle was determined to confront Clyde before he escaped. On second thought, it might be better to follow him to his source. She had trouble believing he was bright enough to be the leader.

She filled J.O. in on her strategy while Mitch dressed. "Give me until noon. If you haven't heard from me by then call your friend." In case of trouble, Gayle wanted back up. She suspected once Kara and Elliot read her emails, they would be hot on the trail, and the agency didn't need a safari following Clyde.

41

Gayle parked outside Clyde's apartment building. She tugged the baseball cap low over her face, the short brown wig she wore peeking from beneath. With the engine off and the windows closed, the car was stifling, but the less attention drawn to them the better.

In the passenger's seat, Mitch flicked the damp hair off his forehead impatiently. "Why are we here?"

"To stop Clyde and his partner from vanishing, and to get my life back. I thought you wanted to help."

"How is watching their place going to stop them? Let the CIA handle Clyde."

"To date, their efforts have been dismal at best and almost gotten us bumped off." It was clear to Gayle that Mitch couldn't seem to understand why, prompted by the facts of the case, she'd followed a gut instinct.

He frowned. "The authorities weren't seeing the full picture before. The new evidence you found will set them straight."

"It's also proof enough to convict me. Clyde and his partner have set me up. Should I trust the agency to get it right this time?" She sighed in frustration and retreated into silence. It wasn't like Mitch to be unreasonable.

In the strained silence, he passed the box of croissants he'd grabbed off the kitchen table as they left the house. "Care to try some?" he asked with the semblance of an apologetic smile.

"Sure." She accepted the peace offering, bit into the flaky chocolate croissant and felt better, despite the tension between them.

Mitch was right. She hadn't thought this through and had placed him in unnecessary danger. He wasn't a trained agent. She never should have brought him.

Just when she decided it would be best to take him home, the lights went on in Clyde's apartment, and Gayle couldn't bring herself to leave. Scenario after scenario raced through her mind as she pondered what might play out. Twenty long minutes later, Clyde drove out of the parking garage.

Gayle put the car in gear and tailed him to the warehouse she'd discovered previously. She parked in the shadows. "If I'm not back in fifteen minutes, call for reinforcements."

"I can't let you go in there alone."

She drew in an annoyed breath. "I'm ordering you to stay. I don't have time to argue."

Mitch blinked, looking as if she'd turned on him.

She touched his hand. "I need someone here who has my back. Please, can I count on you?"

"Sure. Be careful in there."

She climbed out of the car and into the darkness, then slipped inside the building behind Clyde *the genius spymaster* who had failed to lock the door behind him.

Gayle walked into a huge open room with partitioned offices and storage units along the peripheral walls. She glimpsed Clyde going into one of the side offices and followed but paused outside the door he'd left ajar. She nudged it slightly open and saw boxes and packing materials scattered about.

His back to her, Clyde reached into his pocket, pulled out a set of keys and unlocked the desk in the corner. Gayle crept forward with her gun in her hand and struck him on the back of the head. Clyde collapsed, unconscious. She stuffed a cloth in his mouth, tied his hands and feet with some rope she found lying about, then checked his pockets, finding little of interest.

Quickly, she searched the desk for whatever he'd been after and discovered a large, concealed panel underneath the bottom drawer with documents and funds. She grabbed as much as she could and slid the items into the lining of her jacket.

She flipped the light off, stepped into the main room and stopped abruptly at the sight of Abby pointing a gun at her. Elliot stood next to her. They must have been in one of the other offices when she and Clyde had entered. How could she have missed the connection between Abby and Clyde? Dismayed, Gayle asked the woman she had once called friend, "What are you doing? What's happened to you?"

"You can stop playing Miss Nice. It's no good appealing to my better side."

"How can you betray your country and your people?"

"I'm also helping to destroy America's narcissistic capitalists who roam the globe acting like they're benevolent gods."

"They aren't all you're destroying. You've chosen the side of tyranny and terror over democracy and free will." Pity and regret welled within Gayle. Abby didn't hate America. Greed had led to her betrayal of country and friends.

Gayle darted an inquisitive glance at Elliot. He must have been at the warehouse all along and therefore missed seeing her email. If only he'd warned her. "You knew about Abby and Clyde working together?"

"Working together? They don't even know each other. We're only interested in Abby." He shifted slightly forward. "We've been on her tail for some time."

Abby laughed. "Yes, Elliot's quite passionate about his work, or at least it seemed so when he was making love to me. He never fooled me, but—"

Elliot whipped a pistol from his pocket. "Put the gun down, Abby, or I'll shoot."

"Not before I've killed one of you." Dominic stepped from the shadows. "Drop it, Elliot. I have you covered."

"Where did you come from?" Elliot asked.

"Does it matter? We have you both covered."

Gayle whirled and stared at Dom, startled anew by the realization that she'd never truly known him. She had created an ideal in her mind and he'd seemed to breathe life into her dream. It was all fantasy.

As Elliot laid down his pistol, Dominic spoke sharply. "Abby, there's no need to shoot them. Let's get out of here."

"Spoilsport." Abby backed to the door, Dominic beside her, then they were gone.

Gayle and Elliot regarded each other suspiciously. "All right Red, you first. Why are you here?"

"What were you doing with Abby before I walked in?"

"My clearance trumps yours, so give."

"I was following Clyde. He's in there, temporarily indisposed." She gestured to the room behind her.

"Let's find out what he knows."

She strode into the side office. "He's gone!"

"Why didn't you tie him up better?"

"I'd planned on leaving the building before he regained con-sciousness." She never imagined Abby, Dom and Elliot would be there. "Where could he have gone? There's no window in here. There must be a back entrance."

"This way." Elliot led.

They rushed out through the backdoor and, finding no sign of Clyde, circled around to the front. Still nothing. A determined search of the area revealed no trace of the man. He had vanished.

Elliot swore. "We'll pick him up, and when we do, the agency will get to the bottom of this"

She agreed half-heartedly. It was hard to remain optimistic.

Elliot frowned. "I'd better get to the office." The distance between them had burgeoned into a river of annoyance he couldn't or wouldn't forge.

She understood. He had to give his superiors an account of what had occurred there. The agency needed someone to blame. And she was expendable. Gayle walked toward the car and found Mitch standing beside it, locking the doors.

"I was coming in to make sure you were okay. How did it go?" Mitch asked, opening the car door for her.

She slid into the passenger's seat. "Not exactly according to plan. Clyde got away, as did Dominic and Abby." She studied Mitch. He looked as if he'd been in a tussle. "What happened to you?"

"I went to check on you after the fifteen minutes were up," he said wryly "and caught Clyde sneaking out of the warehouse. He's in the car on the floorboard, tied up and prepped for questioning. I was about to go look for you when you and your friend arrived."

"He's a colleague." Gayle had underestimated Mitch. "Nice job nabbing Clyde," she said admiringly.

He started the car and drove down the street. "Any particular direction I should be headed?"

"Let's get out of here ASAP. You know the CIA has a watch on this place. You were probably spotted abducting Clyde." Gayle knew the agency maintained video surveillance and likely hadn't missed any of what had transpired.

"Gee, thanks. On top of everything else, I could be wanted for kidnapping." Mitch didn't appear frightened and seemed to be enjoying the challenge.

"If the bureau wanted to stop you, they would have. The agency has granted us enough leeway to break him. If we fail, who knows what they'll do. We will have to try to lose them."

"Maybe you should take over the wheel."

"You're doing fine. Remind me to tread lightly in a fight with you. How did you get Clyde in the backseat?"

"Easy. I knocked him out cold. He didn't have any say-so. And he's going to stay disarmed as far as I'm concerned." Mitch glanced across at her. "Where to?"

Gayle had been brainstorming for a place and finally hit on an idea. "There's an old CIA safe house no longer in use. Keep on this road until . . ."

They drove on, each busy with their own thoughts. She considered all that had happened at the warehouse and was anxious to learn what the papers hidden in her jacket contained. She suppressed a twinge of guilt at keeping the discovery from Mitch and Elliot. The agent in her insisted on verifying what was in the documents first.

Gayle wanted to repay Mitch for the risks he'd taken on her behalf but wasn't sure how. She pressed his arm. "I'm sorry I got you into this."

"Hey, none of that. We're on the same team and I trust you."

"I can't imagine why. I've gotten you shot at, chased, and now up for possible kidnapping charges."

He cackled. "I still think our problems are somehow linked."

"The research does seem to suggest a tie-in. If we only had more to go on."

"Concentrate on the evidence and where it leads."

Gayle believed the raiding of Transway's marketing division pension tied in with the terrorists' funding. With her out of the way, Clyde and her nemesis had gained unfettered access to the accounts, snapping up the opportunity to funnel money into their own coffers. Worse, the Machiavellian impostors had tried to frame Gayle as the embezzler. But she would find the evidence to convict them. The necessary proof might even be in her jacket lining. "This is the safe house," she said, directing Mitch.

He turned in and parked. They got out of the car, then he unloaded Clyde and hoisted him to a standing position. Mitch eased forward with the trussed-up prisoner in front of him.

The door to the place was slightly ajar. Gayle waved Mitch aside and cautiously drew her gun.

Elliot appeared in the entry. "Nice to see you made it, Red."

She lowered the pistol. "You're always popping up."

"What can I say? Keeps you on the qui vive."

Mitch came up beside her, stumbling a bit with Clyde. "Where do you want him?"

"Let's get him inside," she said.

The men hustled Clyde into the building. Gayle followed and bolted the door behind them. She raised her eyebrows at the bevy of people inside. She greeted Kara and Francois, nodded to the other agents and introduced Mitch.

"Surprised to see us?" Kara asked.

"I expected you to track us here, not be waiting. You've got my moves down to a science."

"There was nowhere else nearby you could have taken him," Elliot said.

Gayle walked across to one of the tables, realizing the situation was rapidly spinning beyond her control. She slipped her jacket off, unzipped the lining and removed what she hoped was evidence, spreading it out as everyone gathered around. "I found this concealed in Clyde's desk and brought what I could carry."

"Good work," Francois said.

Gayle handed Kara the envelope of cash. "Count this and verify it's legit."

"I'm on it." She pulled out a chair and sat, resting her elbows on the table. "The rest of you might as well grab something and help go through the pile."

Francois picked up a bundle marked *père*. "I'll start with Clyde's father's letters."

Elliot chose the stack marked *fraternite* for brotherhood.

Gayle pushed a journal toward Mitch. "See if you can make any sense of this."

She was drawn to the letters marked *soeur*, the French word for sister. The first one was from Clyde's half sister Sara. After Gayle had read several pages, a picture emerged of two siblings, unknown to each other until diabolically brought together by their father, Harri, a leader in the Muslim Brotherhood. Could he be the same Harri Malone she and Mitch had stumbled across in their investigations? The one in the import and export business who was a client of both Transway and Carey International? If so, that linked Harri to the diamond heist, the plane crash and the embezzling.

Gayle read on. Sara was the impostor! Her father Harri had masterminded the plot she and Clyde carried out, bilking Transway of millions. Their motive—helping to finance the three-pronged attack set to take place simultaneously in Paris, London and New York in the fall. Gayle shuddered. Autumn was almost upon them.

Apprehensive, she read through the letters. "It's all here. How Clyde's half sister Sara pretended to be me. Proof of Clyde and his sister's embezzlement of Transway funds and the plot to destroy Paris."

"Perhaps you haven't heard, Sara's been murdered," Francois said.

Elliot added, "We suspect Abby shot her shortly before leaving for Vienna."

Stunned, Gayle confronted Elliot and Kara. "You knew it was Sara impersonating me all along?"

"We couldn't tell you," Kara said. "There was a great deal at stake."

"You didn't trust me," Gayle said, hurt.

"We wanted to protect you. The less you knew the safer you were."

Before Gayle could respond, Mitch interrupted. "This journal belonged to an unnamed woman who was a freelance assassin. The Muslim Brotherhood hired her to eliminate Gayle with Clyde's help and afterward to waste him. With Gayle out of the way and Sara set to take her place, Clyde's usefulness must have ended."

"One presumes Clyde knocked off the assassin instead, since her journal was found among his possessions," Kara said. "There's about twenty million here in cashier's checks. Gayle, you traced more than seven million that was stolen from Transway. It's possible Clyde cleaned out the assassin's accounts after he'd dispatched her. It would explain where the rest of the money came from."

"Remember, my savings was looted too," Gayle said.

"Interpol found those listed separately among Sara's assets," Francois said. "Once the investigation is ended, everything will revert to you."

Gayle smiled in relief. "Praise the Lord! That is wonderful news."

"I think it's time we interrogated the suspect." Elliot rose.

"Hold on," Gayle said. "What was in the brotherhood and father files?"

"Leave it for later," Elliot said.

"No. I insist that you read us in on the intel we brought." She straightened her shoulders and met Elliot's annoyed look. "No one has been more affected by this than Mitch and me."

Francois said, "I concur, mademoiselle. You've earned that right. Harri has revealed much of the terrorists' plans in these letters. There's proof he masterminded nefarious schemes to dredge up the finances necessary to wreak mass destruction. On behalf of France, please accept our gratitude for helping to prevent this." He pressed his hand to his heart and said, "You had the foresight and courage to collect this evidence and persist in the fight against evil."

Gayle read the sincerity in his gaze. "Thank you." She waved her arm to include him and those around the table. "But we've all had our parts to play."

"Did you come across any information relating to the Carey International crash?" Mitch asked.

"Oui. Monsieur Carey. The terrorists sabotaged the plane and its flight crew," Francois said. "I'm sorry you were drawn into this and sad also to inform you that none of the preflight external check crew survived. You are, however, acquitted of any wrongdoing or liability."

Mitch drew a deep breath and looked away. "Ryan was a particularly close friend. Can you tell me how he died?"

"My understanding is Ryan was shot while trying to save the men in his crew from being kidnapped. They were on the flight to Oklahoma, which landed at CI's facility in Tulsa. Evidently, Ryan received a call asking them to fill in for some sick crew members there. During their final external check before the return flight to Houston, Ryan and his crew must have noticed that someone had tampered with the mechanics of the plane. Before they could tell anyone, they were dead. Video cameras in the area showed Ryan attempted to stop the kidnappers and was killed. Two of his crew escaped, only to die in suspicious car accidents that same day. Ryan didn't suffer. His death was instantaneous. Your friend died a hero."

"Has his wife been told?"

Elliot said, "I thought you might want to break it to her personally."

Mitch swallowed. "Thanks. I'll do it now." He pulled out his cell and walked away from the group to a quiet corner.

They waited, observing several moments of silence for those who had died, until Mitch returned. "She was quite brave."

Gayle took his hand. "I'm sorry, Mitch."

He gave her a quick hug.

Gayle felt as if her heart would burst, it was so full. Still, she knew the attacks had to be prevented or many more would die. "Elliot, what have you learned about the Muslim Brotherhood?"

"Clyde and Sara were brought into the group by their father Harri, who also organized the diamond heist and the Carey crash. His mission was to raise the funds to attack and destroy New York.

Clyde's contribution was to embezzle funds from Transway to finance the annihilation of Paris.

"London's fireworks were to be arranged by the Muslim students from Munich. There's no mention of how. The information could have been above Clyde's pay grade. We do have leads on the sleeper students from the jewel heists, but Francois might be better informed on this."

Francois said, "British Intelligence is handling their end. Let's move on to the interrogation. We can revisit this later when we know more."

Gayle started to rise as a commotion at the door caught her attention. She was shocked to see J.O. walk in with two men. Her scrutiny passed over the tall hunk to his left, and narrowed on the shorter, nondescript fellow on his right, who was trying to fade into the background.

J.O. saw her and hurried across the room with his entourage.

She arched a brow at the friends he'd neglected to introduce. "What are you doing here? How did you know where I was? And how did you even get through the door? Let me guess." With a keen sense of satisfaction, she motioned to the shorter of the two. "You must be my brother's mysterious friend in the upper echelons of the agency."

"You're very astute, Ms. Regan. What gave me away?"

"The low profile was a bit overdone."

A gleam of appreciation lit his eyes. "The problem is, I came straight from one of our ops."

J.O. said, "Have you forgotten we have a meeting with the lawyer this afternoon?"

"The appointment isn't until two." She turned to his friend. "I want to thank you for your help. It has meant a lot, sir."

He studied her for a moment, then nodded. "Glad to be of service. I understand a lawyer might be redundant by the time we finish here."

"I hope so."

"Really? What's going on?" J.O. asked, as his friend moved to greet Francois.

"Give over, Big Bro. I've suspected you were with the agency for some time." She spoke in a low voice to keep the others from hearing.

"The crazy ideas you get! Are you ready to leave?"

"Not a chance. After what I've been through, I want to be in on Clyde's interrogation." Gayle followed the others to the back room where the questioning would be held.

<h1 style="text-align:center">42</h1>

For hours, Gayle watched Francois and Elliot interrogate Clyde. Handcuffed to a chair in the middle of the room, he refused to speak. Now she approached Clyde, determined to make him talk.

He sprang at her, furious, but was stopped by his restraints. "You!" His fingers retracted claw-like. "Why couldn't you have died like you were supposed to? Allah knows we tried to kill you." He cursed, spittle flying.

Francois's cold, flat stare threatened retaliation. "Shut up and listen. You are *fini*."

She moved closer. "Harri's plans were doomed to fail. Sara is dead. Your father has fled and left you, his own son, to take the blame."

She dropped the bundles of letters on the table for him to see. His correspondence had been held back until now in an effort to gain the most leverage from the evidence. "We know all about you. There's only one way out of this and that's to talk."

His sullen glare rested on her. "My sister is dead because of you. I have nothing to say."

Francois's lip curled. "Enough. Sara died because one of your affiliates, her partner in treason, murdered her."

Gayle opened one of Clyde's letters and read several salient paragraphs. "You admitted to doing away with your accomplice, following the attempt to finish me off." She picked up another letter and glanced down the page. "Here you confess to embezzling from Transway to help destroy Paris."

"I want a lawyer."

Gayle continued. "We know Harri is the architect behind the planned attacks. He used and discarded you like garbage. Where is Harri staying? Who else is working with him?"

"I have nothing to say."

"Haven't you any pride? This man abandoned you and your mother."

"Shut up. You don't know anything."

"He left you in an orphanage until he could use you. He didn't want to be bothered raising you. His Arab wife and children aren't even aware you exist."

"Stop it! I hate you! You ruined everything."

"Who is your contact when Harri's not here? Who are you working with? When are the attacks planned to take place? Where . . . ? Why . . . ?"

Her questions were met with silence.

"If Harri considered you a true son, he would have invited you to meet his family. Maybe taken you in. Instead, he let Abby shoot Sara. All he cares about is revenge. You're nothing to him. Harri Malone isn't even his name. He's really Harri Bustani. Did he ever tell you that?"

"Get her out of here," he cried, his voice breaking.

"Who were you supposed to buy the explosives from? Who was told to detonate them?"

"I don't want to hear anymore. Leave me alone. Just leave me alone."

"Clyde, I'm not the enemy. What have I ever done to you?"

"You're an American capitalist who stands for everything we hate. You were investigating the pension fund fraud and would have had me arrested for embezzling. I had to get rid of you or Harri would have murdered me."

"I understand. You were only helping your father, but Harri doesn't care and we do. Talk to me."

"No. There can never be anything but hate between us."

"I've never hated you. Work with me, please." She talked until he finally broke, his bravado crumbling as she read more of the documents and the ramifications of the evidence against him sank in.

"I want immunity before I talk."

Gayle said, "The best you can expect is leniency from the court, which could save your life."

"You're lying to me. The death penalty was abolished in eighty-one."

"There are prisons worse than execution." Her voice was hard. "Where does Harri stay when he's in Paris? How do you contact him?"

Gayle picked up the two phones on the table which were in Clyde's pockets at the time of his arrest. She held up the burner phone. "Will I get Harri if I press redial?"

His look of terror convinced her she was right. "Either you speak now or I'll tell Harri you're cooperating with the CIA."

His hands trembled and he seemed to have difficulty breathing. "Harri's staying at the Residence Foch Hotel, on rue Marbeau, number ten, near le Porte Maillot Métro. Room sixty-two. If he finds out I told you, he'll kill me."

Francois's eyebrows narrowed into a pucker. "Not much of a father, is he?"

Clyde stared down at the floor. "He's all about destroying the West."

"Why does he hate us so much?" Gayle asked.

"An American soldier raped his daughter."

"I remember the case," Francois said. "The American was charged. He's dead now."

Clyde mumbled, "Doesn't matter. Hate has its own life span."

Sadly, he was right. Hate outlasted people like Harri and lived on through those they'd infected. Gayle sighed and continued. "When are the attacks scheduled?"

"In September, on the day of le Grande Classique."

Her thoughts raced. The annual Paris Versailles 16K Race was one of the most popular in France. Le Grande Classique started at the foot of the Eiffel Tower, wound along the banks of the Seine, through the Forêt de Meudon, and ended at the Chateau de Versailles.

"There will be about twenty-five thousand participants, along with thousands more who will be lining the streets, watching," Francois said.

"Surely we'll arrest him long before then."

"Let's hope so." He pulled out his cell and ordered a unit to Residence Foch to arrest Harri.

Shortly afterward, the team reported back that Harri had left the hotel earlier and hadn't returned. At the news, Francois and his men went to Interpol's central office in Paris.

Gayle, J.O., Mitch and her agency colleagues relocated to CIA headquarters to track down leads. Investigative teams were searching the warehouse, Clyde's office at Transway and his apartment for evidence. London and New York were scrambling to prevent the looming attacks.

Hours passed without any new leads. Harri and his accomplices were in the wind. It was past midnight when Gayle looked up from the desk where she'd been working and spoke to Mitch. "I'm worried. What if the terrorists have learned of Clyde's arrest and have escalated the strike dates to present time?"

"I sincerely hope that's not the case."

She googled *Paris August events* on her laptop and clicked enter. "Tomorrow afternoon, the two-day Feast of the Assumption of Mary begins."

"Most of France is on vacation. How many Catholics can be there?" Mitch asked.

"More than half of the French are Catholic, and visitors from around the world come for this event. About one hundred and fifty thousand people are expected to show up."

Kara spoke from the doorway. "It's a national holiday and has been since Louis XIII consecrated France to the Virgin Mary and asked her to give him an heir for the throne. His prayer was soon answered."

Mitch's forehead wrinkled. "How do the people celebrate?"

"Both days begin with mass at Notre Dame Cathedral," Gayle said, "then tomorrow, an evening procession along the Seine and around the two Îles of Paris. The next day, there'll be a grand procession downtown that starts at Notre Dame."

"Catholic clergy with a life-size silver statue of Mary holding the Infant Jesus, and thousands of followers will parade from Notre Dame down the streets to celebrate the Assumption of Mary," Kara said.

Gayle chimed in, "King Charles X gave the statue to Notre Dame in the eighteen hundreds. The church bells will ring and a large group will carry candles. When they reach the Seine, the statue and thousands of pilgrims will board the boats to begin a floating procession."

"The boats go around the two islands of the Seine, the Île de la Cité on which the Cathedral of Notre Dame is located and the neighboring Île Saint-Louis," Kara added.

"Observers, singing and praying, line the bridges and quays to watch the Procession Fluvial," Gayle said.

"And all this is in anticipation of the huge celebration to follow on the next day," Kara said. She yawned. "Go home and get some sleep. There's nothing you can do until more intel is in."

Gayle could tell Mitch was as reluctant to leave as she was, but they were both exhausted. They hadn't slept in a couple of nights, and it was almost two in the morning. They wouldn't be much help if they didn't get some rest. "She's right. Let's go, Mitch."

"Are there any taxis this late?" he asked.

Kara tossed him a set of keys. "Take my car. It's the blue sedan out front. We'll phone you if anything new happens."

Gayle patted her shoulder. "Thanks. You need a break too."

"I'm going to bed down in my office. It won't be the first time."

"Sounds like a plan." With a yawn, Gayle waved and walked with Mitch to the elevator. They got off on the ground floor and strolled outside.

Mitch said, "I've forgotten my mobile."

"I'll wait here while you get it. The air feels good."

At his hesitant look, she said, "I'm in plain view of the security guard inside. If it makes you feel better, ask him to watch me."

"Okay. I'll be right back."

She sat on a nearby bench, tempted to go sleep in someone's office. They could always toss her out when the day-staff arrived. Mitch could bring her a change of clothes. She stared up at the crescent moon and stars twinkling above. Hardly a car in sight.

At a faint shuffling sound behind her, Gayle stood. A hand covered her mouth and she struggled until a gun pressed against her back. The assailant dragged her into the shadows, then tugged her down the street and shoved her inside a van.

A shiver ran down her spine. She knew him from photos as Harri Malone, a.k.a. Harri Bustani, the mastermind behind the three-prong attack the agency was investigating. He was on the CIA's and Interpol's Most Wanted Terrorist Lists.

Her body jerked as the driver tore down the road. There were four swarthy Middle Easterners in the van, two in the front and two in the back. One of them roughly frisked her, confiscated her cell phone and tossed it out the side window. The man gagged her and tied her hands and feet.

"*Was machen wir mit ihr zu tun?*" the driver asked in German.

Harri grunted in the same language. "She's our insurance out of here in case of trouble."

Clearly, Harri was the leader. Others must have bungled his orders badly for him to be personally involved. The men either assumed she didn't speak German or it didn't matter what she heard, because they planned to murder her when her usefulness ended.

When the van stopped, Harri untied her and removed her gag. "Play along or you are dead." He urged Gayle out of the vehicle and slid his arm around her waist, pulling her close like a lover.

She recognized the small neighborhood of shops and markets in Babres known as the Arab Quarter in the fifth arrondissement. Harri pushed her inside the backdoor of the Mosul Café, then led her to the basement, through a trap door and into a tunnel below.

It opened into a large work area. Gayle gasped at the plastique explosives and detonators on the table in the center of the room. It looked like enough to blow up a large section of the city.

Harri's eyes gleamed with satisfaction at her distress. "As you can see, there's no stopping us." He gagged her again, then retied her hands and feet. "This is where you'll be sleeping. You won't bother the rats too much." He switched off the light.

She heard the door close and a key turn. Despair washed over her as she thought of Mitch, her brothers and others in the city destined to die. There must be something she could do. *Lord, show me your plan. Once again, I've come to the end of my strength and need your guidance and deliverance.* Eventually, she nodded off.

43

The pain radiating from her bound wrists and ankles awakened Gayle. Her throat was parched and her body chilled from lying on the hard ground. She arched one shoulder and rubbed it against her cheek, struggling in vain to loosen the gag about her mouth.

She couldn't tell if it was day or night or how long she'd slept. It must have been past three in the morning when Harri had dumped her there. After her captors left, she'd thought and prayed for what seemed like hours before finally falling asleep.

Her stomach rumbled and she guessed it might be about noon. J.O. and Mitch would be anxiously searching for her. The CIA was already using all their resources in pursuit of Harri and the terrorists. Would the agency find him in time? Could they stop the massive attacks? And rescue her?

Gayle needed to save herself. But how could she outsmart the terrorists? There were so many lives at stake besides her own. She supposed Harri's weaknesses were rooted in his hatred and arrogance. In her brief glimpse of the explosives last night, she noticed that the detonators weren't attached yet.

The terrorists must be planning to strike tomorrow, during the Feast of Assumption celebrations. The festivities would start at ten with morning mass at Notre Dame Cathedral, followed by noon prayers, and then the two-hour afternoon procession. If Harri wanted to cause the greatest devastation possible, he would trigger the devices to blow up in the afternoon.

She felt sick at the thought of the massive threat to 150,000 or more people and the destruction of Notre Dame Cathedral and other historical landmarks. Dear God, what could she possibly do to avert such a catastrophe? In her mind, a plan began to take shape.

Gayle cringed when Harri and his comrades returned. It must be morning, and as she had feared the first day of the feast. The men set to work, attaching the percussion caps to the plastique explosives. They packed each bomb into an individual worn cloth shopping bag, added three small pipe bombs in a separate bag and then carefully set all twenty-one bags into a cardboard box.

Gayle figured each unit had the potential to demolish a four-way intersection and any individuals and buildings in the surrounding area. The way the pipe bombs were assembled was nowhere near as deadly. She studied the room carefully while the lights were on, seeking a weapon to protect herself later, when they came back to kill her. She glimpsed a utility knife on the table half-buried beneath some cellophane wrappings.

The men ignored Gayle and her needs for food, water and to use the bathroom. They turned out the lights and rushed out with the deadly weapons, stopping only to lock the door behind them. "Please God, let them return before setting off the bombs," she prayed. Gayle planned to be ready.

She scooted on her side, inching toward the knife she'd seen earlier. After several attempts, she managed to kneel at the table and brace herself to stand. Then she pivoted and leaned against it, sweeping her tied hands along the edge, feeling for the knife.

Her fingers grasped it, and she strained to cut the rope, wincing as it slipped and nicked her wrists. Gayle kept sawing until her hands were free. Quickly, she cut the binding around her ankles and stuffed the knife in her back waistband. She removed the gag and flipped on the lights to search for another weapon.

All she found were wires, fuses and stray electronic parts until she reached the small water closet built into the corner of the room. A large rusty wrench was under the sink in a plastic bucket set there to catch drips. Gayle heaved a sigh, relieved herself, drank from the tap, then turned the lights off and hid behind the door in anticipation.

As she waited, the fallacies in her plan became more obvious and worrisome. What if Harri failed to return? And if there were more than one of his men, how would she defend herself? There had to be a better way.

She flipped the lights on again and hunted through the electronics on the table. Gayle grabbed two detonators, a battery charger, a long cable with two leads and duct tape. Her plan was to arrange enough of a bang to open the door without hurting herself. She taped one of the blasting caps above the knob and the other below it, then attached the wire leads to the two fuses.

With slow, cautious movements, Gayle pulled the opposite end of the cable and the battery charger across the room. Her heart racing as if it would explode, she connected the leads to the charger and covered her head. A loud boom shook the door. Smoke filled the room, causing her to cough.

It was finished in seconds. She picked up the wrench and grabbed the hole where the knob used to be, pulling the door open. She found her way out of the tunnel and upstairs to the deserted café. The terrorists could return any moment. Still, Gayle had to warn the bureau.

Shaken, she called Kara from the wall phone in the kitchen and briefed her on Harri's plans, describing the bombs and the men. "I'm leaving for the feast procession now."

"It's too risky. Walk two blocks over and head toward Notre Dame. I'll send Mitch to pick you up."

Gayle agreed and hung up. She checked to ensure the knife was in her waistband, stuffed the wrench in a shopping bag and left. About fifteen minutes later, Mitch pulled alongside, sprinted out of the car and hugged her tightly. "I've been worried sick. Are you all right?" he asked, looking her over carefully.

"I'm fine, but we've got to hurry if we're going to intercept Harri." They clambered into the vehicle.

"Okay," Mitch said, "how about filling me in during the drive?"

She filled him in and by the time they reached the cathedral, Mitch knew as much as she did.

"The agency hasn't made much progress in preventing the strikes or finding Harri, but they're doing everything they can."

Gayle sighed. "If only there were more time."

"Yeah, if only. What's in the bag?" Mitch asked.

"A wrench for protection. I also have a knife in my waistband."

"Your gun is in the glove box. Kara knows you too well to think you'd sit this one out."

"I don't suppose she gave you a weapon?"

"I'll take the wrench." Mitch parked and they mingled with the others lining up for the procession. "Tell me if you spot them."

She nodded, craning her neck to find Harri. "He's probably somewhere far enough away not to be affected by the blast. Let's search the bushes alongside the streets for bombs. Harri stashed them in shopping bags."

"Won't they be too dangerous for us to handle?"

"Not if we disconnect them before he detonates them."

"A mighty big if."

"You're right. The CIA will have agents on this. They'll be dressed as civilians to keep Harri from knowing that we're on to him. We're not in this alone."

Their gazes met for one long moment, then he hugged her tightly and gave her a quick tender kiss. "I don't want to lose you."

She touched his cheek gently and drew back. "Let's find Harri. Take this side of the street and I'll watch for anyone suspicious."

While Mitch inspected the bushes, Gayle surveyed those in the procession and on the sidelines. There were a number of tall, lean, tanned men, but none of them had Harri's hard brown eyes, long angular chin, aristocratic nose and deadly air.

Gayle and Mitch had feverishly covered about half of the parade's route when they heard a blast that sounded like a bomb exploding a mile or so ahead. Smoke and soot rose in the air. The hysterical crowd ran back toward the cathedral, screaming and trampling others underfoot.

She reached for Mitch. "Hoist me up onto the base of that lamppost so I can see." Gayle was worried that Harri was maneuvering the huge crowd toward Notre Dame for his own deadly purposes. Her feet secure on the base, she wrapped an arm around the lamppost and scanned the surrounding area. Relieved to be able to see above the crowds, Gayle was alarmed at the sight of the destruction up ahead. He must have set off one of the smaller pipe bombs. This fueled her determination to find Harri before he could detonate the larger explosives.

She spotted him standing alone in a park across from her. Harri glanced down at a paper in his hand and then started dialing his phone.

Gayle shouted, "He's dialing to set off the next bomb." She aimed for the spot between his eyes and fired. Harri slumped and fell. She jumped down from the lamppost and ran to where he'd fallen. She picked up Harri's mobile and powered it off. Gayle gently opened the back cover, removed the battery and slid the SIM card out.

She grabbed Harri's list as Mitch ran up and handed her his mobile.

"Kara's on the line," he said.

"Thanks," she mouthed the word. "Kara, I've killed Harri and deactivated his phone. Here's the list of numbers they're using to set off the explosions. The first one is. . . ."

She hung up the phone, reassured that twenty-two numbers would be almost instantaneously shut down.

Gayle shivered and looked at Mitch. "That's twenty-two bombs intercepted and tens of thousands of lives saved today. But what about tomorrow and all the future tomorrows? How will we ever stop them all?"

44

It was a month before the various cells were ferreted out, arrested and charged. The pending investigation against Mitch was dropped and Gayle's possessions restored.

The scene at the Paris Central Intelligence auditorium was jubilant. Gayle stood center stage unable to stop beaming as J.O.'s friend, CIA bureau director Neil Rochey, presented her with the Intelligence Medal of Merit on behalf of the department.

"Gayle Regan, this badge of honor is hereby awarded to you for meritorious service and achievements beyond your normal duties, all of which contributed significantly to the success of the CIA's mission."

She raised her hands in a gesture of appreciation at the scattered applause. "Thank you. And a special salute to the colleagues, family and friends who stood by me and, in part, made this celebration possible. Though this medallion is not mine to keep, I am honored and humbled to accept it." The medal would be displayed in an area where only those with top security clearance could view it. She slipped it into Director Rochey's hands and returned to her seat.

Gayle's heart sang. Her mission could have ended disastrously. Yet, God's sustaining hand and the support of family and friends had helped her pass through her wilderness. It hurt that both Abby and Dominic were branded traitors. Abby had chosen greed as her god, betraying her country. Dominic opted for duty, giving France his all and entering into deep cover.

Gayle found it difficult not to question her own judgment, having once trusted Abby and Dominic. Obviously, Gayle wasn't as adept as she'd once believed at distinguishing between truth and appearances.

She studied the crowd. Francois and Ari were pretending to be crushed by Dominic's deception. The two needed to be careful and not overplay their parts. Francois drew her aside. "Can you spare me a moment?" He led her into a small room and closed the door. "There's someone here who wants to speak with you."

She looked across the room, surprised to see Dominic approaching. "Despite rumors to the contrary, I understand he's not the treasonous villain he's purported to be."

"Off the record, he's one of our top agents," Francois said.

Dominic stopped before her, emotions playing across his face, uncertainty, concern . . . was that shame? "I'm glad you're all right," he said.

She tapped a loose fist against her heart to keep the moment light. "I seem to be fine."

"Am I forgiven, chéri?"

Gayle nodded. Initially, her sorrow at his desertion had turned to rage, then somehow along the way her anger had melted into sympathy. To withhold forgiveness would leave her bitter and weighted down by all the negative forces she wanted to be free of.

"Are you sure?"

"You have my forgiveness, but not my trust."

"That's fair enough. I haven't earned it, have I?"

"No, you haven't. Dom, I wish you the best in the Middle East."

He bent and murmured softly for her ears alone. "You would have been mine if not for our family motto. 'Unto whom much is given, much more is required.' You understand?"

"Yes, it's one of my favorite passages in Luke." It seemed to her Dom had missed its essence, taking up the mantle of duty while foregoing the joy of salvation. She prayed someday Dom would experience the spirit of adoption that freed God's children to be joint heirs with him.

They parted and she drifted back into the auditorium. It was heartening to see how Pia clung to Perry's hand, and the reassuring grin he gave her in return. It wouldn't be long before the two realized they were in love. Gayle shuddered at the thought of what Pia had endured. She deserved happiness.

Gayle's three brothers and Mitch approached, smiling with pride. She couldn't have made it without them. Mitch brushed against her, and she met his warm gaze. She sensed he was waiting on a sign from her before speaking again about the future. She was too uncertain to trust her feelings.

"Ride with me to the house?" he asked. She nodded and they all walked out together. Mitch said to her brothers, "We'll meet you at Gayle's place."

She read the approval on their faces as she and Mitch climbed into the taxi.

The driver stopped at her home and they got out. "Let's sit in the yard a while and talk," Mitch said. He opened the gate and they went through and sat together on a cushioned wrought iron bench.

The horse chestnut trees were in bloom, all pink and white. "Aren't the flowers lovely?" Gayle said. "And now, I'll finally have time to enjoy them."

"It is nice back here. After all the turmoil we've been through, it's tranquil."

They relaxed, enjoying the calm and watching the birds, fluttering on the branches among the blooms.

"Hey, I wanted to congratulate you on the intelligence medal. You earned it. I'm so proud of you."

"We did it together."

He took her hand and held it. "What will you do now?"

"I'm not sure. A vacation at home in the States. Time with my parents. How about you?"

His clear gaze turned stormy, breaking over her.

"What's wrong?"

"I leave for the US tomorrow. I can't put off getting back to the company any longer."

She turned toward him and her heartbeat quickened. She wasn't used to seeing Mitch in a suit and tie. It emphasized his tall, lean strength. "I'll be returning soon too. We'll both be in Houston, for a while anyway."

"Gayle, we haven't known each other long, but I've never met anyone like you." He let go of her hand and his arm slid around her. "You're smart and beautiful—strong, gentle—focused, yet easy to be with."

Her stomach fluttered as she looked into his eyes, warmed at the goodness in their depths. Still, she wanted to take it slowly and be sure this time. "Mitch, a lot has happened in the brief period we've gotten to know each other. I care about you and can't imagine how I would have survived if you hadn't been by my side."

He pulled her closer and took her chin. His lips met hers in a long kiss. "I don't want to lose you, and I'm not asking for any promises. Let's give what we have a chance to grow."

She smiled, her tension unfurling as a sense of destiny filled her. "I'd love that."